SISTERS STORM

GLEN W. CHRISTEN

VOLUME 2 OF THE MARSHALS STORM TRILOGY

Green Ivy Publishing
1 Lincoln Centre
18W140 Butterfield Road
Suite 1500
Oakbrook Terrace IL 60181-4843
www.greenivybooks.com

Sisters Storm/Glen W. Christen
ISBN: 978-1-946043-84-9
Ebook: 978-1-946043-85-6

TABLE OF CONTENTS

PART 1

SARA

PROLOGUE

Sara stepped down from the closed carriage into mid-morning sunshine, concentrating hard because of the unfamiliar green traveling dress she was wearing. When her feet were planted firmly on the ground, she said, "Good morning, Miss Harrison. Are you ready to leave?"

Miss Harrison was dressed in a plain gray dress Sara had arranged to have delivered the day before. "Yes. My trunk is ready. We can leave as soon as it's loaded." She bid goodbye to the two women from the staff who had accompanied her to the service entrance at the back of the embassy.

The driver loaded the small trunk into the luggage compartment before helping Edwina into the carriage. Sara stopped him with a raised hand and spoke quickly. His eyebrows rose before he gave her a grin, repeating her instructions to make sure he understood, before helping her into the carriage.

The two young women sat in silence for some time, listening to the clip-clop of the horses' hooves, before Sara broke the silence. "We're going to have one of those unannounced changes of plan I warned you about. We're going to be leaving this carriage in a few minutes and changing to another. You'll need to be ready to move in a hurry."

Edwina glanced sharply at Sara before she asked with amusement in her voice, "Does anyone else know about this change of plans?"

Sara grinned unrepentantly. "I told our driver about the change of plans when I boarded. I'm glad his instructions were for him to do what I told him, no matter what."

A few minutes later the driver slapped the side of the coach with his hand. Sara ordered briskly, "Get ready. When we stop, follow me out as fast as you can. When you hit the ground, go straight ahead through the door in front of you. When you get inside, wait for me. We'll only have a few seconds, so don't dawdle."

The carriage stopped. Sara shot out the door, spun on one foot and helped Edwina down. She ran for the door while Sara flipped up the lid of the compartment and grabbed a trunk in each hand, yanking them clear. The lid slammed shut and both young women were through the door and out of sight less than thirty seconds after the carriage halted.

Edwina gawked at her new surroundings and found herself in a small, cramped, very dirty office. The unmistakable odor of a livery stable assaulted her nose. She stared in consternation when Sara dropped the trunks and pulled the door shut behind them while the sound of the carriage retreated.

Sara dropped a bar across the outer door before she circled the grungy desk filling most of the room. She dropped the bar on an inner door and turned to the trunks waiting on the floor, lifting hers to the desk-top. She opened it before she stripped her dress off, pulling it over her head. Handing it to Edwina, she directed, "Hang on to this while I change."

Sara grabbed a small bolt of plain cotton cloth from the trunk, and wrapped it tightly around her chest, flattening her breasts before she quickly donned the man's white shirt and black trousers she had bought so long ago in Denver.

Edwina stared in amazement when Sara wound her shoulder-length hair into a bun and pinned it to the top of her head. When she donned her battered Stetson, her shoulder-length hair disappeared. Next, she slipped on her new vest, momentarily turning the left lapel inside-out to display her marshal's star.

Edwina was speechless at the transformation. The young woman she had accompanied in the carriage had been transformed into a tall and lean young man. She gaped, dumbfounded, when Sara exchanged her now-folded dress for a large handbag from her trunk.

Sara kept one hand in the bag while she raised the bar on the inner door. Pulling the door slightly ajar, she glanced outside and snapped, "Take the bag. Our new wheels are waiting."

A horse harnessed to an open buggy stood waiting in the open alleyway. Sara grabbed a trunk in each hand and with two steps stowed them behind the seat.

Edwina followed, still dazed by the transformation. Sara helped her into the seat before climbing in herself. When she gathered the reins in her left hand, the dappled gray turned its head to eye her curiously. She was about to reach for the whip in the socket beside her knee when some sixth sense made her reach for the handbag instead. She placed it on her lap with her right hand inside before gently flicking the reins across the horse's rump with her left.

The carriage began to move toward the open door

some distance away. They were almost to the doorway when a man stepped from the deep shadow, a gun in his hand. He raised it, aiming at Sara's chest, sneering with exaggerated courtesy, "Miss Storm, I presume?"

Edwina squeaked in terror.

Sara said nothing when the gunman continued conversationally, "The ghost of Theodore Preston is smiling on me today, because I am going to kill you."

Sara's voice was inhumanly calm. "Why?"

"Because your death will punish your bitch of a mother like nothing else could." He smiled in delighted anticipation, raising the gun slightly as he shifted his aim to Sara's head.

Her ready gun hand was hidden by the bag on her lap. When she squeezed her trigger finger slightly, her Colt roared twice. Both slugs slammed into the gunman and he was thrown backward, his own gun discharging one slug into the haymow floor above.

CHAPTER 1

Bright sunshine bathed the mountains but its warmth was tempered by the chill of high altitude. Springtime had come to the Colorado Rockies, causing snowmelt to be everywhere as rivulet joined rivulet, until the rumble and roar of flowing water could be heard for miles.

The small town of Wilford almost filled a level space Mother Nature had carved into the side of a mountain. Businesses were crowded together between the railroad tracks following the outer rim of the notch, and the mountain. A small depot, homes, a church and a school filled most of the remaining level area, stretching to the rising slope. A tumbling snowmelt-fed stream flowed in its channel through the town at one end, swollen to many times its summertime flow.

Doc Madison was only a few paces from the depot when a distant whistle echoed back from the surrounding mountains. He increased his pace slightly, his seventy-plus years showing in the slight shuffle of his feet. He knew he would have only a few minutes to share with the young woman he could see standing by herself, waiting.

Sara Storm was bursting with excitement and anticipation as she paced back and forth in the shade of the awning, as nervous as a young colt in the path of a thunderstorm at the sound of the whistle. She stooped to pick up her traveling bag just as a familiar voice observed, "Sara, I see you're going traveling."

She wrapped her arms around the elderly gentleman, giving him an affectionate hug. Her glance swept over the white hair and a face whose eyes were crinkled with laugh lines, grinning at her. "Did Ma send you down to see me off? I know she's told you more than once I've always wanted to try my own wings someday."

Doc Madison affectionately eyed the young woman standing before him, as dear to him as his own granddaughter. She was slender, as slender as he remembered her mother at the same age of eighteen, yet even taller. Sara towered over him, standing a lithe two inches over six feet in her bare feet, thanks to the genes inherited from two equally tall parents.

She was wearing her usual rider's boots, whose high heels added another two inches to her height. The boots were part of her usual rider's outfit of battered Stetson and a faded chambray shirt, which emphasized her full figure. Jeans clung to the curve of her hips and thighs, the cuffs tucked into the tops of her boots. A gun belt with full bullet loops and a holstered Colt .45 on her right hip completed her attire. The whole image set her much apart from most of the women of the West in the year 1911.

Doc eyed her familiar face, seeing the deep tan and the sun-bleached hair. *She looks so much like her mother.* "No, Sara, your mother didn't send me. I just know you so well I've been expecting this for some time."

"I've wanted for years to go see some of the places Ma and Pa told us stories about. They probably told you I tried to get them to take all of us to see some of the sights a couple of years ago. Ma just laughed; said if I waited until I was eighteen I could go on my own." She laughed. "I know now I wasn't ready to be let loose when I was that young."

Another whistle blast drowned out any chance for conversation as the locomotive pulled into the station. When the echoes died away Sara concluded conspiratorially, "Don't tell Ma unless she were to ask, but I took her old marshal's star without telling her. I thought there might be a time when it would be handy to have."

She was startled when Doc snapped, "Promise me you won't use that star unless you have absolutely no other choice!"

Her eyes met his for a moment, astonished by his vehemence. "I promise."

He relaxed somewhat. The word of any Storm was their bond. She would do as she promised, but the old cliché *young and foolish* certainly came to his mind.

Doc was startled by a gentle good-bye kiss on the cheek. She said softly, "I don't know where your mind was right then, but my train is about to pull out."

His eyes were suspiciously moist. "I was just remembering times past. Go. Be careful. Have a good time. Don't try to make it too much of an adventure. I'll want to hear all about it when you get home."

Sara was startled at the intensity of her oldest friend and confidante as she hugged him. She stepped aboard as the engineer loosed a warning blast of the whistle. She found a seat and leaned out the window, waving as long as she could see Doc standing at the depot in the late May sunshine.

He waved back. *I hope she doesn't run into any trouble. She has a level head, but she could still make a mistake just because she is young and doesn't have the experience.* He shook his head with a smile. *You worry too much. If anyone can handle a situation, it's Sara.*

When the train left the sight of Wilford behind at the first bend in the tracks, Sara turned away from the window. Muttering under her breath about the already-cramped quarters, she tried to fit her long legs under the seat in front.

Her thoughts drifted between past and present as she fondly recalled the annual three-day trips her family made to Denver each fall. They'd always spent time visiting friends her parents had known since their days as United States marshals. Part of one day would be spent shopping for one new outfit apiece. The routine of hand-me-down clothing would continue over the years as she and her siblings outgrew their clothes. Unlike almost every other family, older sisters passed jeans and shirts to younger brothers. The last day spent in Denver was always the same when they visited the bookseller, stocking up on books of all types, whether for home schooling or for enjoyment throughout the long winter nights ahead.

Sara fondly recalled those nights because there never seemed to be time to read during the summer months. She had grown up in a saddle, helping her parents operate their cattle ranch from a very young age. She helped care for her three younger siblings as soon as she was able. As she grew older, she took turns with her mother to care for them during the long days, one helping her father while the other tended the ranch house and her brothers and sister.

Sara was accustomed to hard physical labor and dressed in men's clothes for the practicality, equally at ease with a dishpan or a rope, a pitch fork or a gun. She was a crack shot with a rifle before she turned twelve, having been taught by her father, Ted. Her mother Sue taught her to use her Colt .45 when her hands and wrists grew strong enough to control such a weapon.

***

Sue beamed with pride. Sara had just demonstrated her speed and accuracy, resulting in the last of six tin cans bounding up the slope while the echoes of gunfire faded away. "You're faster than I ever was. I know you're fast enough to have beaten most of the old-time gunslingers. I'm thankful you'll never have to face such a challenge."

Sara saw her mother's face suddenly turn bleak for an instant. She asked, "Ma. Did you ever have to face one?"

Her mother slumped down on a nearby stump, silent for several moments. She inhaled deeply. "Yes. I did. It was the day I met your father." She shivered at the memory. "Snake Carson was one of the most vicious outlaws to ever raid and pillage the West."

Sara listened, frightened and fascinated in turn as her mother told her of the first fateful day she shared with her father. Both had been wounded but were able to kill their attackers in the ensuing gunfight, bringing an end to the rampage of the notorious gang of Snake Carson.

The afternoon was almost gone before her mother smiled wanly. "I hope you never have to experience anything like it. We taught you to shoot because we want you to be able to defend yourself under any circumstances, but I pray you never have to face a man with a gun." She admonished sternly, "Just remember, there are other dangers out there in the world."

***

The train arrived in Denver just as the sun was setting behind the mountains to the west. Sara followed her family's habit of walking the short distance to the Drovers' House, where she took a room for the night. The clerk, who was a stranger to her, gave her a startled glance, taking in her unusual attire. He turned the guest book for her signature. At the sight of the neat signature, recognition dawned. "Are you the lady marshal from west of here?"

"No, I'm her daughter."

"Welcome to Denver. Will you be staying long?" He grinned, "Not that I'm worried about your credit. A reputation like yours is as good as gold."

Her spirits rose at the compliment. "Just a day or two. I won't know exactly when I'm leaving town until sometime tomorrow."

She went to her room and was asleep almost instantly. She slept very late; the sun was actually above the eastern horizon when she awoke to street noise outside her window. She lay quietly for several minutes before stirring, strangely reluctant to begin another day. When she arrived at the dining room she was greeted warmly by other diners who were familiar with her and her parents. Breakfast at home had always been relaxed and convivial and this morning proved no exception.

She was in no hurry when she left the hotel, strolling leisurely down one street after another until she stopped at a sign proclaiming AKINS' EMPORIUM AND MILLENARY. A small bell above the door gave tinkling warning of her arrival when she entered.

The interior was illuminated only by the mid-morning sunshine from the many windows, but her eyes adjusted quickly to the sight of the elegantly dressed figure waiting for her. "Elizabeth. I'm so glad to see you. It's always too long between our visits."

Elizabeth Akins smiled. "You look just like your mother did the first time I met her. And just as she was, you are a real beauty."

Sara blushed.

Elizabeth examined her figure critically. "I have the two dresses you ordered ready for you. I'm sure they'll fit perfectly because I've already incorporated the changes you sent me."

"I don't think it's possible for you to ever make a mistake regarding clothes. Let's see if you're right again."

Elizabeth led the way to the back of the store, where she took a dress from a rack and held it up for Sara's inspection. She admired the handiwork. "You've really outdone yourself this time. It's absolutely beautiful."

"You go try that on and you'll see a real beauty in the mirror."

Sara left her gun belt and Stetson on the counter and disappeared into the dressing room. When she returned, she went directly to a floor-length mirror fastened to the wall and was stunned at her own reflection. The long dress was bright red, trimmed in white lace. The bosom emphasized her full breasts, while the neckline was cut low to offer a glimpse of cleavage. Her arms were encased in long sleeves to the wrists, while the skirt belled out from her waist and brushed the floor, hiding her rider's boots.

"Elizabeth. I've never seen a prettier dress!"

"It's not just the dress. It's who's wearing it."

Voices chimed in from behind them, echoing Elizabeth. Sara blushed as red as the dress.

Elizabeth spent several minutes carefully examining the fit before she nodded in satisfaction. "I won't have to make any alterations at all. I'll have this one ready for you in a few minutes. Then we'll have you model the other one as well."

Less than a half-hour later Sara finished packing her new clothing in the small trunk she had purchased. The red dress and a dark green traveling dress were tightly folded and packed on top of an outfit from Andrew Akins' men's store next door; a man's black trousers, vest, coat and white ruffled shirt.

They had talked all the while about many subjects. Elizabeth asked, "Is there someone special waiting for you when you get home from your trip?"

"I'm very fond of my neighbor, Andy Franklin. He's sweet on me, but he's always known I want to see some of the world before I'm ready to settle down."

"When you decide if he's the right one for you, don't hesitate," Elizabeth advised gently. "Life's too short to not enjoy all of the happiness you can. I very much hope one of these dresses will be your wedding dress."

***

The delivery wagon had departed with her trunk before Sara bade goodbye to her friend and started walking back in the general direction of her hotel. All of her previous visits to the city had been with her family and she had never just wandered by herself to explore. Today was different and she decided to make the most of the opportunity.

Several hours had elapsed since breakfast and Sara began to feel hunger pangs as she strolled along another previously unexplored street, focusing on the signs showing in windows or hung from awnings on both sides of the street. One window was painted TONY'S CAFE.

The interior of the cafe was very neat, with immaculate place-settings waiting at each table. A clean, polished counter sported a row of stools huddled next to it. A row of hooks beckoned to her Stetson. The hour was well past noon and the room was empty of other customers. A man and woman who were obviously the owners stood behind the counter, staring at her with such intensity she instinctively checked the Colt in her holster.

Sara tensed when the man started to move toward her as if in greeting but stopped and asked anxiously, "Are you the lady marshal?" She was startled by the unexpected question. A few seconds later his disappointment was obvious. "Ah. No. I can see you are too young to be the marshal."

His tone was so dispirited Sara relaxed. "My mother was a marshal before I was born. Is it possible you've mistaken her for me?"

The smile on the man's face spread from ear to ear. "You are the daughter of the Marshals Storm?"

"Yes, I am. I ask you again, why do you want to know?"

She did not think it possible for the smile to spread any wider but it did.

"I am Tony Benito. Everything I have and everything you see I owe to your mother. Did she never tell you the story?"

She gawked at him. "No. My mother never told me anything about you."

Tony stepped from behind the counter. "I would imagine you came to us because you are hungry. Sara, put something together for this young lady. We are going to be closed while I tell this young woman about the angel who is her mother."

They were soon seated at a table, a heaping plate of food sitting in front of Sara. Tony said, "I must first introduce my wife, Sara. Then please tell me your name because I haven't stopped talking long enough for you to tell me."

She grinned and said, "You'll have to specify which Sara you're talking to because I'm Sara Storm."

"Then you will be Sara and my Sara will be *Dear*."

Both women laughed as his levity faded. "Sara. I only met your mother once, when I was nine. My father and I were living in one room of a flophouse here in Denver at the time.

"We were awakened one morning just before dawn by two strangers in our room with drawn guns. My father was terrified because a crooked policeman in Oregon had shot my mother to death just a few months before. Pop was trying to shield me from the intruders when one told the other they'd made a mistake."

Tony drew a deep breath. "That was your mother. The sound of a woman's voice lessened our fear. She apologized and told us they had the wrong suspect. We learned later your parents had been nearly murdered in their hotel earlier in the night. I was never sure why my Pop was on their list of suspects; but he was, so they came to our room first."

Sara was startled, never having heard any of the tale.

"My father never held it against your mother. When I was old enough to understand, he explained it to me. I never held it against your mother, either."

Sara relaxed.

"As I said, when they found they had the wrong suspect, your mother apologized to us. When she left, she did something which has been forever burned into my memory.

"She put something in Pop's hand, saying '*This is not charity. This is a gift from one motherless child to another. Use it well.*'" He paused, retreating to a scene only he could see. "The gift she gave us was two gold coins."

Tony's eyes were moist at the memory. "I never understood exactly what she meant. I'm hoping you can explain." He swallowed hard. "Those two coins were the seed that kept Pop and me here in Denver. They bought this cafe, brought me my dear Sara, and allowed my father to see his grandchildren before he died. Pop swore we had seen an angel that morning. I believe with all my heart he was right." He cleared his throat noisily. "Sara, we owe all of our happiness to your mother."

Sara's own eyes were moist and she swallowed. "You asked what my mother meant when she said it was a gift was from one motherless child to another. She was an orphan herself. Her mother died when she was four and her father when she was sixteen. She'd been running her own ranch for two years when she met my father and was deputized as a United States marshal. They were both wounded in a gun fight. The reward she was paid for killing the outlaws made her a wealthy woman. She would have been eager to help someone who obviously needed it."

Sara spent the rest of the afternoon with Tony and Sara. The day was almost gone when she apologized, "I hate to leave but I have to get a ticket for a train leaving tonight." She grinned at the thought of springing her discovery on her parents at some point in the future. "I'll be sure to tell my mother what I've learned about her hidden past."

Sara Benito held her close for a moment, the top of her head barely reaching Sara's shoulder. She looked up at the much taller woman. "The Spanish have the perfect goodbye for this situation. Via con Dios. Go with God. Take care, Sara Storm. We'll remember you and your mother always."

She smiled as she waved goodbye from a bend in the street and the cafe disappeared from sight. *Ma and Pa sure never told us about every adventure they've had.*

CHAPTER 2

Sara purchased a ticket and made arrangements for her new trunk to be picked up before she hurried back to the Drovers' House. Taking time for a quick supper, she went to her room to try for a few hours of sleep.

It was nearing midnight when her train rolled away from the station. Hours later, she watched in fascination while the miles rolled by under the light of a full moon. As the train chugged eastward, the terrain slowly changed from familiar mountains to slight ridges and shallow valleys. Dawn was beginning to lighten the sky when the land began to change to rolling hills marching off into the distance.

She had managed to doze fitfully while the night passed, rousing to fully awake in the light of dawn. When the sun rose above the unfamiliar horizon, her intense interest was obvious to her fellow passengers.

A traveling salesman sitting behind her teased, "You haven't seen this country before, have you?"

"Was I so obvious?"

He laughed.

"You're right. I've never been east of Denver before."

Passengers began to exchange names and pleasantries as the light increased, but Sara was uncomfortable and stood to stretch her muscles. When she started to move around the car, her gun belt and holstered Colt were visible to the occupants of the seats behind her.

The salesman, who was returning to Chicago from his latest trip, stared in consternation when he realized the young woman, dressed in man's clothes, was armed. Two of the other passengers recognized her family name. Knowing of her parents and their reputation, they began to tell true stories which made Sara uncomfortable.

The salesman began to suspect he was regarded as a gullible dude and was being taken for a ride. One of the story-tellers recognized the signs and hastened to explain. "We're not making any of this up. This young woman's mother was a sworn marshal when she out-drew one of the worst killers in the entire west not so very many years ago."

The sincerity of the storytellers finally convinced him and he belatedly introduced himself. "Miss Storm. I'm Matt Hazlet. I'm delighted to make your acquaintance."

Sara was fascinated by the rolling vistas of prairie grasses stretching from the broad Platte to the horizon in all directions, dotted here and there by small towns. They stopped frequently, taking on fuel and water, or switching cars into and out of the train.

The day was well spent when the train rolled into the outskirts of Omaha at the easternmost border of Nebraska. Mr. Hazlet knew the city well and explained to Sara, "Omaha is one of the biggest and most important rail centers in the States. There are lines coming into the city from virtually every point of the compass. It's always been such an important rail hub it was chosen as the eastern terminus for the first transcontinental railroad, completed way back in '69. They did such a good job choosing the route then, the rails we rode in on use the rail bed laid down at that time."

***

Sara found a room in a boarding house not far from the station and was asleep almost before her head hit the pillow. Exhaustion, a very short night, and a very long day all combined to make her sleep soundly until shortly after dawn when a chorus of locomotive whistles startled her awake. She languished for several minutes, listening to the first stirrings of traffic on the street outside her window. The nearby rail yard continued to rouse, with the shriek of steam whistles near and far signaling a new day as the night retreated before the rising sun.

She scrubbed her face and hands in the wash basin in her room before repacking the few items she had not checked at the station. She gathered her belongings and descended the stairs to the dining room, where other guests and several workers from the nearby Union Station filled most of the tables. Sara worked her way through the crowd to an empty spot at a table on the far side of the room. She tried not to smile when the stunned silence turned to low-voiced murmurs as the observers realized the young woman in man's clothes was wearing a gun.

When Sara boarded her train about an hour later, she was startled to be greeted by Mr. Hazlet. "Good morning, Miss Storm. I didn't know I would be sharing your company again today." He continued his geography lesson of the day before. "This isn't the most direct route across the state from Omaha, but this Chicago Northwestern Express is by far the fastest. There are only three stops in Iowa, and then it's a straight run into Chicago. I'll be home tonight."

She responded, "I'm just following instructions on what route to take. Ma and Pa gave me directions. I'm on this train because they said so. Pa told me to change trains at Marshalltown and go northeast. I'll still have to change trains a time or two, though, before my final stop in his hometown of Canada."

Shortly after departing from the station, their train crossed high above the Missouri River on a double-track bridge. Mr. Hazlet said, "The original route was only a single-track line but was expanded to double-track sometime back in the 80's. Now we don't have to worry about sitting on a siding waiting for trains going in the other direction. That's the reason this line is so much faster than other routes between Omaha and Chicago."

Sara stared in fascination as she watched the broad valley of the Missouri disappear behind them. A sharply defined series of low hills changed to more gently rolling prairie. Farms and homesteads now dotted the countryside amidst a sea of grass.

Her stomach knotted and her face tightened when they thundered over one particularly high bridge spanning another river valley. Mr. Hazlet teased her, "We're only about 150 feet above the river. You shouldn't worry so much. The Kate Shelley Bridge hasn't fallen yet."

"Thanks. I think."

It was less than an hour later when they rolled

into the rail center of Marshalltown in central Iowa, where their train was crowded by other waiting trains sitting on parallel tracks. Mr. Hazlet explained, "Three rail lines intersect on the west end of the city, and a fourth on the east. They're all busy with so much traffic the switchmen in the control tower are busy around the clock."

When they braked to a stop at the station, Sara joined the line of disembarking passengers as Mr. Hazlet bade her goodbye. "I'll be getting off here for a few minutes while they switch locomotives. I'm glad to have met you, Sara Storm."

"I've learned a lot about Iowa from you. Thank you for everything."

She walked to the station and waited in line to claim her trunk from the baggage car. The station clerk said, "You don't have to pick up your trunk here. We'll transfer it to the Great Western depot for you."

"That'll save me a lot of trouble. Where's the other depot?"

The clerk grinned, "Through the station to the street, turn right and it's about two blocks. You have about an hour before your train is due to depart. If you want something to eat while you're waiting, the best place in the state to eat is Stone's Restaurant, just across the street."

Sara watched for a few minutes until her luggage was loaded on the transfer wagon before walking across the street to the wood-framed building. Her eyes swept the room while savory aromas wafted around her. A hat rack on the wall to her right took her Stetson. There was an empty spot at the counter, where she straddled the tall stool. There was little room to spare and the butt of her revolver bumped the man on her right. "Excuse me. There wasn't as much room as I thought."

"No harm done."

Sara's eyes widened when she realized her neighbor was wearing a blue uniform and a police badge. His eyes dropped to the gun butt protruding from her holster. "Young lady, would you mind explaining why you're wearing a gun?"

The room waited in dead silence.

"I don't mind at all. Let me show you." She slid off the stool, slowly slipping her left hand into her gun belt. Her fingers drew out an object she laid on the counter in front of the officer.

Everyone in view stared at the U.S. marshal star that Sara had 'borrowed' from her mother. "Is it against the law to wear a gun here?"

"No. It's just not something we see very often." His eyes met hers. "Officers usually wear their badges where they can be seen."

When she offered no explanation, he changed the subject. "I'd say from your accent you're not a local."

Sara nodded. "You're right. I'm from Colorado, about a day west of Denver. I'm just passing through to visit kin."

When conversation resumed she gave her order to the waitress who had witnessed everything. A few minutes later a heaping plate of food was placed in front of her, diverting her attention from the curious crowd. She ate steadily in spite of questions being directed at her while the clock on the wall kept moving. "I don't mean to be rude but my train leaves in a little while. I don't want to miss it." She paid for her meal, settled her Stetson on her head and bade the curious crowd goodbye. She could hear murmuring break out behind her as the closing door cut them off.

CHAPTER 3

Sara could barely contain her eagerness when the conductor walked through the car. "Canada! Next stop is Canada. All passengers for Canada." He stopped at Sara's seat and grinned. "That means you. You're the only passenger getting off here today."

The sun was near the horizon and the shadows were lengthening when Sara stepped down from the car, her eyes sweeping her surroundings. A short distance away, hills climbed steeply along the river valley where the small northeastern Iowa town sprawled. Trees hemmed in the station with a thick carpet of deep green on either side of the track.

When she turned toward the red clap-board depot, she saw a young couple waiting next to the building. Raising her voice enough to be heard over the noise of the locomotive, she called, "Melissa! Is that you?"

"Sara Storm! It can't be anyone else!" The young woman rushed to her, throwing her arms around Sara in a welcoming hug. They embraced for several moments until she stepped back to survey the much taller Sara. Her voice quivered with delight. "I'm so glad to finally be able to meet you after all these years."

Sara's own voice was unsteady as she looked at the much shorter Melissa. "I'm glad to finally meet you, too."

Melissa stepped back an arms-length, turning to the young man standing close beside her. Her face was aglow when his arm encircled her. She bubbled, "Sara. I'd like you to meet my husband, Wade Grant."

Sara's eyebrows rose as she offered her hand, scolding, "Melissa! You never wrote to tell me you were getting married."

"We were married two weeks ago last Saturday. When I got your last letter and learned you were coming to visit, I decided to surprise you." She smiled and giggled, "I'm so happy you decided to come visit us."

The train began to move with a rush of steam and a blast of the whistle, making conversation impossible until the noise receded. When quiet returned, Sara admitted, "You certainly did surprise me."

Melissa explained to Wade how she and Sara had become pen pals, making it easy to recognize one another. "I was too young to understand when Mother first tried to tell me about the mountains out West. She finally gave up and told me to write my cousin who lived there. Maybe *she* could make me understand."

She laughed delightedly, "I don't remember for sure if Sara ever did make me understand, but it was the beginning of years of letter-writing."

Melissa gazed up at Sara for a few seconds, as though asking herself a silent question. "My mother told me many times about meeting your mother for the first time." Her smile widened. "I think I'm seeing exactly what she saw, except you're not wearing a marshal's star."

Sara laughed nervously. "Please don't tell anyone else. Ma doesn't know it, but I sort of *borrowed* her star when I left home. You'd be surprised at how many arguments it's already prevented."

The station master interrupted, "Miss Storm, do you want your trunk stored here or do you want to take it with you?"

"I'll carry it," Wade offered. "It's only a couple of blocks." He followed the station master around the building while the two young women trailed behind.

The newlyweds' home was a small, white-painted bungalow crowding the street. A one-horse barn behind the house backed against the alley, next to a small fenced area making a corral for a sorrel gelding. Melissa explained, "My folks gave us the buggy for our wedding present. Wade's folks gave us the horse."

She swept her hand in an arc. "Canada is practically two towns. It was originally founded just east of here where Otter Creek joins the river. You can't see many details from here because it's almost a mile. Wade works at a grist mill tight against the river bank. They built it there so they could use the water power for the mill.

"The railroad came through where we are now because the river had formed a big oxbow and they had to avoid it. After that, the town really started to grow. Years later, another mill was built at this end of town, next to the creek for power. The town is so long and narrow, it's almost as though it were two separate towns."

Melissa drew Sara a few feet to one side for a better view as she pointed. "If you look just right, you can see the belfry on the school house, which marks the middle of town, and is the biggest building around."

Sara's eyes followed her pointed finger. Parts of an impressive two-story brick building showed above a cluster of trees in the distance. "That's quite a school. It makes Wilford's school house look positively puny."

Melissa beamed with civic pride at the compliment. The newlyweds' pride in their new home was also obvious. The house was small, with a kitchen and pantry opening onto the parlor, while two small bedrooms were connected by a short hallway.

Wade lit the kerosene lamps in each room while the cousins prepared the evening meal. Sitting out of the way, he grinned at the constant flow of conversation. When they were done eating, he chuckled, "Don't mind me. I can tell the two of you won't miss me if I go for a walk."

Melissa stared at him guiltily for a moment, smiling sheepishly. "You're right. We've left you out of the conversation."

The evening sped by. When Wade returned Sara greeted him, "I have something I want to show both of you." She opened her trunk, searching for a moment before she found a thick envelope. Selecting two folders, she handed them to Melissa. "These are for you to keep."

When Melissa unfolded the first folder, she exclaimed in delight. The Storm family stared back at her, dressed in their Sunday best. She admired the picture for several moments with Wade looking over her shoulder.

"There's another one." When Melissa opened the second folder, they both gaped in astonishment. The Storms were posed as before, but were now dressed identically in jeans, chambray work shirts, vests and Stetsons. Everyone sported a holstered revolver on their right hip. Melissa gawked, recognizing her Aunt Sue and Uncle Ted, both of whom had a marshal's star pinned to their vests.

"Ma wanted a traditional family portrait to share, plus one that shows us as we really are," said Sara. It should be obvious who's who," she pointed, "but that's Ma, Pa, Tim, Tom, Sally, and me. The pictures were taken last fall. The other kids are growing so fast it won't be long before they're all as tall as, or taller, than I am."

The next morning Melissa was cooking breakfast when Wade came in from caring for the horse. "Do the two of you have a plan for today?"

"We don't have a plan and haven't decided on anything yet." Melissa was flustered in a moment of indecision.

"Should I harness the horse to the buggy before I leave? You'll need it if you're going visiting."

Sara cleared her throat. "I don't want you to think I'm bragging, but I can handle the harnessing. I've worked with horses all my life."

His eyes widened. "Then I won't worry about the horse. The two of you can plan your day by yourselves. I'll see you after work."

Melissa knew word of her unconventional cousin would spread widely in the community; she had left both portraits at the local newspaper office, on display for several days in the front window, beneath the caption *Beth Storm's Son Ted and Family.*

The old woman's eyes were bright and twinkling, glistening with unshed tears. She stroked Sara's cheeks with her wrinkled fingers before embracing her. "I'm so glad you came to visit me." Sara's grandmother's voice was soft and lilting. "You look exactly like I remember your mother when your father brought her home to meet us. You're as beautiful as she was."

Tears of joy trickled down her withered cheeks as she gathered both young women into her arms. "Melissa, you're a dear to bring your cousin to me. I know all of our relatives are eager to meet her, too." She kissed both young women on the cheek.

Sara and Melissa drove many miles over the next few days, visiting their many relatives. Uncles and aunts were astonished by how much Sara resembled her mother. Cousins of all ages were open-mouthed with astonishment at her unconventional dress, especially her holstered Colt.

Melissa insisted they spend Saturday in town. Canada was like Wilford in that this was the day most of the surrounding population came to town for supplies and social gatherings. Canada's business district was only two blocks long, extending westward from the grist mill sitting on the river bank. The town's businesses ranged from a ramshackle wooden carpenter's building to substantial brick buildings, each bustling with customers on such a mild summer day.

The cousins staked claim to an iron bench in front of the millenary, where friends, relatives, and the curious stopped all afternoon to greet them.

Too soon, the week she had allotted for the visit

had flown by, and Sara waited at the station again with Melissa. She gave a teary Melissa a goodbye hug. "I'm so glad I could visit you and the rest of the family. If we never see each other again, I'll still remember these few days for the rest of my life." She brushed tears from her own cheeks. "I'll write and tell you about my travels when I get home. It'll likely be several weeks."

Melissa returned a goodbye hug, watching in fascination as her cousin's gun-belted figure disappeared aboard. Both waved as long as they could see each other, until the track curved and vanished into the screening trees.

CHAPTER 4

Sara changed trains at a junction less than a half-hour from Canada, near the edge of the Iowa prairie. Her new route followed a small stream which wound its way downhill into another river valley. The train was a local, comprised of a locomotive and tender, one passenger car and one baggage car. It clattered alongside the stream, stopping occasionally for a lone passenger standing along the track, for a solitary business sited in a clearing in the woods, or a small town crowded next to the winding river the stream had joined.

The valley was narrow but widened as the miles rolled slowly past before again beginning to narrow and deepen, the river growing in volume when many small tributaries added their flow. Sara was fascinated to see the tree-covered hillside converge and steepen toward the vertical, forcing the track ever closer to the river.

The train twisted around a sharp bend and stopped at a small depot. She gazed out the open window at the building, perched on a spit of ground overlooking the tracks and the confluence of two rivers. Another passenger observed, "We're less than ten miles from the Mississippi. This station is the last on this line."

Shaking her head, Sara said, "This state has a lot of surprises. I'd never have guessed it would have anything that looked so much like mountains."

A laugh. "There are bluffs along the Mississippi

where you could fall most of five hundred feet before you wound up in the river. That's why this area is known as the Switzerland of Iowa."

They rattled along beside the meandering river, the cars rocking gently while miles passed slowly. They rounded one particularly towering bluff and the horizon suddenly fell away, revealing the broad expanse of the native Americans' Father of Waters, the Mississippi, to the east.

Sara stared in awe when the river they had been following dwindled to insignificance, merging with the waters of the Mississippi and disappearing, leaving no trace. The conductor called, "End of the line! All passengers must disembark."

Gathering her luggage, Sara joined the few remaining passengers who got off, and stood beside the locomotive puffing smoke on the west side of another tiny station. A main-line set of tracks swept past on the east side of the depot. When the agent returned from unloading the mail and freight, he asked, "Where you bound for?"

"Peoria, Illinois."

He took the ticket she offered and glanced at it. "The next southbound is due in an hour and a half. You'll take it to Davenport and change for Peoria. If you're hungry and want something to eat, there's a hash-house just up the tracks."

The shadows cast by the towering bluffs lengthened on the surface of the river while Sara watched from an uncomfortable hard wooden bench. She was fascinated by the sight of watercraft of many types, creeping northward against the current, or hurrying swiftly southward with the current's aid. The station was deep in the shadow of the bluff to the west when a whistle from upstream sent her scurrying back to the station.

Night fell while her train rattled ever southward, the darkness total before she arrived at the depot in Davenport. She checked the schedule board to find her next train was due to depart at 2:06 in the full darkness of morning. She had checked her luggage through to Peoria so she found an unoccupied bench, leaned back with her head against the wall, and promptly went to sleep.

Her internal alarm woke her some time later. A glance at the huge station clock told her she had about fifteen minutes before departure. When she arrived at the platform the conductor was calling, "All aboard! Peoria and points south. All aboard!"

The empty car was dimly lit by kerosene lamps when Sara selected a front seat that allowed her to stretch out her long legs. After the conductor punched her ticket, she made herself as comfortable as possible, pulling her Stetson low over her eyes, falling asleep in a few minutes.

Much later she was awakened by a hand on her shoulder. A timid voice asked. "May I sit here?" She swept her Stetson aside to see an elderly woman standing in the aisle, watching her apprehensively.

"Of course. Just give me a moment." Full sunshine was streaming through the windows across the aisle when she stood to stretch sleep-stiffened muscles and adjust her gun belt. Eyebrows rose throughout the car.

"You're a woman!" the now-seated elderly lady gasped.

"Yes, ma'am. I am." While stretching, she had seen that the car was virtually full and apologized, "I'm sorry to have kept you standing. It was very late when I boarded and I went straight to sleep." She introduced herself. "I'm Sara Storm and headed for Peoria. Could you tell me what time it is, and where we are?"

Her companion smiled, "I'm Mildred Black. We're on schedule. It's just after eight and we're about an hour from Peoria."

Mildred was fascinated and plied Sara with questions about herself and her unusual dress. She responded with no hesitation and had no problem overhearing the low murmur of voices as her replies rippled from one row of passengers to another behind them.

Sara asked, "Do you live in Peoria?"

"I've lived there almost all of my life. I'm on my way home from visiting my son in Eagleton."

"If you've lived in Peoria for many years, you may have known my great-grandmother."

"What's her name?"

"Ruth Ashworth. She died a few years ago. One of her daughters owns the newspaper, *The Peoria Reporter*. I'm on my way to visit her and the rest of the kin I've never met."

Mildred's eyes glistened. "Aye. Ruth was a friend for many years. You must be June's granddaughter. I remember well the day your mother and father came to town, both of them wearing their marshal's stars. That was an event talked about for many a day."

Sara smiled as she could hear the gasps quickly travel the length of the car and someone exclaimed, "Her *mother* was a marshal!"

When they arrived in Peoria, she was the first to step down from the train. She then turned to help Mildred from the car, and bid her goodbye. Mildred shook her head. "My son is here to pick me up. Let us give you a ride to the newspaper office." Before Sara could say anything, Mildred brushed her objection aside. "Please don't refuse me. I owe it to the memory of an old friend to show her kin around."

Sara was soon standing on a wide sidewalk in front of a substantial brick building, waving goodbye to Mildred and her son. There was a brightly painted sign in the window identifying *THE PEORIA REPORTER*. When she walked in, an excited voice greeted her, "Sara Storm! Welcome to Peoria!"

A gray-haired woman rose from her desk along the back wall, hurried toward her, and enveloped her in such an enthusiastic hug it lifted her heels off the floor. "I'm your great-aunt, May. I'd imagine your mother has told you all about me."

They exchanged broad grins. "She has. Many times," Sara replied.

May released Sara as four younger women gathered around them. "These ladies are only some of your relatives. My daughter, Lucy, my nieces, Ellie and Anne," she smiled as she pointed out each woman. "The youngest is Anne's daughter, June. She's named after your grandmother."

They were interrupted by a burst of noise when a door opened in the back of the room and a man entered the office. The sudden clatter of machines died with the closing door. "May, we just finished today's run." He offered Sara his hand in welcome. "I'm Marvin, Lucy's husband. You must be Sara Storm." He grinned widely. "May never leaves the office before we finish the day's print run. She thinks she's our good-luck charm and nothing will break if she's here. It's now safe for her to leave."

***

Sara stayed at May's home, which she shared with Lucy and her husband, Marvin, the chief press operator for the newspaper. When the dishes were washed, dried and put away, they moved to the open porch surrounding the house to enjoy the cool breeze after a hot day.

Sara squirmed in her chair until she was comfortable before speaking. "I doubt there are very many women who run a newspaper, much less own one. How did you accomplish it?"

May thought for a moment, then said, "My future husband, Norman, hired me as a women's society reporter. We were married a year later. I was widowed young, left with two small daughters to rear, and was faced with the decision to sell the paper or run it myself."

Her smile was thin, her eyes remote. "Everyone expected me to sell out because they didn't think a woman could run a successful newspaper, even if it was only a small weekly at the time."

"That sort of attitude made me mad. I decided

I was going to make a success of the paper and rub the doubters' noses in it." She scowled briefly before smiling and continuing her story. "Over the years, several city and county officials ignored the power of a female editor. I've helped put more than one in jail for graft and corruption. I guess I'm a lot like your mother; I was too mad at the idiots of the world not to fight back. I made a success of my life and my business."

Sara's smile matched May's as she recalled stories her mother had told her. "It sounds to me as though you are exactly like my mother. You both have done your best to make this a better world. The only difference is you used a pen instead of a gun."

May nodded in agreement. "I never thought of it in quite that light, but you're right."

Sara had planned to spend a week in Peoria and the time seemed to evaporate like smoke. Still another morning brightened to find her at the depot, with May, Ellie and June there to see her off. A waiting locomotive puffed softly in the background while freight and passengers were loaded and unloaded.

June's admiration was shining in her eyes as she bubbled, "We have something we want you to take with you." She handed Sara a folded newspaper, her anticipation obvious.

When Sara unfolded it, she gasped at the picture centered on the front page. It was the portrait of her family dressed in their work clothes with their guns. The accompanying caption was under May's byline:

The arduous task of an editor

rarely allows one an opportunity to

brag to the world about your own

family. This is one of those rare occasions.

Many of our older readers may yet

recall when my niece Sue and her

husband, Ted Storm, both U.S. Marshals,

graced our city with their presence almost

twenty years ago. Their legacy lives on, and

my own family has been blessed the last few

days by the presence of their eldest, Sara.

The conductor called, "All aboard!"

Sara choked a farewell before boarding, giving a last wave as the whistle shrilled and the train began to move.

CHAPTER 5

Sara stood at the head of one of the many stairways opening onto the lower platforms of Chicago's LaSalle Street Station. She unobtrusively stretched, trying to loosen travel-stiffened muscles, while watching, fascinated, the mass of humanity flowing to and from a multitude of waiting trains.

She gathered her bags before resuming her trek toward the central ticketing area but stopped abruptly when a uniformed policeman blocked her path. She asked mildly, "Is there something I can do for you?"

The officer was visibly tense. "Young lady, are you aware it's against the law to carry a gun here?"

"No, I wasn't aware. However, let me put your mind at ease."

The officer's brows rose when Sara set her bag on the floor, his eyes growing wary when her hand moved to her gun belt. She extended her right hand, the marshal's star in the palm of her hand reflecting the available light.

He stared, dumbfounded. "Might I suggest you wear it where it people can see it. You've already caused a near-panic among some of our local population."

Sara smiled and pinned the star to her vest. "I'll do so. Thank you for your advice." At his nod, she continued on her way, glancing back once to see him standing where she left him, a bewildered expression on his face.

Later, she was waiting her turn in line to escape the crush filling the ladies' powder room when she became aware of angry voices filtering in from outside the door. The loudest penetrated through the open doorway, demanding, "You must clear the way! Mrs. Hollingsworth demands her privacy!"

Mrs. Thomas Wilson Hollingsworth IV, Grande Dame of Chicago's North Side social elite, seethed in disgust while her retinue tried to force their way to the head of the line. Her face was serene from a lifetime of practice as she followed, silently cursing the great unwashed crowd of peasants blocking her way. She was almost at the doorway when a tall figure in man's clothes suddenly appeared from inside. She exploded, her voice rising in a screech of indignation heard throughout the rotunda. "Young man! How dare you use the ladies' powder room?"

Sara glared at the red-faced dowager, keeping rein on her own temper. "If you think I'm a man, you'd better get your eyes checked!"

Mrs. Hollingsworth stared at the apparition, horrified and shocked into silence. Her mind struggled to accept the fact the tall figure facing her was a young woman wearing man's clothes, a gun, and most horrendous of all, a marshal's star. Her genteel world of stability and tradition collapsed; she swooned.

Watching in dismay that rapidly turned to disgust, Sara saw hands surreptitiously break the dowager's fall at the last instant. She turned and forced her way back into the powder room, where she filled her Stetson with water from the faucet, making as much noise as possible. The mob of other women watched, mystified, when she poured the water down the drain.

It was only a short time before Sara was back outside. The attendants had moved their charge to a sitting position against the wall and she offered her Stetson, suggesting, "Here, take this. Pour it over her head. That'll bring her around."

Winifred Hollingsworth leapt to her feet, screeching, "Don't you dare!" She exploded in a tirade, aimed at the crowd of unwashed trash surrounding her. Sara and the crowd watched in icy contempt until the combined efforts of the embarrassed attendants finally staunched the outburst.

Sara had held her Stetson high while a rumble of rising anger erupted from the crowd. Fear began to creep into Winifred's eyes as realization of the precarious situation she had gotten herself into began to dawn. Sara glared at her while the crowd quieted, waiting. It exploded with laughter when she righted the empty Stetson and settled it on her long brown hair.

She raised her hand and the laughter died. "That's all, folks. Let's break it up." Her cold eyes met Winifred's. "I'd suggest you get out of here before you dig yourself in any deeper."

The watching crowd began to drift off. Winifred was consumed by rage and tried to stare down the young woman who had so humiliated her. She managed to hold her tongue as she glared at her tormenter, suddenly becoming aware of the eyes that glared back at her; cold, alert and totally unafraid. She shivered, her own eyes dropping before she spun on her heel and stormed off in a fury, headed for the main exit while her retinue trailed helplessly behind.

***

The next day, in the office of *The Peoria Reporter*, Sara's cousin Lucy was busy at her desk, skimming the many newspapers they subscribed to, and on occasion reprinted stories from. She suddenly sat up, calling to her mother, "I think you'd be interested in this article, whether we print it or not." May joined her, reading from the society page of a Chicago paper:

Unnamed sources report a

certain member of society from the near-

north side was overheard loudly

declaring in public her contempt for the

common people. The incident occurred

in the LaSalle Street Station yesterday,

where she was promptly rebuked by an

unnamed female U. S. Marshal.

May grinned and said, "It had to be Sara. She knows how to stir people up, just as her mother does."

***

Sara was sitting at a window, watching passengers scurry to and from the train as it sat on a siding in Gary, Indiana. The warning wail of a whistle was sounding when a portly man staggered toward the front steps of her car. Close behind, but obviously not traveling with him, she could see a young darkskinned woman, burdened with luggage and trailed by two small children, hurrying across the platform in his wake.

The portly man clambered aboard and staggered down the aisle, sinking heavily into the seat immediately ahead of hers. He ignored his surroundings, rolled his head back, and stared at the ceiling. The mother and children took the sole remaining seat immediately in front of him.

Sara watched when he tipped his head forward, suddenly uttering a curse. "You worthless trash! Get out of here." The car was suddenly silent. The mother flinched as though she had been whipped.

Sara's alto carried clearly. "Mister! You have thirty seconds to apologize or get off this train."

The drunk sneered, twisting toward her; a blast of whiskey-laden breath hit her in the face. "Who's going to make me?"

Sara sprang to her feet, her revolver in her hand, the front sight digging into the underside of his jaw. "Me and my Colt. You just made your choice. On your feet! You're leaving."

His florid face paled as he attempted to protest. The blast of the whistle and the conductor's *All Aboard* from the next car cut him short. When Sara pressed harder, the drunk twisted away from the gun sight and staggered to his feet, stumbling for the door. They were at the top step and the platform was starting to slide past when he tried again to protest. "You can't do this to me! I'm..."

She dropped the revolver into her holster, grasped the drunk by the collar and the seat of his pants, and heaved. He was still upright when his feet hit the platform but his momentum and lack of equilibrium combined and he pitched forward on his face. Sara winced at the sight when he rolled over and sat up, blood pouring from his nose.

She returned from the steps to the now silent car and quickly surveyed the watching passengers. Some avoided her glance; others nodded approval; a few glared. She greeted the three faces in the front seat and smiled. "He won't be bothering you anymore. Where are you headed?"

The mother's voice trembled. "Lagrange. Thank you for saving us." She introduced her small family. "I'm Anna Brown, and these are my children, Rebecca and Jason."

She gently patted the woman's shoulder. "I'm Sara Storm, and headed for Philadelphia. I'll ride with you until you get off." The hum of conversation in the car resumed. She moved her things forward to the now-vacant seat, placed her ticket in the holder at the window, and tried to find a comfortable position.

The conductor entered the car a few minutes later, calling for tickets. Following previous stops, it had usually taken only a few minutes for him to check and punch tickets. This time it seemed to be taking much longer than usual, as Sara could hear many low-voiced conversations from behind her.

"Miss, I'd like to talk to you for a minute."

Sara turned from the window to see the conductor, his face twisted in a scowl. Her stomach tightened.

"What can I do for you?"

"I understand you threw a man off this train. Do you have any idea who he is?"

"No. I don't know and I don't really care! He was falling-down drunk and abusing other passengers." The conductor goggled at her as she continued. "I suppose I could've waited until we left the station and then arrested him for disturbing the peace."

The conductor's eyes blazed in anger until he focused on the star pinned to her vest. His eyes widened in astonishment. When he noticed her revolver, his jaw dropped.

A gentle voice interrupted, "Excuse me, but I would like to say something about this young lady's actions." Both turned toward the speaker.

Sara's jaw dropped. Three women were standing in the aisle, dressed in long black dresses and white hoods.

The conductor sighed, "Go ahead, Sister."

Sara realized the trio must be nuns, the first she had ever seen.

The eldest nun spoke for the group, "We don't want to interfere, but we feel this young woman has demonstrated our Lord's command to care for the helpless, even as did the Good Samaritan." She smiled serenely. "We believe there should be no repercussions directed at this young woman because of her defense of the helpless."

Sara flushed, realizing her own impetuousness.

The conductor stared at the nun for a moment, glared at Sara, and grumbled, "Oh! All right! When you have support like these there's nothing I can do." He shrugged. "You might want to know the man you threw off back there was United States Representative Wilson Rawlings from Illinois. He might prove to be a bit upset."

When the conductor moved on to collect the last of the tickets, Sara sank heavily into her seat, her throat dry and her knees weak.

One of the nuns asked, "Would you mind if I sat with you?"

Her voice was suddenly raspy. "You're welcome to sit with me."

CHAPTER 6

The eldest nun moved up to sit with Sara, while her two companions occupied the seat she had just vacated. "I'm Sister Mary Elizabeth. This is Sister Mary Anne, and that's Sister Mary Ruth."

Sara nodded in acknowledgement at each introduction, trying to keep her nervousness from being obvious.

"I wish more people would stand up for the oppressed, as you did, and as our Lord instructed us to do." An impish smile showed momentarily. "In spite of the fact you didn't turn the other cheek, as we were also instructed."

The nun continued with a laugh. "I'm not scolding, mind you. I have to admit His admonishment to us is a goal few people often attain. Where're you from? You certainly don't dress like most young women your age."

Sara began to relax as the nuns' questions encouraged her to tell of her home in the mountains of Colorado, and how her mother had been a marshal since before her birth. The nuns were good conversationalists, drawing her into topics as widely diverse as religion and the wildlife in her familiar mountains.

The small family under Sara's protection disembarked when the train stopped in Lagrange, Indiana. The young mother took her hand for a moment, her eyes misty. "Bless you. We will never forget your kindness."

Sara reddened. "I don't like bullies of any stripe. No one has the right to do something like that to you." The children shyly smiled and followed their mother from the train.

Sister Mary Elizabeth's serene face hid a broad mental smile. *This young lady is a perfect example of Max Golden's credo.* She fondly recalled the battered face of one of her more outspoken parishioners, whose nose had been broken several times in his bare-knuckle fights in the ring. *As direct and effective as a hard right to the chin. This young woman is such a paradox. So confident and capable, able to handle a dangerous situation, but innocent and naïve. It obviously never occurred to her someone could hate another person simply because of the color of their skin.*

The time passed swiftly for Sara and she was surprised when the train pulled into the station in Toledo. She knew she would have to change trains, resulting in an extended layover; but she was in no hurry, and she continued chatting with the nuns while other passengers filed off.

When she stepped onto the platform she was immediately accosted by two men wearing railroad detective badges. "Hold it right there, Miss. You're under arrest for assaulting a United States Congressman."

She bristled and snapped, her voice and eyes frigid, "Do you think you can arrest a U.S. marshal? That damn fool congressman has immunity from assault charges only when he's on the floor of the House."

Her new friends moved to form a human barrier between Sara and the detectives, while the officers gaped at the star pinned to Sara's vest.

Sister Mary Elizabeth's gentle voice was firm. "Gentlemen. There is no need to be so uncivil. This young woman simply defended a young mother with two children from a drunken, ill-mannered lout. I would suggest you report back to the congressman any attempt to cause further distress for this young woman would be extremely detrimental to his career."

Chastened, the detectives retreated in confusion for an extended argument. Finally surrendering with poor grace, they settled for statements from Sara and the three nuns before retreating into the crowd.

Sara watched them until they disappeared, scolding herself for her intemperate behavior. When Sister Mary Elizabeth turned to her, she apologized. "I'm sorry if I caused you any trouble, and ashamed of myself for having done so. I appreciate your standing up for me."

The Sister waved the apology aside. "You have nothing to be ashamed of," she said as she grinned widely. "Although you didn't say so in so many words, you made it plain you're not much interested in organized religion. Your acts of compassion, even if somewhat unorthodox, are a better sermon than most delivered from any pulpit." She hugged a red-faced Sara. "God be with you, Sara Storm."

***

Sara's arrival at the Philadelphia station was uneventful except for the stares directed at her unusual attire. She had claimed her luggage and was carrying it across the rotunda toward the main entrance when a young woman about her own age hurried in the door.

Sara watched warily, ready to dodge to avoid a

collision. The other young woman abruptly altered course directly toward her, her face hopeful. "Would you be Sara Storm?"

"Yes, I'm Sara. You would be...?"

She offered her hand. "I'm your cousin, Heather White." Her own relief was obvious when she apologized. "We got your telegram yesterday telling us on which train you'd be arriving. I was supposed to be here an hour ago, but a runaway team caused a wreck and tied up traffic. I'm sorry I was late getting here to meet you."

Sara smiled. "I know too much about runaway horses to let it bother me."

Heather tried not to stare at the cousin she had met for the first time. Her gaze took in the star pinned to Sara's vest before dropping to the revolver in her holster. Her eyes widened. "You're a marshal, just like your mother?"

Sara found herself caught in a quandary of her own making. She didn't yet know her cousin, so she lied, feeling guilty. "Yes."

Heather stared in silent awe for a moment before laughing nervously. She led the way to a hack waiting at the curb, still chattering nervously. When the driver finished loading the luggage, the two young women climbed aboard.

Heather continued a non-stop monologue, describing the many points of interest they passed until Sara interrupted softly, "Heather, I know you're my cousin, but just how are we related?"

Her face reddened. "Forgive me. I've been babbling. I don't usually do that." She was silent for a moment, thinking. "Your great-grandfather was my father's much older cousin. When your mother refused to stay in Philadelphia and take over running the factory, he persuaded my father to go to work for him. No one else in the family wanted anything to do with the factory, so Father held out until he got a written contract stating he would inherit the company."

Heather's face darkened. "Don't hate me, but my father was never as happy as the day the old man died. He was mean, domineering and vindictive. Your parents were very wise indeed they didn't stay to work for him."

Her set face lightened. "Your great-grandmother was a saint to have lived with him as long as she did. In fact, my own parents gave me her middle name in her honor." She sobered. "I just hope I can live up to her reputation."

During Sara's visit in Philadelphia she was escorted all over the city, accompanied by a gaggle of fascinated cousins of both sexes, intent on showing her the many famous sites scattered throughout the city. She stood, awed, as she felt the solemn silence of Independence Hall and stood before the majestic Liberty Bell.

The morning of her last day in the city she approached Heather's father, who was sipping a cup of coffee in his study. "I have a letter my mother asked me to give to you."

Warren White eyed her somewhat warily despite the fact he had come to know her well during her short stay. He took the plain white envelope and extracted a single sheet of paper.

Mr. Warren White,

I want to assure you that my

daughter's trip to Philadelphia is strictly

to visit with her extended family. I pray

you do NOT feel she is in any

manner trying to recover my family's

inheritance. I have absolutely no

interest in doing so.

Best wishes from my family to yours.

Sue Storm.

Warring emotions were evident on his face when he raised his eyes to meet hers. Sara explained, "Mother let me read the letter before she gave it to me. She told me to assure you that she is happy with her own life, and all the money in the world could not make her happier. She was very adamant and wanted me to emphasize she has no interest in the factory."

The tension faded from his eyes when she continued. "I'm sure Heather didn't fully realize what all she was telling me when we rode here from the station. She confirmed to me that anyone who ever worked for my great-grandfather deserved every cent they ever earned from him."

He eyed her for several moments before extending his hand, his lips curving into a smile. "Your mother is a very astute woman. Please thank her for me."

***

Sara's first sight in Washington was the tip of the Washington Monument, showing above the trees in the distance, shining brightly in the sun of the late June day. The young woman who had been her seatmate caught a glimpse of the pinnacle at the same time and asked, "What in the world is that?"

Sara explained, "It's the Washington Monument. The tip is 550 feet high and dominates the entire Capitol. You can climb the stairs or ride an elevator to the top and view the whole city."

An older man was sitting behind them and had been conversing with them all the way from Baltimore. He smiled and said, "It sounds as though you've been here before."

"No. I haven't," she admitted sheepishly. "My parents visited Washington before I was born and told me and by brothers and sister about it many times. I'm looking forward to seeing everything for myself."

I hope the years are as kind to you and you can share this memory as well. It's nice to see a youngster so excited about Washington, the gentlemen thought to himself before responding. "I hope you enjoy your visit to the Monument. I'm afraid it would be a bit beyond me to climb the stairs."

They continued chatting while the spire grew closer until it was blanked from view by a massive roof.

Sara joined the line of passengers to exit the crowded car, following them along the platform to wait at the baggage car. After claiming hers, she headed through the crowded terminal to the street with a bag in each hand.

She hailed a hack whose bored driver was half-asleep. When he realized the young man awaiting him was really a young woman, he started fully awake. His jaw dropped and his eyes widened at the sight of her gun and marshal's star.

"Is the Harmon House still a good place to stay?"

"Aye, it is. You've been here before?"

"No. My parents stayed there years ago."

The hack dropped her at the Harmon House a few minutes later. The driver offered, "I'll wait while you check to see if they have a room for you. If they don't, there are similar places which would treat you right."

"I appreciate the ride. If they have a room I'll stay here. If I need a hack to get around town, who should I ask for?"

"Just tell the desk you need Ellie Smith. They'll know how to get in touch with me."

When the gray-haired clerk looked up, Sara asked, "Could I get a room for several days?"

The eyes in the lined face widened in amazed recognition. "Mrs. Storm. It's a pleasure to have you back with us."

Sara's spirits lifted. "You're not quite right. I'm

her daughter."

The old man's smile remained. "You are most welcome here, as she would be." Bob Whitmore beamed, "I do have a room for you. I'd throw someone else out in the street to make room if I didn't."

Sara laughed, "I'm glad you don't have to. I'll take the room as soon as I send my driver on his way."

CHAPTER 7

Sara spent some time in her room, changing from her rider's clothing to her green dress and matching hat. Refreshed and relaxed, she left the hotel carrying the handbag she had borrowed from her mother. The bag was heavy and she held it tightly on a strap over her shoulder. Secreted within it were her traveling money, her mother's marshal's star, and her gun belt wrapped around her Colt.

She turned west when she left the Harmon House, heading for the Washington Monument. The tip of the monument winked in and out of view, hidden by screening trees and buildings. In no hurry, she stopped often to window shop.

Traffic was heavy, both pedestrian and vehicular, and after several blocks she took shelter in a small alcove to get out of the crush for a few minutes. Fascinated by the constant bustle of traffic, she was mystified by the many inquiring stares directed her way.

A passing middle-aged woman stopped and asked, "I don't want you to think I'm nosey, but I just have to satisfy my own curiosity. Are you from out West?"

"I'm from Colorado, and I have a question of my own. Why does it seem so obvious to you I'm from out of town?"

"Young lady, there are several clues. It's obvious from the tan line on your face you've spent a lot of time in the sun, but the line doesn't match your hat. Other clues are the way you stand and the way you walk. Being almost a head taller than most of the men in this town also draws everyone's attention. Everything about you marks you as an unusual woman.

"Now, my curiosity has been satisfied. I'll not embarrass you any further."

Nonplussed, Sara watched the curious but good-hearted lady continue her way down the street.

Her first full view of the beauty of the Mall made her catch her breath as she took in the grassy expanse extending westward from the Capitol. When she reached the monument, she joined a line inching its way toward the entrance at the base of the tower. The sun was hot and she was grateful when she reached the shade of the monument as she waited in line for entrance to the elevator.

The steam-powered elevator took twelve minutes to reach the observation deck. Voices of other visitors erupted in awe and wonder as they crowded to the windows to overlook the city and Capitol grounds so far below. She waited patiently for her turn at the tiny windows. When it was her turn, she eyed the vista below, comparing it to her memories of the stories told by her parents. She started when a voice next to her ear asked, "Have you ever been here before?"

She turned to face a uniformed guide. "No, I haven't. My parents visited the monument before I was born. The stories they told us made me want to see it for myself."

He nodded. "There are more people than you might think who come through feeling the same.

Whatever their reasoning, a lot of people are drawn back again and again."

***

Sara spent several days exploring the buildings and monuments scattered around the Capitol which were so much a part of her country's history. One mid-afternoon, she was passing the portal guarding the main entrance to the Department of Justice when she yielded to a sudden impulse and turned to go inside.

The light was subdued, requiring a few moments before her eyes adjusted enough for her to gaze in wonder at the soaring ceiling above her. The rotunda was surrounded by multiple levels of balconies, all dwarfed by the dome rising above them. Taking time to absorb it all, her eyes moved from one carved marble edifice to another.

When her gaze returned to the main floor, she could see signs identifying many different branches and offices of the Department of Justice. Scanning each in turn, she spotted a booth with the sign *Information* in the middle of the rotunda floor.

A steady stream of people flowed between her and the booth, with an attendant background hum of voices. She started toward the booth at an angle, but the first sight of the man behind the counter caused warning flags to fly in her mind. The young man's cold face was stamped with an arrogant sneer. He was dressed in what she presumed to be the height of fashion.

His eyes met hers but he ignored her approach until she asked in a voice that carried clearly, "Could you tell me if any of three men still work for the Marshal Service? Their names are Leonard Hopkins, Wilbur Anderson, and Abe Swanson."

Mister Arrogance sneered, "Never heard of them."

Her temper rose at his instant dismissal, but she kept her voice even. "Where might I find someone who would know?"

He snarled, "Who wants to know?"

Her tone was cold, "I'm Sara Storm. Both my mother and father were once U. S. marshals and worked with all three of them."

He snorted in disbelief.

Sara had moved within arm's length; now her hand shot out and her fingers twisted deep in the fine material of the man's fancy shirt. Years of hard physical labor had given her tremendous strength in the hand and arm that suddenly dragged Mister Arrogance from his stool and half-way across the counter, his face only inches from hers.

When she twisted harder on the fabric, threatening to choke the breath from him, his face changed from red to white. She scolded him in a voice the more menacing for its gentleness. "Listen to me, you horse's ass. You'd better learn some manners real fast or you're going to get that fancy tie shoved down your throat. Sideways."

Mister Arrogance found himself staring at eyes which would make ice seem warm. He tried to twist away as the pressure on his throat increased, unable to speak because the unbelievable power in the woman's grip held him mute and helpless.

Sara's fingers were twisted tightly in his shirt, waiting for a response, when a mild voice interrupted. "Excuse me, Miss Storm. I couldn't help but overhear your name, and the names you asked about. If you would come to my office I believe I could help you."

She turned to meet the eyes of a man about her father's age. "Mister?"

"The name's Bailey."

She met his unwavering eyes before turning to her victim, whose face was starting to turn blue as his hands vainly tried to break her grip. Her cold stare held his eyes for a few seconds before she threw him in the direction of his chair without another word. He crashed into it but missed the seat and fell to the floor. Crumpled on the floor, his shuddering gasps echoed in the now-silent rotunda.

"Well, Mr. Bailey, why don't you lead?" She ignored the shocked stares from the onlookers and followed him toward the nearest stairs.

Her guide said nothing while they climbed several flights of stairs. A long hallway led to a door with a sign, *Marshal Service, Special Services, R. Bailey, Commander*. She followed him into a large office.

He instructed the clerk behind the desk at the front, "Don't disturb us. I'll get my messages later."

She followed him into an inner office and waited while he closed the massive door. Indicating a chair, he said, "Miss Storm, please sit down. I'll be happy to tell you about the men you asked about."

Sara felt the entire situation was rather odd, but the comforting weight of her Colt in her handbag gave her confidence. "Thank you."

Mr. Bailey waited until she was seated before moving to a chair behind the massive desk facing her. "First of all, Leonard Hopkins retired about five years ago and moved to a somewhat more temperate climate in Pennsylvania. Abe Swanson was promoted to an administrative position and is working in another department here in Washington. Wilbur Anderson was killed in the line of duty a few months after your parents left Washington."

"You knew my parents?"

"No. I was never fortunate enough to have met them. Twenty years ago, when they were here in D.C., I was the most junior of junior agents and I wasn't allowed anywhere near them. I wish I had been able to meet them because I've always admired their integrity." His demeanor abruptly changed from warm and friendly to harsh and penetrating. "Does their daughter share that same integrity?"

Sara was startled but not intimidated. Holding her tongue, she tried to account for the sudden change of attitude. "I'm their daughter. That fact should satisfy most people."

"That's true, but I have a very good reason to know everything about you. I need to know if you are a short-tempered, damn-fool youngster, or a level-headed, inexperienced, foolish youngster who lost her temper downstairs. Why don't you tell me about yourself?"

Sara flushed, but after a moment of reflection, she condensed her life and experience on the ranch into a few sentences. "I've always wanted to see Washington after hearing the stories Ma and Pa told us. I've always wanted to meet relatives I've seen pictures of and exchanged letters with. My parents told me I could do both when I reached eighteen, so here I am."

She was still flushed at his implication. "I suppose it was foolish, but I *borrowed* my mother's marshal's star, thinking it would help keep me out of trouble." She elaborated how she used it with two policemen and how it cowed the grand dame in Chicago.

He chuckled at the fake swoon and hatful of water, but scowled when she related the ejection of the Congressman from the rail car. "I have two things to say." He grinned wickedly. "First, ignorance can be cured."

Sara reddened.

"Stupidity cannot, but it certainly doesn't apply here." He leaned back in his chair, staring at nothing for several moments while she waited nervously. "Are you as good with a gun as your mother and father?"

Still pink, she answered soberly. "Ma told me once I was faster than she ever was."

"Could you demonstrate how fast you are, preferably as soon as possible?"

"Would right now be soon enough?"

His eyebrows rose.

She picked up the handbag by her chair and

opened it before unwinding the belt from around the holster, buckling it over her dress before carefully drawing the gun. "I've never worn my gun while wearing a dress before, but I can give you a good idea of my speed."

Approaching the desk, she broke the action. Ejecting the bullets from the cylinder, she laid them on the desk. Showing him the empty cylinder, she slipped it back in her holster. She smiled. "I was taught that it's always good etiquette to prove you can't accidently shoot someone."

She stepped back from the desk before turning sideways to Mr. Bailey. Flexing her knees slightly, her hand moved to her side before flashing downward and upward, faster than his eye could follow. The click of the falling hammer echoed in the room.

He stared at her, unable to believe she could move so fast.

She returned to his desk, gathering the cartridges before reloading her revolver in seconds. She spun the cylinder, placing the hammer above the empty chamber. Slipping it back into her holster with one fluid motion born of long practice, she unbuckled the belt and returned it to her handbag.

"Sara, would you like to officially become a United States marshal?" Mr. Bailey beamed. "You could join your mother in your own right as one of the very few women who have ever been federal marshals."

CHAPTER 8

Sara gaped in open-mouthed astonishment for several seconds before she could recover her voice. "I've always admired my mother and what she's been able to accomplish in her life. Of course I'd be honored to be a marshal, just like she was!" She gave him a suspicious glare. "What's the catch?"

Bailey smiled and answered, "I may have a job for you, but I must emphasize at the moment it's only a possibility. If you're willing to be sworn in, subject to the approval of the other parties involved, I have a mission you would be uniquely qualified for."

He picked up the telephone sitting on his desk. "Operator. Would you please connect me with Director Hodges' office?"

She was still bewildered when he spoke again, "This is Mr. Bailey. If the Director is in, I'd like to come over for a few minutes."

After another moment, he hung up, nodding in satisfaction. "Let's go visit one of the concerned parties. We'll find out right now if he still has need of someone with your special qualifications."

Ten minutes of walking the hallways within the building brought them to an office door labeled *United States Secret Service: V Hodges, Director*. A young clerk greeted them, "Mr. Hodges is expecting you. Go right in."

They entered an inner office where a man somewhat younger than Mr. Bailey was staring at a map on the wall. He turned to greet them, his eyes widening upon seeing Sara.

Mr. Bailey made the introduction. "Vic Hodges, this is Sara Storm. She's visiting from Colorado." He grinned at the other man's obvious confusion. "Vic, do you remember the discussion we had a few days ago about our limited options in the Harrison situation?"

"Of course. Have you found a solution for our dilemma?"

"I just introduced you to the solution to our joint problem."

Visibly startled, Hodges eyed Bailey before his eyes shifted to Sara. "Miss Storm, don't be insulted if I seem doubtful about your abilities. You look mighty young to be of any help to the Secret Service."

Sara said nothing, leaving everything to Mr. Bailey.

"Let's sit down and I'll explain everything." When they were comfortable, he continued, "Vic, think back about twenty years to when we were both new offi-cers. Do you remember a lady marshal and her hus-band from Colorado who came to the city? They broke the case open against old man Preston and his hench-men." He smiled. "They are this young lady's parents."

"I remember, now that you mention it. Their pedigree gives Miss Storm a good background, but still doesn't tell me what she has to do with Miss Harrison."

Mr. Bailey smiled. "It's very simple. I'll deputize Sara and she'll escort Miss Harrison to San Francisco for you."

Mr. Hodges' gaze shifted back and forth as he considered the ramifications, his face betraying his interest. "Miss Storm, would you mind waiting in the other office for a few minutes? Mr. Bailey and I need to discuss this in private."

"Of course. I know people talk a lot plainer if there're no witnesses."

The two men waited in silence until the door closed and Bailey could fill in the Director. "Sara Storm is definitely young. When I accused her of being young and foolish, she admitted the possibility. However, she's wise beyond her years and has been exposed to the law all of her life. I believe she is as honest as her parents. If your worry is whether she could handle herself and Miss Harrison, I believe she is fully capable. I interviewed her rather harshly. The mistakes she has made are those of youth, not of incompetence."

He reviewed his interview with Sara, not glossing over her deception of using her mother's star to pose as a marshal. "She didn't brag about it, but she didn't dodge the issue, either. I think, no, I know, she's capable of making it safely to San Francisco with Miss Harrison."

A lengthy silence followed before he continued. "I gave her what amounts to a final test, if you will, by asking her to show me how fast she is with a gun. I was astonished! She is extremely fast, so fast I couldn't follow her hand, though I knew she was going to draw.

"Her speed is a tremendous asset. No one would ever suspect a woman, especially as young as she is, to have that sort of skill. I also gave her high marks because she unloaded her gun and showed me the empty cylinder before she demonstrated, said it was only good manners. She's no blowhard, but she can make a point when she needs to. Do you remember all the problems we've had since we got our newest political employee in the information booth?"

Hodges rolled his eyes and groaned in agreement. "Do I ever! I'd like to strangle the politico who hired him."

A choked laugh answered him. "Well, we either won't have him very much longer or we'll have a major improvement in his attitude. Sara almost strangled him and threatened to shove his tie down his throat if he didn't improve his manners."

Hodges' eyebrows rose when he heard what had happened. He chuckled but didn't let go of his skepticism.

Bailey pressed his case, "You know as well as I do a lot of our cases depend on nothing but a gut feeling. My gut tells me this young lady can handle the assignment we want to assign her."

"You know I trust your instincts. I'll agree to her if the Brits will. If they're willing to talk, let's get started." He reached for the telephone on his desk. "Operator, would you connect me to the British Ambassador?"

***

Sara waited in the outer office for some time before the door opened and the two men emerged. Both were smiling and a knot in her stomach began to unravel. Mr. Hodges explained, "Miss Storm, there are other people involved who would like to meet you. Would you mind going with us?"

"Just lead the way."

He took the lead through several corridors and stairways until they exited to the exterior where a closed carriage waited.

Bailey opened the door and helped her in. "Where you're going is outside my bailiwick, so Mr. Hodges will be in charge. If the other parties who are involved agree to you being an escort, I'll swear you in and take care of the paperwork when you get back. Good luck."

Mr. Hodges gave directions to the driver before he climbed in as well. The team broke into a sharp trot as he settled into the cushions, facing Sara. His face was hard when he spoke. "What I'm about to tell you must be regarded as most secret. You are not to talk to anyone, other than me or Mr. Bailey, about what we discuss." His harsh expression softened slightly. "Mr. Bailey assured me you are a woman of your word. I respect his judgment."

Sara was equally serious. "You have my word."

"Edwina Harrison is the daughter of one of England's finest, although least known, diplomats. She arrived here about two weeks ago, a few days after her father departed by ship to visit several South American countries en route to San Francisco. The voyage is an extensive one and he is supposed to arrive in San Francisco in about three months."

He grimaced. "The problem we have is, a few days after her arrival, Miss Harrison began receiving letters threatening her life, for whatever reason, no one knows. She's been a virtual prisoner in the embassy ever since. The Brits have no idea how to get her safely to San Francisco to join her father once he arrives there."

Sara was mystified. "I don't see the problem. I would have thought they could just send a couple of bodyguards with her."

"If it were only that simple," Mr. Hodges scowled. "The protocols of statecraft forbid any of their people carrying guns while away from the embassy. Neither they, nor I, would even think of having one of our male officers share the responsibility with one of their female staff."

"I'm beginning to get an idea of why Mr. Bailey wanted to talk to me. If they accept me, then you don't have to worry about any sticky romantic entanglements. Even better, you'd have a native who knows at least something about the country. Most importantly, I can pack a gun."

"That's about it. Now we have to sell the idea to the Brits."

After a short drive through the tree-lined streets their carriage was halted at a barred gateway by an armed soldier. Mr. Hodges' identification was closely examined and his appointment with the ambassador verified before they were allowed to proceed. "They've really tightened security around here since Miss Harrison started getting threatening letters."

"If we can sneak her out of here, they'd better keep the security tight for a while. Otherwise they might as well publish it in the paper she's left the embassy."

"An astute observation. I hope the same idea

will have occurred to someone in the embassy if we do move Miss Harrison."

A short time later they were ushered into a large reception room showcasing the power and glory of the British Empire. Paintings, drawings, and statuary abounded, highlighting different eras and locations from around the world.

Sara's gaze swept the room, leaving her impressed and secretly amused by the unsubtle display of power. Their escort announced their arrival, "Mr. Hodges and Miss Sara Storm." The droning voice brought her back to her surroundings and directed her attention to two figures standing quietly next to the massive marble fireplace.

"Good afternoon, Miss Harrison, Ambassador Starr. It's good to meet you again."

Sara waited silently while the two men exchanged pleasantries, her eyes taking stock of the other woman, a woman only a few years older than herself, the crown of whose head would be little higher than her own shoulder. Miss Harrison's face was pale, untouched by the sun, framed with curly auburn hair. The fit and material of her dress told even an unsophisticated Sara it probably cost more than most working people would earn in many months.

After the introductions and pleasantries, Ambassador Starr explained, "Our time is limited. Let's go into my office where you can explain to us what sort of solution you've found for Miss Harrison's problem."

After they were all seated around a massive table, Mr. Hodges explained, "We are aware from the threats you have received that Miss Harrison is in great danger outside this embassy. We are also aware it is necessary for her to travel to San Francisco, in spite of that same danger. The problem we have been unable to resolve is to find someone to escort her safely, yet not run afoul of the protocols we both must observe."

He paused to let that information sink in before nodding at Sara. "Miss Storm is a United States marshal and thus uniquely qualified to protect Miss Harrison. We would suggest you consider Sara an able companion to escort her to San Francisco."

Sara was watching Miss Harrison while Mr. Hodges spoke but caught a flash of anger on the sallow face of the ambassador, and deep in his eyes, a burning anger. She blinked, unsure whether she'd actually seen so transient an expression. Alarms rang in her mind.

A sometimes rancorous discussion ensued. Sara answered a few direct questions but otherwise simply listened while Miss Harrison said not a word. During a momentary break, she said quietly, "You two gentlemen have done all of the talking. I would like to suggest Miss Harrison and I go somewhere private, because I have a few questions for her which might make your discussion irrelevant."

The ambassador turned angrily toward her but Miss Harrison spoke for the first time in a distinctly British accent, "I think that is a very good idea. Gentlemen, please excuse us."

The two men rose deferentially, before Miss Harrison led Sara down a short hallway into an antechamber. Finding a remote corner, the young woman turned to face Sara, her face expressionless. "Miss Storm, what are the questions you feel would determine whether anything either of the two gentlemen might have said would matter?"

"How good are you at taking orders?"

The pale face hardened and turned red with anger. "Just what is that supposed to mean?"

"You are obviously accustomed to giving orders. If we travel together, the situation may arise where I have to give you an order which might very well mean your life, or mine. Are you going to obey instantly, or are you going to stand there and argue and get us killed?"

Miss Harrison's angry glare faded. "I see your point." She mulled it over for several seconds. "It would be hard to adjust to, but I believe I could do as you ask."

"Believing isn't good enough!" Sara snapped. "I have to know whether you would obey an order without hesitation or this deal is off. I'm not going to take you on a suicide mission and get us both killed!"

Miss Harrison blanched. "Do you really think we would be in such danger?"

"We both know something fishy is going on." Sara was blunt. "If we travel together, someone else will undoubtedly insist on doing the planning and arrangements. Your life will depend on letting them *think* we'll do whatever they plan for us, but not giving anyone a clue we *might* do otherwise." Her tone softened. "I know when you're hunted you don't do the expected, or you could get yourself killed."

Miss Harrison was silent for several moments, considering the stark choice she had just been offered. She smiled conspiratorially. "Miss Storm, if you are sure you can get me there safely, why don't we go back and tell them we are in agreement."

Sara offered her hand. After a moment of startled hesitation, Miss Harrison extended hers in return.

"First of all, I'm Sara, not Miss Storm. If you were to yell *Miss Storm* at me I wouldn't have a clue who you're talking to."

Her new charge smiled for the first time. "Please call me Edwina."

When they returned, the two men were sitting silently at the table. The ambassador was smiling but Mr. Hodges was frowning. The chill in the air was palatable.

"Gentlemen," said Edwina, "We've agreed Marshal Storm will escort me to San Francisco. Would you please work out the details?"

The ambassador's smile vanished; he was visibly ready to protest.

Edwina continued, "We've reached an agreement. We'll be leaving as soon as possible."

When the two young women were seated, Edwina asked Sara questions about the journey, leaving the itinerary details to the others. "How much luggage will I be allowed?"

"I would say one small trunk. We'll only be a few days on the train. Anything else you'll need in San Francisco can be shipped there," Sara replied. She considered her new charge's appearance carefully. "No offence, but I'll get some traveling clothes for you which will make you less obvious than a peacock in a barnyard. We want you to be as inconspicuous as possible so you won't be such an obvious target. Do you think you'd be ready to leave the day after tomorrow?"

CHAPTER 9

When they were seated in the privacy of the carriage, Mr. Hodges asked with amusement and admiration in his voice, "Did you realize Ambassador Starr had already refused to use you as an escort before you returned to the office?"

"I thought as much, the way he was smiling." Sara shook her head. "I just don't understand his thinking, wanting to keep her here."

"What in the world did you tell Miss Harrison that persuaded her to go with you?"

Sara grinned slyly. "We talked woman to woman for a while. Do you really think I'd give away all of our feminine secrets?"

His grin turned wry. "I guess I asked for that, having warned you about need-to-know."

Mr. Bailey joined them shortly after they reached the office, where she was sworn in as a United States marshal and signed the documents making her appointment official. She accepted the offered congratulations and the star, placing it in her handbag.

The two men discussed details for the trip while Sara listened closely. Mr. Hodges explained, "We'll give you book of warrants for your expenses."

"I don't understand. What are warrants?"

"Warrants are the equivalent of government checks, payable by the federal government."

Sara stared at him in disbelief. "You might as well put signs around our necks that say *SHOOT ME!* We're trying to be as inconspicuous as possible, and we're to pay for everything with government checks?" She snorted in derision. "Make it cash. Small bills or gold coin. When I get to Denver I'll give the Marshal's office there an accounting of our expenses to that point. When I get home from San Francisco I'll give them the rest of the money and an accounting."

She suddenly realized both men were staring at her and she flushed. "You did say young and foolish, didn't you?"

She sat in an uncomfortable silence until a sudden smile blossomed on Mr. Hodges' lips. "I have to agree with Sara. You and I are thinking too much like bureaucrats and not enough like potential targets." He smothered a laugh. "Sara, I'll get you five hundred dollars in cash before you leave. That should take care of any conceivable expenses."

When they were done, Sara asked, "I've been wondering. Does anyone have an explanation why Miss Harrison suddenly became a target?"

Mr. Hodges shook his head. "No one has a clue. I personally think it was because of an announcement in the gossip section of one of the newspapers, just like yours. It's possible someone selected her at random, or has some sort of score to settle with her father."

"What do you mean, *just like me?*"

"You obviously haven't seen the papers," Mr. Bailey replied. "All of the local papers have gossip columns. Your arrival was written up in at least one. My secretary pointed it out to me. Some reporter heard your name and made the connection with your parents. The fact that you're the daughter of the only married marshals ever in the Service makes you a celebrity in this town."

"I guess I made a mistake wearing my jeans and Ma's star on the train."

***

Sara stepped down from the closed carriage into mid-morning sunshine, concentrating hard because of the unfamiliar green traveling dress she was wearing. When her feet were planted firmly on the ground, she said, "Good morning, Miss Harrison. Are you ready to leave?"

Miss Harrison was dressed in the plain gray dress Sara had arranged to have delivered the day before. "Yes. My trunk is ready. We can leave as soon as it's loaded." She bid goodbye to the two women from the staff who had accompanied her to the service entrance at the back of the embassy.

The driver loaded the small trunk into the luggage compartment before helping Edwina into the carriage. Sara stopped him with a raised hand and spoke quickly. His eyebrows rose before he gave her a conspiratorial grin, repeating her instructions to make sure he understood, before helping her into the carriage.

The two young women sat in silence for some time, listening to the clip-clop of the horses' hooves, before Sara broke the silence. "We're going to have one of those unannounced changes of plan I warned you about. We're going to be leaving this carriage in a few minutes and changing to another. You'll need to be ready to move in a hurry."

Edwina glanced sharply at Sara before she asked with amusement in her voice, "Does anyone else know about this change of plans?"

Sara grinned unrepentantly. "I told our driver about the change of plans when I boarded. I'm glad his instructions were for him to do whatever I told him, no matter what."

A few minutes later the driver slapped the side of the coach with his hand. Sara snapped. "Get ready. When we stop, follow me out as fast as you can. When you hit the ground go straight ahead through the door in front of you. When you get inside, wait for me. We'll only have a few seconds, so don't dawdle."

The carriage stopped. Sara shot out the door, spun on one foot and helped Edwina down. She ran for the door while Sara flipped up the lid of the compartment and grabbed a trunk in each hand, yanking them clear. The lid slammed shut and both young women were through the door and out of sight less than thirty seconds after the carriage halted.

Edwina gawked at her new surroundings and found herself in a small, cramped, very dirty office. The unmistakable odor of a livery stable assaulted her nose. She stared in consternation when Sara dropped the trunks and pulled the door shut behind them while the sound of the carriage retreated.

Sara dropped a bar across the outer door before she circled the grungy desk filling most of the room. She dropped the bar on an inner door and turned to the trunks waiting on the floor, lifting hers to the desk-top. She opened it before she stripped her dress off, pulling it over her head. Handing it to Edwina, she snapped, "Hang on to this while I change."

Sara grabbed a small bolt of plain cotton cloth from the trunk, wrapping it tightly around her chest, flattening her breasts before she quickly donned the man's white shirt and black trousers she had bought so long ago in Denver.

Edwina stared in amazement when Sara wound her shoulder-length hair into a bun and pinned it to the top of her head. When she donned her battered Stetson, her shoulder-length hair had disappeared. Next, she slipped on her new vest, momentarily turning the left inside-out to display her marshal's star.

Edwina was speechless at the transformation. The young woman she had accompanied in the carriage had been transformed into a tall and lean young man. She gaped, dumbfounded, when Sara exchanged her now-folded dress for a large handbag from her trunk.

Sara kept one hand in the bag while she raised the bar on the inner door. Pulling the door slightly ajar, she glanced outside and snapped, "Take the bag. Our new wheels are waiting."

A horse harnessed to an open buggy stood waiting in the open alleyway. Sara grabbed a trunk in each hand and with two steps stowed them behind the seat.

Edwina followed, still dazed by the transformation. Sara helped her into the seat before climbing in herself. When she gathered the reins in her left hand, the dappled gray turned its head to eye her curiously. She was about to reach for the whip in the socket beside her knee when some sixth sense made her reach for the handbag instead. She placed it on her lap with her right hand inside before gently flicking the reins across the horse's rump with her left.

The carriage began to move toward the open door some distance away. They were almost to the doorway when a man stepped from the deep shadow, a gun in his hand. He raised it, aiming at Sara's chest, sneering with exaggerated courtesy, "Miss Storm, I presume?"

Edwina squeaked in terror.

Sara said nothing when the gunman continued conversationally, "The ghost of Theodore Preston is smiling on me today, because I am going to kill you."

Sara's voice was inhumanly calm. "Why?"

"Because your death will punish your bitch of a mother like nothing else could," he sneered, raising the gun slightly as he shifted his aim to Sara's head.

Her ready gun hand was hidden by the bag on her lap. When she squeezed her trigger finger slightly, her Colt roared twice. Both slugs slammed into the gunman and he was thrown backward, his own gun discharging one slug into the haymow floor above.

CHAPTER 10

Startled by the gunfire, the horse spooked and broke into a gallop, throwing both women back in the seat. Sara regained her balance quickly but made no attempt to rein in the frightened horse. The nearby street was empty, but startled pedestrians farther down the road heard the clatter of racing hooves and scattered to the sidewalks as they swept past.

When Edwina regained her seat, Sara handed her the now-torn and powder-burned handbag. She gathered the reins in both hands to guide the frightened horse around the next corner. When they were out of sight of the livery, she slowed the spooked horse to a fast trot.

Only then did she turn to face Edwina, whose face was white and strained. She stared back in shock, gasping in horror, "Is he dead?"

Her own face was pale. "I'm sure he is." Sara was surprised at the steadiness of her own voice. "I shot him dead-center."

Edwina wobbled in her seat, almost fainting because of the sudden violence and apparent callousness.

Sara jabbed her hard in the ribs with an elbow. "It was him or us!" Looking at her frightened companion, her voice softened, "This is one of those decisions I warned you about, when I wouldn't have time to ask or explain."

Edwina's face was still pasty white. "I know, but it still terrified me!" She gasped, "Thank you for saving my life."

Sara was shaken and her own face was still pale. "I was shooting for my own life. You don't have to thank me."

***

Three hard-faced men were impatiently waiting in a small room in a nondescript flop-house not far from Union Station. They were a surly group, having been waiting for some time. A muffled knock on the door brought them to tense alertness.

A familiar voice could be heard through the closed door. "It's me." One of the men opened the door. "The big man just called to tell us the carriage left a few minutes ago. They'll be here in about ten minutes."

The three men followed the new arrival to the street below in silence. A few minutes later they were scattered as inconspicuously as possible along the street at the entrance to the train station. Every hack and carriage was closely scrutinized by one or more of the observers. They were still watching and waiting an hour later, snarling in frustration. Their leader drew them together. "Get back to the room and wait for me. I'll find out what happened to our targets."

***

Mr. Hodges' face was scarlet as his fists clenched. He snarled at the agent who had posed as a hack driver for the two young women, "What do you mean she didn't take the train? That was part of the plan."

The agent had difficulty keeping his face expressionless when he reminded his superior, "You told me

79

to do whatever she told me." He handed over the note Sara had slipped to him when he helped her into the carriage.

Sitting in a bull's eye doesn't appeal

to either of us. I'll get us to SF

safely - my way. S Storm

Furious, Mr. Hodges stomped out the door, beckoning to two agents who were working at desks in the outer office. "Come on. We have to find a pair of runaways."

Ten minutes later their carriage halted at the rundown livery barn where Sara and Edwina had disembarked, startled to find several city police already on the scene. Three officers were surveying a body stretched out flat on its back just inside the main door to the livery.

Sergeant Kyle Webster could not keep his surprise from showing in his voice, "Good day, Mr. Hodges. What interest does the Secret Service have in the killing of Bruiser Brown?"

Mr. Hodges snapped at him in frustration, "Who?"

The sergeant was mystified. "You mean you haven't heard of one of our city's most deadly assassins? He's the best the old Preston gang ever had."

He pointed at the two bullet holes in the victim's vest. "He was good, but someone else was better. You could cover those with a half-dollar and have room to spare."

Mr. Hodges was confused. Trying to make sense of the murder scene, he asked anxiously, "Have you found any other bodies?"

"Funny you should ask. We have. The livery attendant had his throat cut and was dumped in one of the stalls at the back. We found a blade on Bruiser showing traces of fresh blood, so we think we've solved that case." The sergeant then asked, "Would you mind telling me what you might know about this situation?"

Mr. Hodges waved for Sergeant Webster to follow him. They moved farther back into the shadow of the livery, out of sight of the curious on-lookers gathered across the street.

"I think your man was gunned down by one of my agents, who then went undercover and disappeared. They apparently traded vehicles here. This bozo somehow got word of where she would be today and tried to..."

Mr. Hodges swore under his breath when he realized what he had let slip. Sergeant Webster's eyebrows rose to meet his hairline. "SHE?" he sputtered.

"You've been around the city long enough. Do you remember a female marshal who broke up the old Preston gang almost twenty years ago? She knocked out old man Preston's son and he wanted revenge, so he sicced a gang of killers on her. That was a huge mistake, because they were killed or captured and he was arrested and convicted."

"She's back?"

Mr. Hodges' thin smile was rueful. "No. It's her daughter," he groaned. "From the stories I've heard over the years from men who met her mother, and what I've learned of the daughter, they're as alike as two peas in a pod. God help us all!"

They returned to the front of the livery where city police and Secret Service officers were questioning on-lookers. One of the officers beckoned to Sergeant Webster, who hurried across the street, trailed by Mr. Hodges. The officer was talking with a young couple. "Would you mind telling us about the carriage that raced out of here?"

"I was just crossing the street when I heard what I thought were explosions." The woman was the first to speak. "I looked up and saw a runaway horse and buggy coming right at me so I ran for the sidewalk."

The young man explained, "Molly just made it to safety before the carriage raced past at a full gallop. The young man who was driving looked like he couldn't control the horse. A woman was slumped down in the seat beside him."

Mr. Hodges asked, "What did they look like?"

The young woman was still shaken by her close call. "I was so scared after getting out of the way I didn't really notice anything."

Her companion was more composed. "From where I was standing, the woman looked young, wearing a plain gray dress and sunbonnet. The man was much taller, wearing a black coat and white shirt."

"You're sure it was a man?"

"Yeah." He fell silent while he attempted to recall the scene. "The clothes looked new, but he was wearing a western hat of some sort that looked old." He paused again, reviewing his memory. "I'm sorry; that's all I can remember. It happened so fast I didn't see anything clearly."

***

Sara brought the horse to a walk in the shade of the tree-lined street, to explain, "I don't want to stop to give the horse a breather. If someone walked past we'd be much more likely to be noticed. This way he can cool down, but we'll hopefully be less conspicuous."

Edwina had recovered her wits enough to comment acidly, "I thought we were going by train to California, which was to take us about a week. Obviously we're not going by train. What sort of adventure do you have planned for us?"

"We'll still take a train most of the way. We just won't get on at a station anywhere near Washington. We won't be going through Baltimore, either. We'll head west from here until we can board at some small town where there's a lot less chance of any hired killers finding us."

Edwina, unaccustomed to not being in charge, fumed silently. When the horse turned at the next corner they left the tree-lined street behind and entered a broad thoroughfare with much heavier traffic. Restraining her fear and anger, she watched closely while Sara kept the horse under easy control, moving smoothly through the mix of carriages and heavy freight wagons.

The traffic remained heavy as they continued westward toward the Potomac, joining a slow-moving line inching across the bridge spanning the river.

Shouts and curses from a multitude of teamsters filled the air, adding to the raucous confusion.

Sara breathed a sigh of relief when she heard the rumble of paving brick when they reached the west bank of the river. Steering the buggy around a slow-moving freight wagon she urged the horse to a quicker pace when they began to climb the hills west of the river.

Badly shaken and horrified by the apparent callousness of her companion. Edwina Harrison sneaked surreptitious glances at Sara. *How can someone be so indifferent? She just shot him and ran, not knowing or caring if he was dead or alive.* Her thoughts were in turmoil as an uneasy silence lay between them. *She's younger than I am by several years, but she's no girl. She's older in experience than I am by many years. She didn't even flinch when that man announced he was going to kill her. I'd have fainted and been dead by now if it had been me facing that gun. What kind of life has she led to make her so callous?*

Several miles passed in uncomfortable silence before she spoke. "I can see it's obvious you've handled horses before. I know nothing else about you. Would you mind telling me about yourself?"

Sara gave her a quick glance before returning her eyes to the traffic ahead. "I don't mind. I was born and raised on a ranch in the mountains of Colorado. I've ridden horses all my life, roped and branded cattle, and done everything that needs to be done on a ranch. I have a sister and two brothers. My parents are both inactive United States marshals."

She steered the buggy around a plodding team hitched to a heavily-laden wagon, waving a friendly greeting to the teamster. The road narrowed, entering a welcome canopy of trees shading them from the direct sun. She wiped her brow gratefully. "It'd be nice if we had shade like this all of the rest of the trip."

Sara let the horse have its head before asking, "Since we're going to be spending a lot of time together the next few days, would you mind telling me about yourself as well?"

Edwina gathered her courage. "I'll tell you about myself if you'll answer one more question first." She gulped and asked, "How were you able to face the man who wanted to kill you and not fall apart?"

Sara's face tightened and her voice became cold. "Do you mean, are you riding with a killer?" Her eyes were icy. "Absolutely not! This was the only time I've ever actually fired at another person!"

Edwina recoiled from the vehemence. Her voice quaked, "I had to know. I could never tolerate a killer as a bodyguard."

Sara glared at her as their horse trotted past an on-coming freight wagon. Her expression eased while she considered the feelings of the woman charged to her care. "I'd guess you've been very sheltered most of your life. In my world, you have to fend for yourself." Her voice was still cold. "I'll tell you how gunplay saved my life once. Then you have to tell me about yourself."

CHAPTER 11

Sara had just celebrated her thirteenth birthday and was excited to be riding in her first roundup. Most of the neighboring ranchers had sent riders as well, although they were all male. The crew swept the canyons and draws, searching for unbranded stock. Her immediate companions varied from moment to moment as the cattle dodged and twisted, trying to escape the determined riders. She was racing her horse down a dry water course in pursuit of a particularly wily steer when the ground in front of her seemed to explode as a maddened bull suddenly charged from hiding.

The attack was sudden and devastating. The tip of one horn smashed into the unprotected chest of her mount. Her horse collapsed instantaneously, already dead on its feet. The body of her mount slid for some distance, trapping her left leg underneath.

"I was real lucky. The streambed was all sand," Sara explained. "Fifty feet in either direction everything was exposed rock. If my horse had fallen anywhere else I would have had my leg badly torn up."

The maddened bull regained its feet after the collision and turned to the downed rider. Sara was lying on her side, her leg trapped under the horse. Her hand swept down to the holster on her hip. When the barrel came level it erupted in flame as she triggered one round after another until the hammer clicked on an empty chamber.

The stricken bull continued its charge but its legs were buckling. She watched helplessly as its momentum carried it closer until it smashed into the body of her horse, the horns barely missing her exposed leg.

Sara was half-stunned and lay still for a few minutes, badly shaken. When she recovered her wits, she punched cartridges from her belt and reloaded. She raised the barrel skyward and triggered off three measured rounds. Waiting another minute, she triggered another three rounds, the reports echoing back from the surrounding canyon walls.

She drew several deep breaths, trying to get her breathing under control before turning her attention to her trapped leg. It was already beginning to tingle from the impaired circulation, but no matter how hard she tried to free it, her foot wouldn't budge. She gave up and started to dig at the loose sand with her bare hands as best she could.

Time dragged as she dug at the sand. She was almost ready to make another attempt to pull free when she heard a trio of gunshots echo from the cliff above her. She triggered an answering trio and the sound of a single shot echoed from the cliff. A few minutes later the distant thunder of racing hooves reached her ears, growing louder as she continued to dig at the sand. She didn't look up until two horses slid to a stop a short distance away. Ben Franklin and Herb Baker leaped from their horses and rushed toward her. She waved reassuringly and called, "I'm okay, but my leg is trapped."

Both men dropped to their knees and clawed at the soft sand, one on either side. When they had dug away what they could reach, Ben grasped Sara under the arms and began to pull as she pushed. Her foot suddenly slipped out of her boot and she was free.

Ben lowered her to the sand, kneeling to massage her leg. The eyes of both men were anxious but she reassured them, "I'm all right. My leg's gone to sleep and it's tingling." Her expression was rueful. "I'm going to be black and blue from ankle to hip, but it could've been a lot worse."

Both men had worked silently while they tore at the sand. Herb gave a sigh of relief at her words. "Why don't you tell us what happened."

Ben continued to massage her leg while she related what had happened. When she finished, Herb walked to the head of the bull, leaned down, and inspected the cluster of bullet holes. He turned, his eyes meeting Ben's. He observed dryly. "You could cover all four with the ace of spades. That's some shooting!"

Herb tied one end of a rope to the body of the bull and dragged it away from Sara's horse. Ben dug more sand from under the body and retrieved her trapped boot. The two men stripped the gear from her dead horse and lashed it behind Herb's saddle.

Ben took Sara's hand to help her to her feet. She was clumsy and winced at the pain. Seeing the two men sharing worried looks, she said, "Nothing's broken, but I'm going to be sore for a while."

Ben mounted and bent down to take her hand while Herb boosted her up. Sara swung her good leg over the rump of the horse and settled behind his saddle, wrapping her arms around Ben's waist. Herb mounted his own horse and both surged forward, heading back to the corral and the branding crew.

***

Edwina was appalled. She gasped, "How could you take a chance riding double with a man? Every man I ever knew would have had his hands all over me, even at such a young age."

Sara stared at her companion. "I would trust both Herb and Ben with my life. Ben's like a second father to me." Her face lit up. "In fact, he's going to be my father-in-law, although he doesn't know it yet." Sara smiled with delight as she said, "I told Andy I'd tell him yes or no when I got back from this trip. It will be yes!

"You still have to tell me about yourself. Your life has to have been entirely different from mine, if you're so leery of riding double with a man."

Sara halted the horse beside a small creek meandering alongside the roadway. She stepped down from the buggy and turned to help Edwina down. The horse snorted in gratitude for the break and the shade of the overhanging limbs, ducking its head to drink its fill.

Edwina was also thirsty. Wondering if there was a cup she could use, she stared when Sara dipped her battered Stetson into the water and drank her fill from the improvised ladle. When Sara offered her hat, she flinched away. When Sara's expression tightened, Edwina belatedly took the Stetson and began to drink.

Sara turned toward the buggy, her face stiff and cold. Unpinning her hair, she let it fall free before climbing to the seat.

Edwina reached out to intercept her, her eyes meeting Sara's. "I'm sorry if I offended you by not taking your hat. Forgive me. I've neither seen nor done anything like this before. My life has been totally different from yours."

Sara's scowl softened.

Edwina climbed into the carriage, facing her, letting her eyes roam the tranquil scene in silence. "While I was growing up, Mother and I followed Father from one embassy to another. I've never had a permanent home, although my family's ancestral estate is in England. I've lived in Australia, Hong Kong, Canada, Singapore, and India, to name some of the countries where Father was posted."

Her face stiffened, watching the swish of the horse's tail stirring the buzzing flies. Her voice was flat, bitter, and barely audible. "My mother died in India when I was fourteen. I was the only English child my age in the embassy, so I didn't have any schoolmates or friends."

She began to cry, tears trickling down her cheeks. "The adults kept telling me, 'Don't let down the side. Stiff upper lip, child.'" She tried to suppress her sobs. "Because my mother had died, Father had me take her place at all the diplomatic functions he attended. I started to grow up and the men began to take an interest in me." Edwina choked, "No one ever, ever, ever, asked *me* how I *felt!* Everyone just kept telling me to do my duty, for God and Country."

Sara draped an arm across her shoulders. "I think I have some idea how you felt. My grandmother died when Ma was four, and she was orphaned at sixteen. She told me how much it hurt and vowed she would make up the lack with her own kids." Sara's tone was rueful. "I thought sometimes she overdid it, but when I was old enough to understand, she explained her reasons. That made it easier to understand, even if I still didn't like it."

The unexpected sympathy and understanding were too much for Edwina. Unshed tears from years of anguish and loneliness flooded her eyes.

Sara held her gently, providing a sympathetic shoulder until the paroxysm of sobbing tapered off. The shadows had shifted significantly before Edwina drew away, dabbing at the remaining tears with the edge of her sunbonnet.

She lifted her gaze to the younger but much taller woman seated beside her. "I've never been able to talk to anyone about how I felt. We British women are supposed to carry on, no matter what. The men, old and young, stationed at the embassies only wanted to paw me. That's why I couldn't believe you would chance riding on the same horse with any man."

Climbing down from the carriage, Edwina knelt at the flowing water and washed her face.

Sara checked for traffic in both directions before slipping out of her vest and man's shirt. She unwound the confining cotton and slipped back into her shirt and vest with a sigh of relief. Reaching under the seat for her gunpowder-stained handbag, she removed the heavy gun belt and revolver and buckled it around her waist. She finished the transformation by pinning her star to the vest.

***

Late in the afternoon of their third day, the travel-worn carriage crested a hilltop overlooking a small, bustling town. Travelers that they had met on the road had told them Froelich was in Maryland, although Sara was not sure of its exact location. She halted the tired horse and they surveyed the valley below. Both were eager for the first sight of the railroad they had been informed followed the banks of the river.

Edwina was the first to spot the twin ribbons of rail bisecting the business district. "I can see the tracks from here. We'll be able to catch a train for the rest of our trip."

Sara's attention was directed elsewhere, her eyes scanning rank after rank of mountain crests as the Alleghenies receded to the horizon. She said, "We won't be able to head straight west because of all the mountains, but it'll still be a lot faster than this buggy."

The shadows from the late-afternoon sun were long and the sun was barely above the horizon when they drove into town. Both women scanned the businesses on either side of the street. Edwina was the first to spot a small sign proclaiming ROOMS. A few minutes later they halted in front of a modest inn.

Sara stepped gratefully from the buggy, ignoring tired and aching muscles as she strode into the small lobby. The room was empty, shrouded in shadow, lamps yet unlit. A small bell sat on the counter, ringing surprising loudly when she tapped it. She waited, surveying a room that was clean and neat, though modest. A doorway opened to her left, obviously a small dining room from the savory smells. A few minutes passed before footsteps sounded on the stairs. She turned to espy a woman of middle age at the foot of the stairway.

"Hello. I'm Mrs. Olsen. Can I help you?" said the clerk.

"Would you have a room for two for the night?"

The woman halted as though she had run into a

wall. Her surprise was apparent as she realized the silhouette of a man wearing a gun was in reality a woman. She managed a strangled response, "Yes. I have a room. Let me light some lamps first."

Mrs. Olsen scurried around the lobby lighting lamps, gasping in astonishment when lamplight reflected from the shiny star pinned to the faded blue shirt.

They were shown to a comfortable room on the second floor where a double bed filled most of the floor space. A nightstand in a corner near the head of the bed held a pitcher and a wash bowl. A small table in another corner held a kerosene lamp. Sara placed the two trunks against the wall, beneath the window.

"Miss E has a condition that caused her to lose her voice." She elaborated on the subterfuge they had agreed on to hide her distinctive British accent. "She'll need something to write with if you need something from her."

Mrs. Olson nodded.

Sara asked, "Where'd I find a livery?"

***

Ezra Williams was standing just inside the door of his livery stable, trading tales and gossip with his good friend and employee, Miriam Hensley. They heard the familiar clip-clop of a horse's hooves and moved to the doorway as a carriage drew to a halt in front of the livery. They watched with idle curiosity while a very tall figure stepped down from the buggy. The gathering darkness reduced a holstered revolver on the right hip to a dark blur.

The figure was shrouded in shadow, face partially hidden by a wide-brimmed Stetson and framed by shoulder-length hair.

Ezra asked, "Can I do somethin' for you?'

Both men were shocked into stunned silence when a woman's voice answered. "I sure hope so."

He stared in disbelief. "What is it I can do for you?"

"I'm looking for a buyer for this rig."

The horse-trader in Ezra surfaced happily. He stepped down to examine the horse and rig in the dim light before spitting a plug of tobacco juice into the dust. "I'll give you fifty bucks for the nag and outfit."

The woman tipped her head back and roared with laughter. Still chuckling, she looked him squarely in the eyes. "I could have gotten a better offer from a horse thief." Her eyes were alight with laughter. "What're you really going to offer me?"

Ezra growled at the young woman and began to haggle, learning quickly that this woman really knew horses. Miriam listened in admiration while both hagglers traded insults and offers in equal measure before reaching agreement.

"Done!" Sara offered her hand. They shook on the deal.

"Let's step inside where there's some light," Sara suggested. "I'll give you a bill of sale for this magnificent gelding you insulted by calling a nag."

The dim light of a single lamp left deep shadow in

the cramped office. Ezra took his cash box from a drawer and counted out the payment. Both men watched the young woman clear a space on the desk and write quickly.

She handed the sheet of paper to him. "Is that satisfactory?"

Miriam read over his employer's shoulder.

Received from Ezra Williams for

clear title to one gray gelding and

buggy, $425.

Sara Storm

United States Marshal

Both men stared in disbelief as she turned from the desk, lamp light reflecting from the star on her shirt. She nodded once and disappeared through the door into the darkness.

Both men stared at each other before Ezra exclaimed, "I'm damn glad you were my witness! If I told someone I'd seen a woman wearing a marshal's star, they'd accuse me of being a damn liar."

CHAPTER 12

Much refreshed after a good night's sleep, they walked the short distance to the depot. Sara was wearing her green traveling dress, while Edwina was wearing another nondescript dress and sunbonnet. Edwina carried the battered handbag, holding the door open while Sara carried the two trunks inside and set them on the floor not far from the doorway.

The small waiting room was empty. At the ticket window, Sara requested two tickets to Cincinnati. The clerk filled them out without comment and passed them across the counter before he asked, "Would you be the two women someone is searching for?"

Edwina's shocked gasp echoed in the small room.

Sara tensed, shooting a cold glance at the clerk. She asked with steel in her voice, "Who wants to know?"

"I don't, but there was a hard case in here yesterday. He asked if I had seen two women, one of them very tall." After a moment, he added. "He left on the westbound yesterday morning. I don't know where he was headed."

Sara held the man's steady gaze until she was satisfied with the level look he returned. She beckoned to Edwina. Taking the handbag, she removed the hidden star. "I'd appreciate it, if anyone were to ask, you haven't seen us."

The clerk's eyes widened at the sight of the star.

"I haven't seen two women traveling together for several weeks, much less anyone who looks like you do."

"We thank you, sir."

***

Mr. Bailey was at his desk, dealing with the constant flow of paperwork crossing it. He sorted the pile that had collected in his *IN* basket, into piles for immediate and deferred action. He was almost done sorting when his eye fell on an envelope marked *Personal*, with no return address. Curious, he opened the envelope and removed several sheets covered with fine handwriting. He shuffled through them, stopping at the second page when he read the signature, *Sara Storm*. He chuckled, remembering the sulfurous comments his friend Mr. Hodges had shared when he explained what had happened to his plans for the travel of the two young women. He skimmed the entire missive before dividing the sheets of paper into two piles. Carefully rereading them, he devoted extra attention to the first section, an official report submitted by Marshal Sara Storm, present address unknown.

To Whom it may concern

On this date, the exact time unknown, but between nine and ten o'clock in the morning, Miss Edwina Harrison and I were accosted by a man in the doorway of the Wheelock Livery on Willow street, Washington, D.C. The subject was of medium height, clean shaven and dressed in modest fashion.

The man announced he was going to kill me, and the ghost of Theodore Preston would be smiling this day. I asked why, and he said it was to punish my mother. (I have to assume he had something to do with my parents' visit to the city nearly twenty years ago.)

When he raised his revolver and aimed at my head, I knew I had no choice and would have to shoot him in self-defense. I fired first, two shots which could not have missed at such short range. I have to assume he is now dead, and submit this report as an explanation for his death.

I did not stop to report this action to anyone in authority because I felt the safety of my charge, Miss Edwina Harrison, took precedence over any other responsibility.

signed: Sara Storm, United States Marshal

witnessed: Lady Edwina Cornwall Harrison,

obedient servant of His Royal Majesty,

The United Kingdom

He read the rest of the pages, containing the same information, but written in the hand of Miss Harrison. Her statement was witnessed in turn by Sara Storm. Mr. Bailey grinned. *Sara's parents sure did a good job of instilling a sense of legal responsibility in this young woman. I just wish some of my more experienced agents were as thorough with their reports.*

He completed his review of the two reports, then directed his attention to the remaining pages. They proved to be a letter, rather than a formal report. His interest rose at Sara's reasons for their diversion from the route planned by the Secret Service. He grunted in dismay at the discovery someone was still trying to intercept them even after they left Washington.

Edwina and I agree there's something rotten in the Embassy itself. We've reviewed everything that's happened since she arrived, which, by the way, we determined was never reported in the gossip columns and had to have been obtained some other way. We suspect the ambassador himself is the rotten apple. I realize we can't prove anything in a court of law, but you might have someone start checking on his activities.

Edwina thinks it may have something to do with the sudden departure of her father. She found out from talking to some of the staff, her letters to her father arrived in the mail room but her father never received them. We're sure that is the reason he didn't wait the few extra days for her to arrive to accompany him.

As I said, something smells funny but we can't prove it from here. We'll be in touch, but if you need to contact us, send any messages in care of my home office. We'll stop there on the way home, where we'll stay for as long as needed before heading for our final destination.

Sara Storm

***

The rail bed twisted and turned as they clattered over bridges, dove into tunnels, and puffed up and down switchbacks behind the laboring engine struggling across the Alleghenies. The train was a small local, with only one freight car and one passenger car trailing behind the engine and tender. The surrounding mountains echoed back the thunder of pounding pistons on upgrades and the tortured scream of steel-on-steel when the brakes were applied on steep downgrades. The mountainous terrain forced the train to travel at little more than the pace of a trotting horse and frequent stops slowed its pace even more.

Sara and Edwina shared the single passenger car with only a few other riders, most of whom were residents from the immediate area. The locals were curious and friendly, willing to share their knowledge of the mountains to the visitors.

When they rolled into Elkport, Kentucky, the conductor stopped at their seat. "End of the line! Ever'body off. You'll need to change trains here, but you won't be able to leave town until Monday. Most of the stations in this part of the country are small. Their schedules are all *Daily except Sunday*. Since tomorrow is Sunday, ever'thin's shut down for the day."

The latter part of their journey had passed through more-populous towns, where they picked up greater numbers of passengers, filling the car almost to capacity before they halted amidst a burst of escaping steam.

Sara was sitting next to the window, her eyes sweeping the two sets of tracks between their train and the depot. She observed dryly to no one in particular, "This must be a busy junction. Except on Sunday."

The passengers streamed slowly from the car, chatting noisily. Sara followed Edwina down the stairs, the handbag gripped in her left hand, onto an uneven layer of ballast, which forced them to be careful of their footing as they moved toward the station.

A distant squeal of steel on steel drew her attention. Her head snapped up, eyes sweeping her surroundings. She followed a pair of rails that angled to the left and up a steep incline before disappearing in the gathering shadows. Her hand flashed to the

handbag and she whipped out her Colt, pointed it skyward, and triggered off a round. In the stunned silence,
she bellowed at the top of her lungs, "Runaway train!
Clear the tracks."

People scattered, dropping their possessions
and running for their lives. She gave Edwina an urgent
shove toward the depot and turned back to view the
onrushing railroad cars, approaching rapidly but still
several seconds away.

She turned to flee and gasped in horror. A young
woman, heavy with child, had tripped and fallen flat
astraddle a rail only a few feet from her. Helplessly
sprawled across the track, a crying child huddled on
the ground beside her.

Sara dropped her Colt and the handbag and
leaped across the intervening space. She scooped up
the toddler, literally throwing it to a man who had
turned to look back upon reaching the safety of the
station platform. His face blanched in horror as he realized what happened, but still had the presence of
mind to catch the terrified child.

Sara grabbed the fallen woman, lifting her with
adrenalin-fueled strength, and dashed for safety,
barely clearing the tracks before the runaway rail cars
thundered past. The blast of wind from the cars threw
Sara and her burden off-balance and they crashed into
the mass of humanity watching in horror.

Total confusion ensued while the crowd attempted to disentangle itself. The young mother was
shrieking hysterically in terror and grief, unaware her
toddler had been rescued. Sara was unceremonious-
ly yanked to her feet, while the expectant mother was

helped more gently. Her shrieks subsided into grateful sobs when the toddler was returned to her arms.

Edwina worked her way through the crowd to Sara's side, exclaiming, "I'm so proud of you!" While the rumble of the runaway rail cars receded, she realized Sara was trembling violently. Alarmed at her pallor, she threw her arms around Sara and hugged her close, willing support and sympathy from her own body. She clung tightly until color began to return to Sara's face and the trembling subsided.

Sara gave a shuddering sigh and inhaled deeply, slowly filling her lungs with oxygen. "Thanks! I needed that." She shook her head in disbelief. "I've never been so scared before, even back at the livery."

They were suddenly swamped by the crowd, wanting to shake Sara's hand and offer congratulations. A passage opened through the crowd, allowing the young mother to approach, her whimpering child clutched tightly in one arm. Looking up at the much taller Sara, her voice trembled. "We owe you our lives and I can never repay you." Gratitude shone in her eyes. "Would you please tell me your name? If my baby is a girl, I'd like to honor you by naming her after you."

Sara flushed scarlet while the crowd waited silently. She swallowed to ease the sudden dryness in her throat. "I'm United States Marshal Sara Storm."

Astonishment and disbelief flashed across the faces in the crowd, remaining so until Edwina handed Sara her Colt and the battered handbag. Late-afternoon sunshine reflected from the marshal's star pinned to the bag as her distinctive English accent added emphasis, "I did not think you would like to leave these lying around. I was afraid what might happen if someone unfamiliar with guns were to find these."

***

Elkport was a small town and most of the passengers who had ridden in with Sara and Edwina were residents. News of her actions spread quickly and a thank-you potluck supper was soon organized in spite of both young women's attempts to dissuade the townspeople.

The parson of the little church was the master of ceremonies and talked at length. Sara sighed in unobtrusive gratitude when he concluded his oration, but it was short-lived. "We've heard from many of our neighbors, relating the courage of this young woman," he smiled broadly, "but we haven't heard from our guest of honor. Miss Storm, would you share a few words with us?"

She tried not to show her apprehension. Wearing her best, the red and white dress she had bought in Denver, she faced the crowd silently, her height dominating the room. Lantern light reflected from the star pinned to her bodice, the golden light dancing on the walls. Her throat was dry as she faced the crowd. They listened quietly, waiting, as she nodded to the parson. "I felt more comfortable when I was afoot facing a charging bull."

The crowd dissolved in laughter and she waited until they quieted. "I only did what anyone else would have done, if they'd been the first to see the runaway.

"I have a request for all of you. It is possible someone will pass through asking questions about two women who fit our description. If it were to

happen, we'd appreciate it if you had never heard anything about us. I'm afraid that's all that I can tell you,
but I've heard tell mountain folk like you know how to
keep secrets."

CHAPTER 13

Several more days of travel on locals and an occasional express found Sara and Edwina steadily rolling closer and closer to the Missouri River town of Saint Joseph. The past many miles had been through a forest of mixed hardwoods and softwoods, roughly following the twists and turns of the historic river through the state of Missouri.

Edwina's flagging spirits rose when Sara said, "Tomorrow night we'll be in Denver. From there, it's only a day's travel to my home, where we'll be as safe as if we were in church. We'll hole up there for several weeks while we wait for your father to get to San Francisco. When we hear from him, I'll take you the rest of the way."

Edwina asked, "How will we be able to find out if he's arrived without taking the chance of someone finding out where I'm staying?"

"I've been pondering the problem," Sara replied. "I think the safest way will be to send your mail to the Denver Marshal's office, then have them forward it to the San Francisco office. They can deliver it by hand to the consulate, or just mail it. That way no one can find out my return address."

"Sara, you're devious enough to have a career as a spy."

"I don't think so." She grinned. "A spy needs to be less conspicuous than I am."

As they entered the fringes of the city known as

Saint Joe, Sara told Edwina of some of the area's history. "This area was the home of one of America's most infamous desperadoes, Jessie James. His career started in the tension before our Civil War. Even without an actual war, he didn't hesitate to ambush and shoot down in cold blood, anyone he or his gang disagreed with.

"His depredations continued through the war. After the war, he went into thievery full time. He and his gang robbed banks and trains all over the country. He met his end in his own home when one of his fellow gang members shot him in the back while he was hanging a picture. I guess the man wanted the reward."

Edwina blanched. "How perfectly awful!"

"A lot of people in this area looked on Jessie as a local Robin Hood. He survived the war because of help from like-minded people. Later, most called his killer a hero, especially his victims."

Saint Joe's station was bustling with traffic when they arrived. One of the other passengers explained, "There's far more traffic through here than you might expect from a town this size. This was the original jumping-off point for the Oregon Trail, which got people accustomed to shipping through Saint Joe. Businesses here handle thousands of tons of freight every year, although most of it now goes by rail instead of by wagon."

Sara led the way when they left the train, keeping her gun hand free. Edwina waited on the steps behind her while Sara scanned the surroundings and every face in sight. Her range outfit, belted gun and marshal's star drew stares as they walked the short distance across the tracks to the station. Her eyes moved constantly, searching every vantage point which might allow someone to view the arriving passengers.

She stumbled when she planted a foot in an unnoticed depression and Edwina asked anxiously, "Did you twist your ankle?"

"No. I'm beginning to think I'm getting paranoid. I thought I saw someone duck behind the building next to the station. It was probably innocent, but I have a feeling our luck is running out. We've managed to dodge our pursuers for too long."

"Why do you think so?"

"There aren't very many different routes we can take to Denver, and even fewer to San Francisco. That narrows their search to a few check points, especially if they know about Ma and Pa from years ago. I have a feeling we're in for trouble and I've learned to trust my hunches."

They checked their luggage at the station before going to the ticket window to check on departures, finding the next express was due to leave for Denver at 8:08 that evening. "I'll take two tickets. Is there somewhere where we can stay for a few hours while we wait?" Sara asked.

"The Downtowner. Two blocks straight out the front door. They rent rooms by the hour for layovers."

"Thanks."

***

The sun was almost on the horizon and darkness

was only a short while away when they left the hotel. The buildings on the street were all brick, crowded wall-to-wall. False fronts faced the street, topped with ornate decorations of many types. The steeply-rising bluffs to the east of the business district were crowned with elaborate homes built by the more well-to-do residents, leaving the wooden homes and shacks of the poorer citizens crowded between the railroad tracks and the river.

Edwina was carrying the handbag to leave Sara's hands free while her eyes swept every nook and cranny, every shadow and doorway. The streets were nearly empty, except for a few people clustered at the distant station. Jumpy and uneasy, Sara halted at each cross street and carefully checked both directions before they hurried across.

A few dying rays of the sun were reflected from windows of the houses on the hill, illuminating the last intersection. One of those random rays spotlighted a furtive movement. Too fast for thought, she rammed her shoulder into Edwina, knocking her to the ground. A gun roared down the street and bullets whizzed over their heads as she dove for cover.

The dive became a roll and her revolver was already in her hand. Flame erupted as she fired four rounds into the shadows from which the gunfire had come. She grabbed Edwina and roughly yanked her into the meager shelter offered by the nearest building.

Muffled curses erupted from the shadows and a thud of footsteps quickly faded in the distance. Sara reloaded, hearing shouting from several directions, one voice much louder than the others. "This is the Law. Freeze!"

Sara's alto carried clearly in the evening stillness as doors banged open all along the street. "I'm United States Marshal Storm. Don't shoot!" Edwina shivered as they listened to the pounding footsteps of the on-coming lawman.

He skidded to a halt a few feet away, swearing lustily before the last of the fading sunlight was re-flected from the star pinned to Sara's vest. He flushed deeply enough to be seen in the dim light and apol-ogized for his language. "Sorry ladies. I've never met a lady marshal before. What's going on here? I heard shooting and came running."

Several more running figures arrived almost si-multaneously. Sara waited while they clustered around the constable.

"Tell us what happened and we'll all help search," offered one of the anonymous arrivals.

Sara said, "We were walking to the depot when we were bushwhacked. Whoever it was, was hidden halfway down the block to our right. I caught a flash of movement and we ducked or he might have hit us. I fired back and I think I hit him. At least I heard him cursing before I heard him beating it down the street."

The constable issued orders to the volunteers and several dashed off in different directions. Two stayed with Sara and Edwina. The constable lit his bull's-eye lantern and adjusted the wick before blank-ing it. He slipped around the corner with the darkened lamp in one hand and his gun ready in the other.

Sara kept a comforting arm around the silent Edwina, whose voice was shaky as she whispered, "I'll be all right, but it was terrifying."

"Marshal! He's gone, but you hit him. There's blood and a gun here."

Sara called back, "We'll come see what you've got."

The constable was thoroughly examining the deep shadow with the lantern when they arrived. "There's not a lot of blood so you probably just winged him. Still, it was enough he dropped his gun before he fled."

"Whoever he is, he's long gone," Sara said. "We've been followed since we left Washington. If you see some dude from the East with a bullet wound, you'll probably have the right man. I hate to run out on you but we have a train to catch in a few minutes. Unless you have a good reason for us to stay, we'd like to be on it."

"There's no need. We can handle it." The constable turned to one of the volunteers. "Harry, you go with these two ladies to the station. Get their names and a statement before they leave. I'll try to follow this bastard's tracks."

CHAPTER 14

Chief Marshal Matt West had been poring over paperwork for most of the morning as a gentle breeze and the summer sun streamed through his open window. He had almost finished dealing with the many reports on his desk when a knock at his door interrupted his thoughts.

His secretary announced with an unusual grin, "Marshal Storm would like to speak to you."

After a moment to organize his thoughts, he asked, mystified, "Is it Ted or Sue?"

"Neither. It's Sara."

His face showed his confusion when the secretary waved Sara and a stranger into his office. He rose to his feet, extending his hand while his eyes took in the star pinned to Sara's vest. "Good morning, Sara. This is quite a surprise, but I'm always glad to see you or your parents." His eyes shifted to her companion. "And who is this young lady with you?"

"Lady Edwina Harrison, please meet Marshal Matt West. My parents have known him for many years. We'd all trust him with our lives."

Sara turned back to the marshal and said grimly, "You are about to be entrusted with Edwina's life. After you've read this letter, we'll try to answer your questions."

Marshal West's eyes widened when she handed him an envelope. After skimming the contents, his respect was obvious. "Sara, I agree with Mr. Bailey. He could not have found anyone better qualified for this assignment than you. What can I do to help?"

She handed him another envelope which had *Hiram Harrison* written in a neat hand on the face. "We need you to mail this to your opposite number in San Francisco. Explain why we need him to deliver it in person to Edwina's father after he arrives at the British Legation. They can return an answer to us the same way. That way we can guarantee no one can trace the letter back to our ranch and Edwina."

"I know your dad often teased your mother about being devious." Marshal West's eyes twinkled. "You sure take after your mother. Your plan is better than any I'd have come up with on short notice. I'll be glad to mail the letter immediately. Is there anything else I can do for you?"

"Not at the moment."

Both young women took turns recounting their trip to Denver before Sara asked, "I have most of our expense money left. Everything I spent is accounted for. Do you think I should keep the cash, or should I give it to you until we come back through on the way to San Francisco?"

"I'll take the accounting of what you've already spent and forward it to Mr. Bailey. You keep the rest of the money until you've completed your assignment. Do you have enough to get you 'Frisco?"

She nodded.

He rose to shake hands with both young women, and followed them to the outer hall to bid them goodbye. As he watched them disappear, he thought, *Sara is one very courageous young woman! Just like her mother.*

***

Sue Storm dismounted from her horse in front of Manlick's Boarding House before handing the reins to her husband. Ted was flanked by their sons, Tim and Tom, astride their own horses amidst the bustle of traffic on Wilford's main street. She watched while they rode off, leading two riding horses and two pack horses. She grinned at her youngest daughter, Sally. "Let's go inside and get a table. They'll be along shortly."

She led the way, forced to duck at the doorway. She was the taller by only a fraction of an inch at six-feet-two in bare feet. Seventeen-year-old Sally was slimmer than her mother, still in the stage between late adolescence and early adulthood. Both were dressed in rider's boots, jeans, chambray work shirts and battered Stetsons. A holstered Colt .45 rode each right hip. The most obvious difference was Sally's bright red hair which cascaded from under her Stetson, unlike her mother's brown hair.

Sue stopped so abruptly Sally bumped into her and started to say, "What the—"

Sue exclaimed, "Sara!"

Sara had been sitting at a table in the dining room, waiting for her family to ride up. She watched her mother and sister dismount and moved to the door to greet them. She hugged her not-so-little sister and was enthusiastically hugged in turn.

She hugged her mother, whose sharp eyes

113

caught the star pinned to her vest.

Sue's eyes tightened as she contained her anger, only to be startled when Sara reached out and placed her own *borrowed* star in her hand.

"The star I'm wearing is mine," Sara whispered. "It's a long story. I'd like to save it until we're on the way home."

She raised her voice, loud enough for both to hear. "Let me introduce you to the lady who's responsible for me being a marshal."

They followed Sara through the crowded dining room as she led them to a table near the back of the room, where another young woman waited. The young woman rose to greet them. The stranger was dressed identically to Sara but Sue's sharp eye noted her clothes were obviously brand-new and she was weaponless.

"Ma, Sally, I'd like you to meet Lady Edwina Harrison, recently of Washington. She'll be staying with us for several weeks." She met her mother's eyes. "I'll be escorting her to San Francisco to meet her father."

A slight widening of her eyes was the only visible clue to Sue's astonishment as she offered her hand. "Welcome to Wilford and our home. We'll be glad to have you stay with us."

Edwina was unprepared for such immediate acceptance and hesitated for a second before offering her own, shaking Sally's as well. "Sara told me a lot about her family. I do hope I'm not intruding."

Sue dismissed her worry with a wave of her hand. "If we were short of room, we'd just add onto the ranch house. We've done so before."

A young girl materialized at Sue's elbow. "Aunt Sue, will the whole family be here?"

"Yes." Sue smiled and gave her a quick hug. "Anna, we'll have this lady as an extra. Unless you two have already eaten?"

"No. We just got here and were sitting down when I saw you coming up the street."

"Then that'll make seven of us." She hugged Anna again. Anna returned the hug and headed for the kitchen, a smile on her face.

Sara spoke quietly to Edwina, "Her mother died several years ago. Her grandmother owns the boarding house and took her in."

Edwina blinked and nodded. "While she's not really her aunt, your mother knows what it's like to be motherless."

The four women were joined a few minutes later by the men of the family, who greeted Edwina as warmly as had Sue and Sally. Everyone was hungry, and when their meals arrived a few minutes later, everyone applied themselves to the hearty meal.

Her brothers began to ply Sara with questions when they had eaten enough to dampen their appetites. They were frequently interrupted when friends and neighbors stopped to welcome her home.

"Yes, Philadelphia and Washington are as big as Ma and Pa told us." She waved at Edwina. "I did meet some very interesting people, but the rest of the story will have to wait until we're on the way home."

Sara's eyes sought her father's. "I'm going to take Edwina to meet Doc Madison. We'll be leaving as usual?"

"I'll take care of getting horses at the livery for you."

"Thanks, Pa."

He smiled fondly at the departing youngsters, then turned to Sue. "She's changed."

"She's more mature. There's something else about her that's changed but I can't define it yet." She grinned. "When I came in, the little minx told me the star she's wearing is her own." She shook her head ruefully. "She never told me she was going to *borrow* my old star, and now she comes home with one of her own. It must be quite a story."

***

Sara and Edwina left her brothers behind as they went their separate way. They walked slowly down the street, as Sara acknowledged welcome-home greetings from most of the people on the street. Edwina was surprised by the many warm welcomes and asked, "Do you know everybody in this village?"

"Just about." Sara laughed. "When you live in a small town all of your life, everyone knows everyone else. There aren't many people here I don't know or who don't know me."

"I wanted you to meet Doc Madison because he's like a grandfather to me. He was at the station to see me off when I left for Washington." Her smile was rueful. "He scolded me good for taking Ma's star, too."

Doc was home and greeted them warmly. His eyes narrowed sharply when he saw Sara's star, remembering his admonishment.

"This one is mine, earned fair and square. Edwina's safety is why I'm wearing it."

He hugged her tightly for a moment before indicating the swing hanging from the ceiling of the porch. "Sit down and tell me all about it. The two of you take that, and I'll take the rocking chair."

Sara hurried over her visits with family on the way to Washington, then explained how she had met and assumed responsibility for the life and safe travel of her new friend. Doc asked a few questions about items that were unclear but mostly let her talk until she concluded, "Edwina will be staying with us at the ranch until her father gets to San Francisco. Then I'll take her there to meet him."

"Sara, I'm proud of you. And glad to meet your new friend. Thanks for bringing her to meet me."

Doc watched the two young women walk away, heading back to the businesses on the main street. The striking similarity between Sara and her mother at eighteen took his memory back to the day he attended to the young woman wearing an identical star.

CHAPTER 15

Doc rode furiously at the head of the posse, silently cheering and cursing the pride, independence, and stubbornness of Sue Mason. *She should have waited until I got back. She'll get her fool self killed!* He drew his rifle from the scabbard and laid it across the saddle. They had almost reached their destination. The dozen riders racing along behind him drew their weapons as well.

A man stepped from behind the rocks some distance ahead, his hands held high as every gun leveled on him. A ray of sunshine glinted from the star pinned to his vest. Doc's mount skidded to a halt and he threw himself off. A few steps later he was in the man's face. He bellowed, "Where is she?"

The marshal prudently kept his hands high and nodded to his right. "Under cover behind the rocks. She's unconscious."

Doc went for the man's throat with both hands, eyes murderous. "Why didn't you keep her out of it? You should have known she'd get hurt!"

The marshal dropped his hands to protect his throat and was forced to use all his strength to keep from being throttled. "God knows I tried!"

The insanity ebbed and Doc relaxed his grip. He admitted, "She can be a bit stubborn at times." Fully regaining his balance, he asked, "How badly is she hurt?"

"A bullet gouge in the side, just above the hip. She's lost a lot of blood. I've patched her up as best I can."

Doc raced for the rocks where the young woman lay, stretched out on a saddle blanket. He whistled in momentary astonishment when a stray ray of sunshine reflected from the marshal's star pinned to her vest.

One of the other posse members approached and asked, "There are a lot of bodies out there. Who were they?"

Marshal Ted Storm grinned crookedly before he stunned them all to silence. "Snake Carson's gang. Sue outdrew him while I was unconscious."

More memories came back, and he smiled as they covered the years from the births of first Sara, then Sally, Tim, and the youngest, another boy. He vividly remembered the day Sue entered his office, her swollen belly making it difficult for her to walk. She sank into a waiting chair with a sigh of relief and looked up with a smile. "I'd like to ask a favor of you, you old reprobate."

Doc's response was in the same vein as always in their private routine. "I know I'm in trouble when you compliment me like this. What can I do for you?"

Sue smiled. "If this baby is a boy, I'd like to name him Thomas in your honor."

Doctor Thomas Madison was rudely returned to the present, suddenly made aware of his surroundings by Hank Smith who was shaking him hard. "Doc. Can you hear me?"

"Sorry. I was wool-gathering and got lost along the way. What can I do for you?"

***

119

Sara and Edwina were walking toward the post office when a familiar voice called loudly, "Sara!"

She spun on her heel as a young man her own age erupted from a doorway they had just passed. "Andy!"

He almost knocked her off feet, as he swept her into his arms and held her tightly. When he kissed her on the lips, they were both completely oblivious to their surroundings.

Another young man emerged from the doorway at a far more leisurely pace and doffed his Stetson to Edwina. "You're a friend of Sara's?"

"Yes. I am. Who might you be?"

He smiled broadly, jerking his thumb at the couple who were lost in their embrace. "Since you're a new friend of Sara's, that's Andy Franklin. I'm his big brother, Mark. What's your name?"

Sara's eyes were shining when they surfaced for air. She whispered in his embrace. "I'll be home tomorrow night if you want to come calling."

His eyes were alight. "You bet I'll be there!"

***

Mid-afternoon had passed before the Storms gathered at the livery. Two pack horses waited with seven saddled horses, their riders preparing to mount. Ted and Sue stood side-by-side, watching unobtrusively while Edwina approached her own horse. They were satisfied with her confident manner which showed she was accustomed to dealing with horses.

Ted said, "I see you're familiar with horses."

"Yes. I've ridden many times, but always side-saddle. This is going to be quite an experience for me." She met both their gazes. "This whole trip has been quite an experience. I've never worn men's clothes before, but after Sara told me how far it is to ride to your ranch, I could see the advantages. Three hours by horse, nine hours by buckboard, or twelve hours by wagon. It wasn't hard to decide."

"You're right about it being a time-saver." Sue's glance accounted for her family. Everyone was present so she slipped her foot into the stirrup and swung into the saddle. The rest of the family followed her lead.

Ted waited while Edwina tried to get her left foot into the stirrup. After several futile tries, he moved to help. "It just takes practice. This time, step in my hands and I'll boost you aboard." He bent his knees, cupping his hands.

She stared at him for a moment before placing her left foot in his hands. He stood smoothly, lifting her easily, until she could swing her right leg over the back of her horse.

Edwina was stunned at the power she felt in his hands, amazed at the ease with which he boosted her into her saddle. She watched with awe when he mounted his own horse with the ease of many years of practice.

Ted led while they threaded their way through streets still crowded with other ranchers and settlers. Wilford was small and they soon left the town behind, following a well-worn trail to the crest of a meandering ridge overlooking the town.

They halted to give Edwina her first full view of

Wilford, sprawled tightly against the mountainside. Businesses crowded together along the rails following the outer boundary of the town. Homes, a church and a school filled most of the remaining level area stretching to the rising slope of the mountain. A tumbling snow-melt-fed stream marked one end of the town.

She marveled at the beauty of the scene. Tree-covered slopes climbed steadily until they were lost in the distance, crowned at even greater distances by snow-capped peaks lining the horizon in every direction. She absorbed the grandeur in wonder. "It's no wonder you wanted to come back to your home. The scenery is magnificent!"

"It is rather spectacular. I've never appreciated the view as much as I do now."

Sue and Ted led off while the young women followed, Sara in the middle.

Tim and Tom brought up the rear with the two heavily-laden pack horses, which followed without need of halter or guidance.

They rode steadily, bunched closely enough to hear while Sara told of her trip, beginning with her first day in Denver. "Ma. Pa. Why did you never tell us about the night when you were nearly murdered on your trip home from Washington?"

Startled, both of her parents twisted in their saddles to stare at her. Her mother snapped, "Where did you hear that?"

"From a young man who believes you are an angel."

An embarrassed flush darkened her mother's cheeks when Sara recounted the story she had heard from Tony Benito. They stayed bunched while Sara told of her visits with their relatives along the way, censoring the account of her run-ins near Chicago, skipping to her arrival in Philadelphia.

While she told of her first meeting with Edwina and their travels across the nation, Edwina listened with one ear, marveling at the beauty of the surrounding mountains. She gasped at first sight of more than one vista as they wound through open meadows and heavy timber, the trail diving into deep gulches and soaring over sharp ridges. Silence had stretched out for some time until they crossed a small bridge over a shallow ravine. Edwina commented, "I see someone has put a lot of work into improving this road."

Ted chuckled. "Everyone using this trail does. There are always repairs and improvements that need to made every summer, so everyone who uses it pitches in. Right now it looks like an easy route, but come winter the snow piles up deep enough to make it impassable. That's when we use the long route if we absolutely have to go to town for supplies." He waved his hand. "For example, this bridge doesn't look like it's needed right now. It's an entirely different story when the snow's melting because the stream turns into a torrent that's mighty cold and dangerous to cross."

The sun was near the horizon when they stopped on another ridge, looking at the scene spread out below. Nestled against a mountainside protecting it from the north winds of winter, a rambling, white-painted ranch house dominated the ranch yard. Slightly downhill from the house, a huge red barn loomed, an island amidst a sea of corrals and smaller outbuildings.

Edwina was amazed, her eyes sweeping the ranch in the foreground, before moving to the backdrop of majestic mountains reaching to the sky all along the horizon. She said, "It's so beautiful it makes my heart ache."

Night was swiftly falling before they halted at the front porch. The pack horses were unloaded, and Sally and her brothers gathered the herd and guided them to the corrals. They made quick work of stripping them of their saddles before turning them loose in the corral for hay and water. The rest of the chores were finished in a few minutes, although full darkness had fallen before they returned to the ranch house.

Supper conversation was lively. Sara wanted to know what had happened on the ranch and in the neighborhood while she was gone, while the rest of the family had many questions regarding her trip. When the table had been cleared, and the dishes washed and put away, she mumbled. "I'd love to stay and talk all night, but I'm so tired I'm about to fall asleep. Would anyone mind if we wait to continue this discussion tomorrow?"

Edwina echoed her and both young women disappeared down the hall to the bedrooms. They had only been gone for a few minutes when Sally remembered the pine cones she had carelessly left on her sister's bed. She tip-toed down the hall, and soundlessly opened the door to peek in. When she returned, her parents looked up, concerned. Sally shook her head in wonderment. "She was already asleep. I've never seen her so tired."

CHAPTER 16

The house was quiet and the sun was high when Edwina entered the parlor the next morning, empty except for Sue, who was sitting at a roll-top desk in one corner. Working on a ledger, she acknowledged Edwina with a glance and a nod but continued her task. She eyed the room more carefully than she had the night before, concentrating on one wall that was almost completely covered with shelves loaded with many books. Moving closer to read the titles, she found they covered a broad spectrum of interests including history, philosophy, math, science, flying machines and many other topics.

Sue finished her last entry and looked up with a smile. "You look much more awake this morning than you did last night."

"I do feel much more awake." Edwina smiled and selected a chair where she could face the desk. "Mrs. Storm. I don't want to be an intruder on your family. What can I do to repay you?"

"First of all, since we're pretty informal around here, please just call me Sue. Secondly, you're our guest." She smiled. "I gathered from what the two of you told us yesterday, your upbringing has been entirely different from Sara's. Before we get into that, would you like something for breakfast?"

"Yes. I'm ravenous this morning."

"I have oatmeal and bacon keeping warm on the stove. If you want something else, I'll fix whatever you want."

"You don't need to. That sounds good."

Edwina found the kitchen much warmer than the parlor. Her eyes followed Sue to the sink where she opened a tap and vapor drifted away from the stream of water. "You have hot water!"

"We always keep a fire going in the stove. It heats the tank on the back, so we have hot, or at least warm, water year-around."

Edwina was awed. "There aren't many homes outside the large cities that have that, are there?"

"No. That luxury was one of the first improvements Ted installed when we were married." Sue grinned widely. "If I hadn't already, that alone would have made me love him." She beckoned Edwina to the window over the sink, which looked out the back of the house, and pointed to the slope of the mountain behind the ranch house. "The spring-fed stream feeds a reservoir part way up the mountain, which gives us pressure. The water is piped underground to the house, where we heat it here in the kitchen. Then some of it is piped from here to the bathroom." She smiled. "We have one of the few homes with indoor plumbing in this part of the state."

She pointed to a spot much lower on the slope. "See the door cut into the mountain? It opens into a cave, which is our root cellar and ice storage."

Edwina's eyes widened and her brows rose. "Ice storage?"

"During the winter we cut blocks of ice from

a small lake around the corner of the mountain. We haul those blocks back here and pack them in sawdust in the cave. The ice lasts all summer and we use it to keep food cold in the ice chest." She indicated a squat cabinet at the back of the kitchen.

"That has to be a lot of work. From what Sara told me, you already have enough work to keep an army busy."

Sue chuckled. "It sure seems like it a lot of the time." She turned serious for a moment. "The entire time we've been married, Ted has gone out of his way to make our lives a lot easier than it is for most families."

She moved Edwina's breakfast from the stove to the table. "You know a lot about us by now. Why don't you tell me about yourself?"

Edwina found it far easier to tell her story a second time, as she had told Sara so much earlier, concluding, "Sara's the only person I ever told about how I felt. It doesn't hurt nearly as much to tell you."

She swallowed hard at the sympathy on Sue's face and received a gentle hug. "I've heard said a sorrow shared is as sorrow halved." Edwina brightened. "Now I really believe the truth of it."

The kitchen was silent except for the whinny of a horse in the distance. "I find it hard to believe how many books are in your library. Does everyone read all of them?"

Sue laughed. "We all read a lot, especially in the winter, but no one reads them all. My mother read to me before she died, when I was a toddler. My father was a professor in his early years and he taught me to read. Many of the books you see were his.

"I schooled our children during the winters when we couldn't travel because of the snow. Every fall we go to Denver and bring home more. We've collected a lot of books on many subjects over the years."

When Edwina finished eating, they sat for a bit in a comfortable silence.

Sue said, "Sara must have been more exhausted than she let on to sleep this late. I'm sure she didn't tell us everything that happened to the two of you. Is there anything you want to share with me?"

"I can't answer for her. I will tell you she saved my life on three different occasions."

Sue's face was somber. "I thought it must be something like that."

Sara's voice came from the hallway. "I heard your question. I'd like to go for a walk with you after I have something to eat."

"I'd like that," Sue replied. She looked up when her daughter bent to give her an uncharacteristic kiss on the cheek.

After breakfast, Sue led the way to the secluded glen where they had shared thoughts and troubles many times before, knowing something was troubling her daughter. Her normally bubbly personality was as flat and subdued as the solid patterns of light and shadow created by the mid-morning sun. Their favorite seat was a sun-warmed slab of stone. Sue slipped her arm around her daughter's shoulders. Silence filled the hide-away while she felt the tension in those shoulders slowly relax.

Many minutes of silence passed before Sara could meet her mother's eyes. When she spoke, it was a flat, lifeless, monotone. "Ma, I killed a man."

"Why don't you tell me about it?"

Sara told of their clandestine departure from the embassy, the gunshots and the flight from the livery. "I knew I didn't miss, but it didn't seem real. When we got to Denver, there was a letter from Mr. Bailey, telling me the man was dead. The coroner ruled it justifiable, something about fallout from an old Preston gang everyone in Washington knew about."

The sun was nearing its zenith before either spoke again. Tears had left their traces on both faces when Sara whispered, "Ma, thanks for listening."

Sue held her daughter tightly, silently cursing the ghost of Theodore Preston, who had reached out from the grave after so many years in an attempt to strike down her daughter. Her own voice was little more than a whisper. "I always hoped to be able to spare you the hurt. You were justified to shoot. I'm so glad I'm here to help you through it."

***

Shadows were rapidly ascending the mountains to the east when the Franklin family rode into the ranch yard, their wagon making enough noise to announce their arrival. Andy leaped to the ground before the wagon had halted and swept Sara into his arms, oblivious to everyone else. Ben, Cathy and Mark stepped down from the wagon and climbed the steps to the porch to greet everyone. Sally introduced Edwina before Sara and Andy reluctantly released one another, slightly embarrassed by the sly grins directed at them.

Cathy followed Sue to the kitchen, carrying the large basket she brought with her. After she set it on the table, she hugged her good friend, smiling broadly. "We got a letter from our Mary yesterday. I'm going to be a grandmother again next spring." They embraced, savoring her joy. When the three younger women joined them to help prepare the meal, the kitchen was crowded, but with so many hands helping the meal was soon ready to serve.

The Franklins insisted on hearing about Sara's travels, enjoying vicariously the sights she had seen in Washington. Once she paused, Cathy spoke up, "Andy told us when he got home you were wearing a marshal's star. Like mother, like daughter. You two are so much alike."

Sara explained about her chance encounter with Mr. Bailey and its consequences, relating the chain of events which brought Edwina to Wilford with her.

Her mother interrupted gently. "You and Andy haven't had any time for yourselves. Why don't you let the rest of us take care of the dishes?"

"Thanks, Ma. We'll be back after a bit."

Andy followed Sara through the kitchen and out the back door, making no comment when they passed a row of gun belts hanging on pegs beneath their owner's Stetsons. A flicker of lamp-light reflected from the star pinned to one belt.

They strolled hand-in-hand in darkness broken only by the faint illumination from the canopy of stars overhead. The night was so still they talked in whispers as they climbed a short distance up the slope behind the ranch house. A solitary tree emerged from the darkness, visible only as a greater darkness.

Andy sat down with his back against the trunk, holding out his arms for Sara to sink into his embrace. They snuggled against each other, silent and motionless, enjoying the closeness of one cheek against the other. When her lips sought his, the kiss lengthened while his fingers began to move, tracing gentle circles through the rough material of the man's shirt over her breasts. Her heart raced, sensation coursing through her body. When the tantalizing fingers finally retreated, her head sank limply against his shoulder as she gasped for breath. When her breathing and heart rate subsided, he asked softly, "Sara. Will you marry me?"

Her eyes met his in the dim starlight. "YES!"

CHAPTER 17

The Franklins were preparing to leave when the kitchen door creaked open and the tardy young couple entered the parlor. Sue's pulse raced in anticipation when Andy and Sara went straight to Ted. She could see Andy take a deep breath as his eyes met the older man's.

"Sir," Andy said formally. "May I have the honor of your daughter's hand in marriage?"

Ted beamed and said, "Yes, you may." His eyes met Sue's as tears of joy trickled down her face. He embraced his daughter. "You have our blessing." Then he turned and shook Andy's hand. "Andy, welcome to the family."

Hours later, Sue snuggled into Ted's enveloping arms, and related what Sara had told her about killing a man in self-defense. "She told Andy all about it tonight while they were on the mountain. She was terrified it might drive him away, but it didn't change his feelings for her. I'll be so happy when she can take Edwina on to meet her father. She said they'll set a date for the wedding when she gets home."

They were almost asleep when Ted whispered, "Mark would sure like to make Edwina Andy's sister-in-law."

"He told you?"

"No, but I could see he was smitten. If there's

time, I'm sure he'll try for her hand."

***

Edwina was up with the others the next morning, to join in the unending daily tasks filling a rancher's life. She lacked the physical stamina of the Storms, who were conditioned by a lifetime of hard physical labor, but she helped with everything she was capable of without complaining, in spite of blisters and sunburn.

She often rode with Sara to check fences or scout for sick and injured livestock. They met Andy and Mark frequently, sharing range chores which shifted interchangeably from one ranch to the other as the workload demanded. None of them fully realized the number of benevolent smiles shared between their parents.

As physically hard on her as the days were, they were the happiest Edwina had ever experienced. Her idyll was shattered one morning at breakfast when conversation died at the sound of a fast-approaching horse.

Ted murmured, "Sounds like trouble."

Tom, closest to the door, left the table and returned moments later with Sheriff Gunderson.

The sheriff was grim. "You need to be on the look-out. I got word last night there's a hired killer headed your way." Shock and anger flashed around the table.

"The sheriff in Denver first alerted me several days ago. One of his stool-pigeons reported some dude was trying to hire someone to kill Sara. The man couldn't get any takers there, but they kept an eye on him. He left Denver yesterday on the train, supposedly for Wilford. He didn't get off, but the sheriff at Long Gulch reported a man matching the description did get off there. He bought an outfit before heading into the mountains in this direction."

Edwina paled as her stomach knotted with fear.

Heads turned to Ted for guidance. He said, "We'll start searching for him. He doesn't know the country and we'll find him before he finds us."

Edwina gulped and asked hesitantly, "I don't know anything about a situation like this, but wouldn't an outlaw expect activity here at the ranch? If everyone's gone, would he be suspicious? I wouldn't be much help out there searching, but I could stay here and do chores. Someone has to do them anyway and keep the ranch looking lived-in."

Ted considered her suggestion which encouraged her to continue, "Might that be important?"

"That's a damn good idea. Yes, it could be critical to drawing him in."

Everyone gulped their breakfast before beginning hasty preparations for the search. When Ted passed Edwina on his way out, he gave her an affectionate hug, exactly as she had seen him do many times with his daughters. "You'll do fine." The simple words were high praise.

***

Edwina gave Sara a last wave before the search party disappeared over the crest of the hill looming

134

above the ranch. Taking a deep breath, she headed for the main barn to finish the morning chores. Her heart sank as she realized it would take her all day to accomplish what four experienced ranchers could do in an hour.

The sun had dipped below the mountains and she was battling total exhaustion when she staggered up the steps to the ranch house. The tasks which seemed so easy when she was helping someone else had proved to be daunting when she had to do them alone. Pride and self-respect had driven her to prove to herself she could do what she had promised.

She forced her aching body to the kitchen, where she gulped a cold roast-beef sandwich and several glasses of water from the faucet. When she had finished eating, she stumbled down the hall to her room, managing to hit the bed instead of the floor when she collapsed. Too tired to change clothes, much less care, she was instantly asleep.

When she woke the sun was up but barely clear of the horizon. She tried to sit up but aching muscles screamed in protest. She tried again, but hurt in so many places she abandoned dignity and simply rolled off the bed onto her knees.

The next half-hour was near-agony as she managed to clean up and fix a more substantial meal than she had eaten the night before. With her breakfast completed, she headed for the barn to begin another day's chores. A chorus of welcoming knickers from the horses in the corral lifted her lagging spirits. She laughed in spite of her aches and pains. "It's nice to have someone appreciate me."

The afternoon was nearly spent when she finished, proud to have completed the chores in markedly less time than the day before. She was about to hang up the pitchfork she had been using when she heard the clip-clop of approaching hoof beats. She froze, her hands clammy as terror gripped her. When she could make her feet move, she sidled to the open barn door and peered out. Her hands clenched the fork handle tightly for reassurance that she had a chance to defend herself.

Her first timorous glance spotted the rider who had entered the ranch yard. He first looked toward the ranch house, but when he turned to face the barn, her knees nearly buckled in relief. "Mark!" she cried out.

He urged his horse toward her and quickly dismounted. She was thankful for having the presence of mind to stick the tines of the fork safely in the ground at her feet before his arms closed around her.

"Are you all right?"

She nodded jerkily, savoring the comfort of his arms, relief holding her silent for a moment. "I didn't recognize your horse and it scared me. I'm fine now you're here." She made no effort to escape his arms and met his eyes. "I'm glad to see you, but what are you doing here?"

Mark belatedly realized he was holding her tightly but could tell she was comfortable in his embrace. He explained, "Sam Davis stopped by on his way home from town. He told Ma about the Storms going on a hunt for a killer. When I got back and learned you were here alone, I figured you could use some help. I came over to help while they're gone."

Edwina raised her hand to stroke his cheek. "I could use the help. I just now finished the chores, but another day like yesterday would probably have finished me off." Her eyes held his, her voice soft and warm as she said, "I'm glad you came." She nestled in his arms for several moments before he reluctantly released her.

***

Any observer would have had no problem realizing the rider was a newcomer to the Colorado Rockies. His seat in the saddle was unstable, the hat on his head a derby rather than the usual Stetson. Alfonzo "The Rat" Scalize clutched a map that had cost several months' pay for most working people in bribes. The map was plainly marked with the location of a ranch.

He was cursing steadily, having been unable to locate the ranch shown on the map, as he had continued to swear for most of the past four days. He cursed his boss, who had selected him for this wild-goose chase simply because he was the only enforcer who had ever ridden a horse. Three days of aimless searching had finally led to the well-worn trail he had literally stumbled upon. His total uncertainty of his location or direction was compounded by hunger, having run out of food the night before. Desperate, he flipped a coin, still cursing the spineless dogs in the Denver gangs who had refused to sign on with him.

The coin came up heads. He turned west, riding off the trail but parallel with it. Guided by the compass he bought along with the map, he tried to stay in cover. Time and miles passed slowly while he made his best effort to move silently.

When the trail disappeared over a slight rise a short distance ahead, his hopes rose at the distant whinny of a horse. Tying his horse to a sapling, he drew a rifle from the scabbard before slowly moving forward, bent low to the ground.

Several minutes passed before he reached the crest of the ridge. He dropped to the ground and crawled forward with the rifle clutched tightly in his left hand. When he cleared the crest, his eyes swept across a ranch house and outbuildings sprawled on the valley floor. *How the hell do I know if this is the right ranch?*

He watched for many minutes before a young woman emerged from the barn and headed for the ranch house. He smiled in grim satisfaction, sure at last of his target. There could be only one ranch in these mountains where a woman wore a man's clothing.

Drawing the rifle forward by the barrel, he started to bring it to his shoulder.

"Freeze!"

The Rat froze, rapidly considering his chances against one man. When he turned his head, his body went cold. Six rifle muzzles were aimed at him from less than twenty feet away, all rock-steady and unwavering.

"Drop the rifle! Put your face in the dirt and your hands on the top of your head."

Alfonzo's hands were numb with shock. Seconds later they were securely tied behind his back.

Ted's face was hard as stone, his voice flat. "You

kids head for the ranch! Ma will help me with this son-of-a-bitch."

The siblings were shaken by his demeanor and departed without argument. They hurried back to the copse of trees where they had hidden their horses before scurrying down the trail for the ranch. When they were out of sight, Ted stalked to his own horse. Taking the lariat from the pommel, his hands were busy. He stooped to yank the captive to his feet and spun the hoodlum to face him. Alfonzo's knees grew weak. *Death* stared at him from inches away, a hangman's noose clenched in his left hand. He tried to shrink away, with no success.

Eyes of stone glared at him. The voice carried absolute conviction, the more terrifying for its blandness. "The only chance you have of being alive five minutes from now is to start talking. If you don't, we'll hang you from the nearest tree and leave your carcass for the buzzards to pick clean."

CHAPTER 10

Marshal Matt West looked up after reading the hand-written confession, studying the trio facing him for a moment before sighing in satisfaction. "You caught a paid assassin, that's for sure. When I first heard of the stool pigeon's tip to the police, I was sure that was what we were dealing with. Why don't you give me the details?"

Ted started with the arrival of Sheriff Gunderson and his warning. "Sue took Sara and Tom with her, while I took Sally and Tim with me. We split up so we could cover the obvious routes from Long Gulch, sure no stranger would know the minor trails.

"Sally spotted this intruder on the second day, but we knew we had to confirm he was the right man, so we followed him in pairs. One team at a time trailed him for the next three days, while the rest of us kept watch on the other trails to make sure we didn't miss someone."

Contempt colored his voice. "It was obvious he was lost. When he finally stumbled on the trail to the ranch, we watched him use a map to try to figure out which way to go. Even then, he didn't know for sure. Sally was close enough to hear him cursing. She saw him flip a coin to decide, but he did guess right and headed for the ranch.

"Tim was riding with her so he came after the rest of us. We caught up with Sally and we all followed until he dismounted and crawled to the ridge above the ranch. When he started to bring his rifle to bear on

Edwina, we knew we had the right man, so all six of us drew on him.”

Sue snarled, “With rifles.”

Matt laughed, sourly. “I’m sure that got his attention.”

“It sure did!” Ted’s lips twitched. “After we tied him up, I sent the youngsters back to the ranch. I didn’t want them to see even the threat of a hanging. When they were out of sight, I told him to start talking or I’d hang him from the nearest tree.”

His voice was icy. “He believed me and started talking, which saved him. I wouldn’t hesitate to kill any man who threatened my family like he did. When we got back to the ranch, Sue wrote everything down and he signed it.”

“We thought at first he was with the bunch after Edwina.” Sue indicated Sara, her voice stern. “This young lady didn’t bother to tell us until then about her two run-ins near Chicago.”

Sara reddened. “I never imagined anything would ever come of them. I obviously stepped on someone’s toes a lot harder than I thought.”

“I’ll talk to the district attorney and see what we can do. I wouldn’t hold any hope of having anyone in Chicago arrest them, if I were you.” He tapped the confession lying on his desk. “Both a congressman and the head of the Chicago Mob will have a lot of friends.”

“You have two inactive marshals who’ll volunteer for the job,” Ted said, his tone dangerous.

Angry, Sara spoke up, “And one active one.” She

fingered her star.

"I know the three of you would be glad to arrest them. The problem is you'd be as far out of your depth there as Alfonzo was here." Matt scowled in frustration. "First things first. Let me see what we can do about getting warrants. If this were only a State of Colorado criminal charge, we wouldn't have a prayer of getting someone extradited from Chicago. Since he was going to attack Sara, I'll file an attempted murder charge on a federal agent. I'm not about to promise something I might not be able to deliver, but I know a man who once worked in the Chicago office that I'd trust. If he's still there, he might be willing to help."

***

Wesley Nance, U. S. Marshal (Retired), stared in disbelief at his companion and sputtered, momentarily unable to find voice for his frustration. He swallowed hard before hissing, "If you think you can just walk in off the street and arrest Thomas Hollingsworth or Representative Rahlings, you're insane. I don't care if you have warrants for their arrest. Those two literally control the law here in Chicago."

He made a throwing-away gesture with his left hand. "I wouldn't give you two cents for your chances of arresting either of them. In fact, I wouldn't give one cent for your chances to live long enough to get anywhere near Hollingsworth. He is one very bad apple and always has at least one trigger-happy bodyguard with him at all times."

"Bear with me for a minute," Ted Storm said with a grin. "I have a secret weapon which will take care of the problems you so graciously pointed out to me."

The two men were sitting at a table in a small cafe in a quiet neighborhood. Marshal Nance had received a telegram from an old friend in the Marshal Service, warning him to anticipate a message he would find extremely interesting. The message arrived the next day via a street urchin, suggesting this meeting place. A sense of curiosity was one of his worst vices and he was now facing a man who had to be certifiably insane.

"Ah. Here they are now." Ted's eyes brightened when he stood. The marshal's eyes followed, and after a moment of amazed hesitation, he stood as well.

Ted politely pulled out a chair for the older of the two women. Nance collected his wits enough to do the same for the younger woman, dumbfounded, as were most of the other diners in the small restaurant. Both women were dressed modestly in subdued colors, but their height, erect bearing, and deep tans marked them as unusual.

Ted introduced them, and explained his plan, "Marshal, we can arrest Hollingsworth and Rahlings and get them out of town for a trial in Denver. We just need to know the lay of the land, who they are, where they hide. For that we need your help."

Nance was glad for the privacy of their table in a back corner. He braced his elbows on the table, covering his face with one hand and groaned. "I'd love to see those two put away for life, but you haven't heard a word I've said. You don't stand a chance because you'll get killed instantly if you try to arrest them. They have too many politicians on their payroll for any local law to give you any assistance. That also guarantees they wouldn't face any charges from shooting you."

"You worry too much," Ted said. "We can do it, and we will do it. Take a look, and I'll tell you *how* we're going to do it."

Marshal Nance shook his head in resignation. When he uncovered his eyes, he was stunned to see United States marshal stars cupped in three hands. Amazed, his gaze darted from one to another.

"We'll take them by surprise, because they'll never expect two women to be carrying guns. We'll have them out of town before they know what hit them."

The marshal shook his head in bemused wonder as a smile blossomed on his face. "I'll be damned! You just might be able to do it with your secret weapons."

"My friends call me Wes. I have other friends, both federal and local, who are still on active duty and are as sick of those crooked bastards as I am. Give me a day and I'll see about getting some *unofficial* help to get you, and them, out of town."

He signaled the waitress who took their order and disappeared toward the kitchen. His dejection had fled. "Let's get one thing straight! You're on my turf and I want the three of you to be invisible until the last moment. Stay off the streets. I'll get in touch with you tomorrow night. In the meantime, for God's sake, keep those stars out of sight!

"We'll have to pull this off as quickly as possible, before someone spills the beans." He glared at his companions. "We're only going to have one chance, so we have to get it right the first time."

***

144

Two days later the closed carriage threaded its way slowly through the heavy traffic in a dilapidated area not far from the bustle of downtown. Run-down brick and stone buildings crowded the narrow sidewalks, which left little room for pedestrians between them and the traffic passing on the street.

They had to strain to hear Wes over the street noise. "That's Thomas Hollingsworth and his hired watchdog. You can set your watch by when they take their afternoon *coffee* at the tavern down the street." His outrage was palatable. "He's so damn punctual because he has so many people paid off he doesn't have to worry. I'll be glad to see him get what he deserves."

They stayed hidden behind the drawn curtains while their driver worked his way through the crowded streets from one target to another. When the carriage halted in a secluded glen in a city park, the three Storms dismounted.

Ted asked softly, "Tomorrow?"

"Tomorrow." Wes pulled the door closed and the carriage rolled away, disappearing into the screening trees.

***

Sara's stomach was aflutter and her throat was dry when she walked out of the seedy millenary shop where she had spent a few minutes to waste time. She stood idly on the sidewalk for a moment, her gaze sweeping the scene, taking in the two men who had stepped onto the sidewalk in the middle distance. She relaxed when she spotted the open buggy and her father. He caught her eye in turn, signaling by touching the brim of his Stetson.

Sara started walking slowly toward the two men, adjusting her pace to allow Ted's local driver, an off-duty marshal, to negotiate the stream of traffic. They all needed to be at the ambush at the correct moment.

Her skin crawled when the eyes of the two men noticed her. Her heart beat harder, shaking her body. The traffic thinned slightly, the street noise diminishing enough so she could hear the two men exchanging coarse comments about her figure. She drew a quick breath as the buggy drew near, altering her path to confront the two men.

The bodyguard was closest to the street and blocked his companion with an arm. She stopped a few feet away, eying them for a few seconds. Her voice was surprisingly steady, even to her own ears, when she said, "Someone pointed you out to me. I need to be absolutely sure. Are you Thomas Hollingsworth?"

The bodyguard sneered, "Who wants to know?"

The other man waved his hand dismissively and said, "Yeah. I'm Hollingsworth. Who wants to know?"

Sara's muscles tensed, readying for action. "I have a message for you." She waggled her fingers at the bag hanging from her shoulder. Both men glared suspiciously. She opened the bag to draw out an envelope, extending it to Hollingsworth. The bodyguard reached for it but she stepped back, steel in her voice. "It's personal. I was instructed to deliver it to your boss, not some flunky. I'm to wait while he reads it."

They stood in a rigid stand-off for several seconds until Hollingsworth snorted derisively. "Hell. What can she do? Ease off while I read it." He stepped toward her with an open hand.

Sara was close enough to give him the envelope. She slipped her hand into her shoulder bag when their attention was diverted. Hollingsworth took the envelope and opened it. Holding the sheet of paper with both hands, he began to read as his face turned a furious red. He glared at her and snorted, "An arrest warrant! For me?"

The bodyguard hesitated for a crucial few seconds, his mouth agape.

Sara slapped a handcuff against each of Hollingsworth's wrists and they snapped shut. Both men were red with outrage when she snarled, her eyes on the bodyguard. "There's a Colt .45 about six inches from your ear. He doesn't miss."

The bodyguard froze for an instant as he turned to see the black muzzle of Ted's revolver inches away. He glared at Sara, his eyes murderous with humiliation and insane rage. He shouldered his charge aside and grabbed blindly for her.

Reacting on instinct, she kicked as hard as she could. Her pointed rider's boot caught him between the legs.

No man could withstand such a blow. The guard's face turned from red to white, then to green as he doubled over, retching. His descending face met her rising knee, the blow smashing his craggy nose and throwing him backwards, unconscious.

Hollingsworth regained his balance to find himself facing another .45, this one in Sara's hand. Coldly, she ordered, "Into the buggy or I'll bend this gun barrel over your thick skull."

Intimidated by the sight of her gun and her voice, he paled and swallowed before obeying. When he was seated under the watchful muzzle of Ted's gun, Sara climbed into the seat of the open buggy behind him. When she was seated, she prodded the back of their prisoner with her own Colt.

Ted commended quietly, "Good job."

The driver flicked the reins across the horses' rumps and they moved off. The bodyguard lay crumpled unconscious on the sidewalk, blood pouring from his shattered nose. The entire encounter had taken less than a minute from Sara's first word. Only a few of the pedestrians in the vicinity had yet realized what had just happened. Of those who had, none had any desire to challenge a woman who could do such damage to a man known to be a vicious killer.

CHAPTER 19

Representative Wilson Rahlings' office was busy, typical of an afternoon at the beginning of the month, *dealing with the affairs of his constituents.* In truth, most of those waiting were bagmen for his many shake-down victims, delivering their monthly extortion payments.

The hulking secretary/bodyguard looked up in surprise when a tall, well-dressed woman carrying a large handbag entered. He was curious, but his manners were his usual surly self. He snapped, "What do you want?"

The woman did not respond but leaned across the desk, grabbing and twisting his ear hard between thumb and forefinger. Speaking as though to a naughty child, she said gently, "I need to see the Congressman. Don't bother to ask why, because it's personal. You can tell him the name is Mason."

The secretary twisted in pain at her grip. When he tried to grab her wrist with one hand, she squeezed even harder. When he tried to grab her wrist with his other hand, the strength of her grip made him realize any attempt would be futile. He snarled in surrender, "Yes, Ma'am. I'll send you in next."

Sue Storm smiled sweetly as she released his ear and said, "Don't forget."

He nearly swore at her, but the cold eyes holding his own forced him to change his response to a barely perceptible nod. She selected a chair as far as possible from the others who were waiting, ignoring their curious glances. Eager to get rid of her, the secretary ushered her into the office of Congressman Rahlings a few minutes later. The hulking secretary was tempted to stay but a cold glance changed his mind and he closed the door on his way out.

Sue's eyes swept the office. The congressman was seated behind a huge desk in a room furnished with no discernible style. Paper was piled on every flat surface, including the floor.

He stared at the new arrival in surprise, obviously unaccustomed to dealing with non-paying constituents, especially a female. Plainly baffled, he waited for her to speak. The silence lasted for several minutes. She was obviously not intimidated and he was the first to speak. "What can I do for you, Mrs. Mason?" Another lengthy silence unnerved him still further.

"I have a document I was asked to deliver to you personally." She drew an envelope from her handbag with one hand, tapping it gently against the other while she waited.

He tried to outwait her. Several more minutes passed before he surrendered, coming around his desk to meet her. He took the envelope, eying her suspiciously. When he began to read, a wave of crimson disbelief flared across his face. "You think you can arrest me? I'm a Congressman!"

Sue's hands flashed out and spun him around. Seconds later the astounded congressman found his wrists handcuffed behind his back. Speechless, he watched her remove a gun belt from her bag, his astonishment turning into apprehension when she buckled it around her waist with the ease of long practice. He turned a sickly white when she pinned a U. S. marshal star to her bodice.

She picked up the dropped warrant, folded it, and stuffed it into her captive's shirt pocket. "You are under arrest for conspiracy to commit murder and assault on a federal officer." Her tone was frigid. "For your information, the law says the only time you're immune to criminal charges is when you are actually on the floor of the House. I'm sure your fellow members will be glad to get rid of a scoundrel like you." She glared at her prisoner, "We're going to walk out through the office together." She patted the revolver in her holster for emphasis. "If anyone is stupid enough to try anything, you get the second bullet."

The congressman's face alternated between red and white when he was shoved through the door, forced into the lead as they moved toward the door. Several *constituents* were still waiting and gaped in astonishment. Disbelief followed the handcuffed figure shuffling toward the door as stunned whispers erupted. The secretary started get to his feet. Sue's hand flashed down and he was faced with the sinister black orifice of her revolver. He sank into his chair, cold sweat trickling down his face.

Sue's calm voice carried clearly, "Don't even think about it. He's under arrest for attempted murder. If you try anything, you both get a bullet."

The ashen prisoner stumbled through the door, where Sue steered him to a waiting open carriage. Dropping her Colt into her holster, she grabbed the manacled prisoner by the collar and the seat of his pants, boosting him up to sit beside the driver. She climbed into the back seat and they moved off smartly.

Bewildered constituents watched in disbelief from the door.

***

It was a long, silent, ride before Ted, Sara, and their prisoner approached their destination, which was heralded in the distance by the frequent shrill of locomotive whistles. The building was an imposing brick and stone edifice, with the name *Wells-Fargo Company* carved over the main entrance. They continued for a short distance down the street, past the front entrance, to a heavy iron gate, which swung open, allowing them to enter the short cul-de-sac of a sally port, a closed and roofed space which allowed the transfer of money and valuables in much greater security. The gate clanged shut behind them as their driver slowed the horse to a walk, halting at the approach of a burly guard carrying a shotgun. When Ted and Sara showed him their marshal's stars, he waved them forward.

A massive inner door creaked open and they drove inside the huge building, where several men were waiting. One man broke from the group, hurrying toward them while the prisoner was roughly escorted away.

Wesley Nance was ecstatic, beaming as he shook hands. "I've never been so delighted to be proved wrong! I still can't believe you actually arrested Thomas Hollingsworth. You'll be glad to know Sue got here about fifteen minutes ago with Rahlings. She's waiting for you in the crew room."

They followed Wesley as he led them to a door a bit farther into the building, where Sue joined them on a large platform. A few minutes later the protesting prisoners were forced aboard an undistinguished rail express car by several carefully-anonymous officers. They were accompanied by two men carrying sawed-off shotguns, one of whom said, "I'm Fred." He waved at his fellow. "He's Ward. Our car will be coupled to our train in a few minutes. As soon as the passengers board at the station, we'll be headed for Denver."

Sara watched from the open doorway while the two prisoners were forced to a pair of bunks along one end of the car, where their newly-acquired manacles and the chains of their leg irons were locked into large hasps bolted to the wall. Half the car's length was sealed off behind a heavy door, next to two large safes bolted to the floor, back-to-back. A now-cold pot-bellied stove was centered in the remaining open space, surrounded by a small table and three chairs.

Fred smiled and said dryly, "It's not like home, but it'll do until you're in Denver. We're glad to give all of you a ride. I'm afraid you ladies will have to move to one of the passenger cars when we get to the station. Mister can ride with us if he wants to."

Sara nodded at the dividing wall. "Can you tell me what's in there?"

Fred shook his head. "You don't need to know." The car suddenly shifted, the clang of coupler meeting coupler ringing through the car. "I might tell you after we get to Denver." He grinned slyly. "Then again, I might not."

***

The Denver station was crowded with curious onlookers when they arrived. Sara had been seated at a window for some time, anticipating her first glimpse of home. When the station finally appeared around a gentle curve, she tugged at her mother's sleeve, pointing to a waiting crowd.

Sue sighed. "Pa and I went through something like this before you were born." She grimaced. "It's a circus, but hopefully it won't last long. Just watch what you say, because if you goof you'll stir up a big controversy."

Once on the platform, they ignored the pressure of the crowd and its shouted entreaties while they pushed their way through a narrow path to the express car, where Marshall Matt West and four deputies were waiting. A few minutes later, the two hostile prisoners were ushered away by the deputies. The marshal shook hands enthusiastically, welcoming them. "Congratulations on a job well-done." He indicated a man standing a few feet away. "I don't believe any of you've met District Attorney George Wayne. I've told him a great deal about the three of you."

While Marshal West led the way through the crowd, they were bombarded with questions by a mob of reporters. Sara took her cue from her parents who simply shook their heads and refused to comment. The D.A. fended off all questions with "No comment," until they reached a waiting carriage. Turning to the crush of reporters, he said, "I know you're all anxious to get the story. After I've talked to the Storms, I'll schedule a press conference to answer your questions."

Sara and her parents were tired and hungry by the time the D.A. summarized their report. He said, "I'm sure we'll soon have an invasion of high-priced lawyers swarming in from Chicago. I'm also confident the judge will refuse to grant bail, or both of them would flee the state. The written confession, and your testimony, will make it easy to convict them. I'll keep in touch as the case develops and let you know in advance about the trial date."

They were almost to the stairs when Marshal West exclaimed, "Sara, wait a minute. I almost forgot, I received a letter from 'Frisco addressed to Edwina." He hurried back to his office. "It came the day before yesterday. I held it here because I knew you'd be back in town today."

Sara's heart sank as she took the offered envelope. "I'm happy for her, but I'll really miss her when she leaves."

***

Darkness had fallen except for the faint afterglow of sunset before they rode into the ranch yard, where they were welcomed by whinnies from the horses in the corral and shouts of welcome from Sara's siblings. Sara and her parents stumbled wearily toward the ranch house while the others took care of their horses.

Edwina was waiting at the base of the steps, back-lit by lamplight spilling onto the porch through the windows and open door. She hugged Sara in welcome but soon realized something was amiss. "What's the matter?"

"A letter for you came from San Francisco. It has to be from your father. I'm afraid you'll be leaving soon."

Her face fell. "I think I'd best go to my room before I read this."

Sue wrapped her in a comforting hug. "We understand. You take as much time as you need."

Edwina's eyes were blurred as tears began to trickle down her cheeks. When she reached the privacy of her room, her hands were shaking so badly the words were hard to read.

My Dearest Daughter Edwina,

I received your letter today, delivered to me by a Marshal Brown

here in the Consular office. I was shocked and horrified to

read of the attempt on your life and am thankful to God

for the young woman who has saved you so many times.

Your suspicions in regard to Ambassador Starr are valid.

He is aware I have documents in my possession proving his guilt

in criminal matters. I believe he would be desperate enough to try to

kidnap you and hold you hostage to prevent my using them.

I believe you would be safest under the protection off the

consular here in San Francisco and insist that you find your way

here as soon as possible. My prayers are for your safe passage.

Your Father

When Edwina returned to the parlor, Sue could see her face was wan and drawn. Drawing her close, she whispered, "Want to tell me about it?"

Edwina nodded jerkily, handing her the letter.

Sue scanned it before beckoning for Sara to join them. "Let's go to the kitchen and discuss this."

When they were seated at the table in the quiet of the kitchen, Sue asked, her eyes meeting Edwina's, "I'd like to know what you *want* to do. I don't mean what you *think* you *should* do, but what you *want* to do."

"I don't want to leave here." Edwina's eyes were moist, her voice trembling. She looked first at one and then the other. "I'm ashamed to admit it, but I feel closer to you and your family than I do to my own father."

"I speak from experience when I tell you family is important," Sue responded gently. The two young women waited expectantly when she paused, collecting her thoughts. "First, my advice would be for you to go on to San Francisco as planned. Second, I have some ideas to discuss in a family meeting."

Edwina's shoulders sagged at what seemed to be her exclusion, but her flagging hopes rose when Sue continued. "In this house, you're a member of the family, so you're obviously included."

The family was soon gathered around the table, where she explained the situation. "I would suggest we - the entire family - escort Edwina to San Francisco. When Sara was sworn in as a marshal, she gave her word she would get Edwina there safely."

Her lips curved in a wry smile. "I doubt anything was said about having help from volunteers. None of us have ever been to 'Frisco. Let's go there for our trip this year, instead of Denver. We could make it a fast trip, only a few days more than to Denver, and be back in ten days or so."

"Sounds good to me," Ted teased, "*if* we can persuade the kids."

Sue grinned at the eager acceptance. "I'm sure we could get Andy or Mark to take care of the ranch. We can find someone else in Wilford to help for a few days, as well."

The five young people stared at one another, dumbfounded at the speed of the decision, with Edwina the most shocked of all.

Ted laughed. "Those in favor, say aye."

Six voices chorused in unison, but Edwina was silent, her head down.

Ted put his hand on her shoulder. "We're not trying to get rid of you. You're welcome to come back with us if you want. We'd love to have you here."

Her "aye" was choked on tears, making the vote unanimous.

Sara's hand found Edwina's. "We'll ride over to the Franklins in the morning. I want to see Andy before we leave, and you can talk to Mark before we head on to Wilford."

"The three of you just got back from Chicago." Sally, the practical one, asked, "Do you need some time here at home to rest up?"

Ted glanced at Sue. She said, "Let's leave the day after tomorrow. Anyone that wants to can pack some things tonight, but we'll have a day to rest. We'll have time to make sure that we don't forget something."

A short time later Edwina stared in disbelief at what was a decidedly miniscule pile of trunks and saddlebags waiting beside the front door. "I can't believe it's been less than half-an-hour since we decided to go." She shook her head at Sue's amusement. "If the embassy staff were responsible, it would have taken at least a week just to pack. Even if we double this pile tomorrow, it's still not a lot of luggage."

CHAPTER 20

Dawn was breaking when Sara and Edwina mounted their saddled horses. The brisk air of high altitude and approaching autumn made both riders grateful for the light coats they were wearing. Sara made a final tally, running her fingers across the marshal's star pinned to her vest before making sure she had the remaining money and tiny ledger safely stowed in her gun belt.

Edwina waited eagerly astride her own mount. At a nod she relaxed the reins and thumped her horse with her heels. Both horses were spirited and eager to run, racing out of the ranch yard with Edwina slightly in the lead.

Sue and Ted watched from the shelter of the porch, smiling with fond amusement. When both riders had disappeared in the faint dawn light, he gathered her in his arms and chuckled when he said, "It's not just the horses that are eager this morning. I'd not be surprised to hear of a second engagement before the day is out."

Sue laughed delightedly. "I won't bet against you."

Sara let her horse set its own pace for a mile or more before reining it in to a trot. The miles passed at a distance-eating pace, one their horses could sustain indefinitely. The sky was a brilliant cobalt blue, the sun working its way from behind the mountains when they topped the rise overlooking the B-bar-F ranch house. They waited side-by-side for a few minutes, watching while a band of light worked its way down the mountainside. One bright beam of sunshine suddenly spotlighted the ranch house, banishing the enveloping shadows.

Sara broke the silence, asking gently, "Have you decided what you're going to say to Mark?"

Her face was momentarily bleak in the early sunshine, finding it hard to speak past a huge lump in her throat. "No, but I think it would be best if I let you tell Andy first. I think Mark needs to make the next move."

Two figures made tiny by distance appeared below them, moving from the barn to the ranch house. They started down the slope, Sara's shrill whistle carrying across the distance. Both figures turned and a raised arm beckoned them onward.

Ben and Cathy were standing near the door, and Andy and Mark were waiting at the foot of the porch steps when the young women rode into the yard. The brothers greeted them, each offering a hand to help dismount.

Sara caught Andy's eyes for reassurance, and said bluntly, "I brought a letter for Edwina yesterday when we got home. Our whole family is leaving today to take her to San Francisco."

Andy's face brightened, knowing that they would be getting married soon after she returned, and he kissed her.

Mark's face fell, a mask of disappointment. "Edwina, can I talk to you alone?"

"I'd like that." She held out her hand, holding his as they headed for the barn and its privacy.

Andy held Sara's hand while they watched the two figures disappear.

Cathy invited, "Come in and have something to eat. You must have left home very early to be here at this hour."

"Thanks. We wanted to have time to talk to you before we take the train today."

They were still eating when footsteps sounded from the porch. Sara held her breath. The front door creaked open and the footsteps moved toward the kitchen, to reveal both Mark and Edwina smiling broadly. "Edwina promised me she'd be coming back from San Francisco." Mark flushed. "She said I'd be welcome to come courting."

Ted was waiting at the livery when the two young women dismounted.

"Mark was getting his horse saddled to head for our place when we pulled out," Sara informed him. "He should be there by now."

He nodded in satisfaction. "Vern Alverson was footloose this morning and agreed to head for the ranch. He's a good worker. They'll get along fine."

Sara agreed, "Vern's a good man to have around."

She dug into her saddlebag, waving the letter she had written the night before. "I need to get this to the post office before we leave. I imagine Mr. Bailey would like a report since we're on the move again. Then we'll be ready to go.”

***

The letter was among others in the IN basket on Mr. Bailey’s desk when he noticed the hand-written notation PERSONAL and scanned the return address. Seeing Sara’s name, he opened it and leaned back in his chair:

Edwina and I will undoubtedly be in San Francisco before you get this letter. She plans to see her father but will be returning with me to Wilford. She has fallen in love with the State of Colorado and with my soon-to-be brother-in-law.

Thank you for introducing us.

Mr. Bailey reread the letter before turning to his files for another letter marked HOLD, from the District Attorney in Denver. Skimming it refreshed his memory regarding the arrests the Marshals Storm had made in Chicago. After reviewing them, he slipped both letters into a larger envelope and summoned his secretary. “Melvin. See that you get this to Mr. Hodges today. I’m sure he’ll find it most interesting.”

***

With a quick glance, Sue accounted for everyone as they waited for the train which was due in a few minutes. When Ted returned with five tickets, she said, “Everybody’s here.”

He laughed, waving in the general direction of the ticket window. “Sara and Edwina will be here in a couple of minutes. Amos was having trouble understanding why *Sara* was paying for two of the tickets.”

The train arrived a few minutes later and several

passengers got off before they boarded, causing a sudden silence among the remaining passengers. One salesman remarked to another, "Hell! I once saw a woman wearing man's clothes. I've never seen four. Three of these are wearing guns. One of those is even wearing a STAR!"

***

Full darkness had fallen before their train reached Union Station in Denver. They clustered in the dimly lit station while Ted checked the departure board for their next train. "We leave in fifty minutes."

Sue responded, "That gives us time to get something to eat. We'd better make the most of the opportunity."

Their next train, an express, departed on schedule, soon leaving the lights of the city behind. Kerosene lamps hanging from the ceiling swayed with the movement of the car, their light reflecting from the few closed windows. It was late and none of the passengers proved to be very talkative. The car was quiet except for the sound of the wheels on the rails.

The entire family was exhausted because of the late nights and began to drift off to sleep. Her siblings and Edwina were asleep when Sara whispered to her mother, "I'll keep watch until we get to Cheyenne. If I get too sleepy, I'll wake Pa and let him spell me."

Sue nodded as she squirmed in her seat, trying to find a comfortable position, savoring the satisfaction of her daughter's devotion to duty, before sleep overtook her.

***

Sara woke the others when the train began to slow, moments before the conductor walked through, announcing their momentary arrival in Cheyenne, where they had an hour's layover before boarding another express bound for Salt Lake City and beyond. Ted and Sue shared the watch while Sara and the others slept for the rest of the night.

At dawn they were still in Wyoming, the locomotive sending thick clouds of smoke billowing skyward as it labored through the mountains, some of it drifting through the open windows. Later, everyone was wide awake but uncomfortable because of the cramped seating when the conductor announced, "Provo! There'll be an hour layover for those continuing on west. Be sure to save your tickets."

Grateful for the respite, everyone got off to stretch their legs during the coaling and watering of the locomotive. The Storms headed for a nearby café, creating a stunned silence when four women dressed as riders entered; although it was not unheard of, it was not common.

Sometime later, the conductor walked through on one of his many appearances. He had seen Tom's interest in his explanations of features of note and stopped to talk. "We're coming up on Promontory Point, where East met West on this, the first transcontinental railroad, back in '69. There's a stretch of track on the western slope, down near the desert, where the original crew laid more than ten miles of rail in a single day. No one has ever come close to breaking their record in all the years since."

Mile after mile fell behind while their train thundered ever westward. They stopped at Reno for a short layover while the locomotive and its crew were changed, before heading into the approaching night again. Dawn found them west of the Donner Pass, slowly navigating the twists and turns of the high mountain tracks as they climbed ever upward. When they cleared the high mountains, the train accelerated down the western slopes to the valleys below. Sacramento had fallen behind as they rolled ever onward toward the fabled city of San Francisco. Elusive fingers of the bay began to appear now and again as the miles passed.

Ted and Sue were as eager as the youngsters, hoping to be the first to sight the City by the Bay. After the train screeched to a halt in Oakland, they gathered their belongings and joined the line of weary riders, following overhead signs and the flow of passengers to the ferry terminal next to the station.

Outside the San Francisco ferry terminal, Ted flagged down a pair of hacks. "Where can we find a good, inexpensive, hotel for seven not far from the British Consulate?"

"The Maple House would fit your needs and their prices aren't out of line."

"Sounds good to me. We'll take it." Ted waved to the others waiting on the steps.

The driver's eyes followed his wave and his jaw dropped when he spotted the armed figures headed toward them. Dumbfounded, he gasped, "They're all with you?"

"Yes."

The afternoon was nearly spent before they left

the hotel, clean and refreshed. Everyone wore their usual range wear except for Edwina who had changed into one of the simple dresses she had worn when she fled Washington. She smiled ruefully at Sue and Sara. "I've experienced many new things since I wore this the last time, but I'm afraid my father wouldn't be ready to see me wearing a man's clothes."

Sara led the way at the point of a loose diamond protectively surrounding Edwina. Sally and Tim were next, with Sue and Tom following. Ted brought up the rear. The wide sidewalk was crowded but oncoming pedestrians moved warily aside, causing Sara to smile at the reactions of the mass of approaching people when they realized the man in the lead was a woman wearing a marshal's star. Some were distracted enough to collide with one another in astonishment. Several others collided with lampposts as they passed. Word of the unusual group spread quickly and more people turned to stare.

It was only a short distance from the hotel to the consulate, where the Union Jack fluttered above the ornate doorway in greeting. Tim held the door while the others stood aside to give Edwina the opportunity to be the first to enter.

CHAPTER 21

Edwina's heart was pounding and her throat was dry as her eyes swept the lobby, anxiously searching for her father. She was disappointed when her first sweeping glance saw only a clerk, seated at a desk behind an ornate railing which separated him from visitors in the lobby.

He looked up, at first showing only mild curiosity, but his eyes widened and he paled when six armed Storms followed her in. He jumped to his feet in near panic, his breath catching in his throat. His terror began to fade though, when his frightened gaze settled on the marshal's star pinned to the vest of one of the armed figures.

"I believe you have been expecting me. I'm Edwina Harrison. I'm looking for my father." Her voice trembled as she turned slightly, indicating the watchful figures standing behind her. "These are my friends and escorts, the Storm family. Three of them are United States marshals."

"Your father has been anxiously awaiting your arrival. If you'll follow me, I'll take you to his office."

Before stepping away with Edwina, the clerk asked the Storms, "Would you like to wait here for Miss Harrison? I would imagine she will be with her father for some time."

"We'll wait for her," Sara said with all the authority she could muster. "Her safety is my responsibility."

***

Edwina followed her guide down the short hallway to a dark mahogany door, brightened by a large window of frosted glass. A gentle knock was acknowledged by a gruff voice. "Enter."

The clerk held the door for her, before closing it behind her as he left. A gaunt figure seated behind the massive desk struggled to his feet.

Her voice broke as she cried, "Father! What has happened to you?"

Hiram Harrison wrapped her in his arms as she hugged him as though she would never let go, breaking down in tears.

He patted her back, whispering, "My dearest Edwina, I'm ill with consumption. The doctors tell me I might recover if I can find the right climate."

***

The sun had set and the lights turned on before Edwina and her father emerged from his office. Because the clerk had warned them of the consumption which had stricken the Special Ambassador, the Storms were able to conceal their dismay when a red-eyed Edwina rejoined them in the lobby.

Her voice was steady when she introduced Sara, "Father, this is my friend and bodyguard, Sara Storm. She has saved my life on several occasions."

The ambassador grasped Sara's hand and choked, "I owe you more than I can ever repay for the life of my daughter! If there is ever anything I can do for you at any time, I will be overjoyed to do it!"

Sara blushed as she shook her head and said,

"When I first met Edwina, getting her here safely was my duty and an obligation." She extended her free hand to grip Edwina's and draw her close. "Now, she's a dear friend."

In a few minutes they were on the sidewalk, moving as a protective box surrounding their two charges. Pedestrian traffic had thinned with the setting of the sun, making it much easier for them to move as a group to the Ambassador's nearby hotel.

The San Franciscan was one of the most upscale hotels in the city with its own security force. After a moment of incredulity at the sight of Sara's star, the head clerk summoned the house detective on duty. When he had recovered from his own startled double-take, he responded to Sara's concerns. "Marshal Storm. I understand your situation and will personally make sure both Ambassador Harrison and his daughter have round-the-clock security while they're living here. You can rest assured no harm will come to them."

"Thank you." Sara hugged Edwina goodbye and followed the rest of the family as they left the ornate lobby.

When Ted asked, "Anybody else hungry?" the response was a chorus of assent. He suggested, "Let's try something different while we're here. I saw a sign for seafood back a block or two."

A dumbfounded waitress stared wide-eyed when they entered. She brought menus to their table and tried to answer their many questions about the different types of seafood. Finally raising her hands in surrender, she suggested, "Why don't I bring samples of everything. When you know what you want, I can bring more."

"That's a good idea," Sue replied. "The only fish we've ever eaten came from a mountain lake."

***

The morning sun found Sara waiting in the lobby of the San Franciscan. She was seated in an overstuffed chair, ignoring the stares directed her way by richly-attired guests as they filtered through the lobby. She was beginning to grow apprehensive when Edwina finally appeared, her heart catching in her throat at the sight of reddened eyes and slumped shoulders.

Edwina shook her head despondently and she spoke in a broken whisper, "I can't talk about it in here. Let's go outside."

Sara led the way in silence to a nearby park overlooking the bay. When they found a small bench under a shady tree, Edwina slumped into a seat, her head drooping.

"Edwina! What's wrong?"

Her eyes brimmed with tears. "Father wants me to go back to England and take care of him. I can't go back to Colorado as I promised Mark."

Sara's eyes hardened and she snapped, "It's time for a talk with Ma. She'll know how to handle a situation like this." She drew Edwina to her feet, practically dragging her as they headed for her own hotel.

***

Ambassador Harrison was seated at his desk, half-heartedly trying to deal with paperwork, when the secretary knocked on the slightly open door. After a muttered response, he replied, "Mrs. Storm to see you, Sir."

The Ambassador scowled at the intrusion but responded pleasantly, "Please send her in." His gaze hardened and his hackles rose when Sue moved a chair close to his desk. Unbidden, she sat and placed her folded arms on his desk, her cold eyes meeting his from inches away.

Silence reigned for several seconds. He glared when she turned his ornately engraved name plate face down, hiding the title AMBASSADOR HIRAM HARRISON.

Her voice was frosty. "You and I are going to have a long talk about a young woman we both love! Your daughter, and mine at heart, Edwina."

***

The three young women waited nervously in the sisters' room as the hour neared noon. Edwina's stomach was tied in knots and her thoughts were in turmoil. "Do you really think your mother can persuade my father to change his mind?"

Sally grinned wolfishly from her seat on the bed. "Is water wet?"

Sara's own smile was thin. "Ma can be very persuasive when she gets mad. She said she'd be back by noon. We should be hearing from her at any moment."

Following a quick knock on the door, Sue asked, "Can we come in?"

"It's unlocked." The trio waited in tense silence.

Sue was wearing a smile when she entered, followed a moment later by Ambassador Harrison. Edwina's father enveloped her in his arms as he smiled ruefully. "I have had the error of my thinking pointed out to me. You have my blessing to return to Colorado to find your own way in life."

His daughter's eyes flooded with tears of happiness. He smiled ruefully and continued, "Mrs. Storm can be very persuasive, and does not hesitate to call a spade a spade. I do believe she was most accurate when she informed me I was a selfish ass to demand you give up your own life." Sue unsuccessfully tried to suppress a smirk.

"She also made me aware of the high, dry, climate in Colorado and its potential therapeutic benefits. So I've decided to take a leave of absence from service to the Crown and move to Denver. I hope moving there will improve the consumption which has so severely affected my health."

He cleared his throat, "Edwina, I would like to host a banquet and dance in your honor this Saturday night before you leave. Would that be acceptable to you?"

Tears glistened in her eyes as she nodded and said, "I would love that."

Harrison held her close as he directed his attention to Sue. "We would be honored if you and your family would be guest hosts with me."

"It would be an honor and a privilege."

***

The consulate was a buzz of activity for the next two days while the staff, the Ambassador, and the Storms helped prepare for the Saturday night celebration. Sara remained a constant shadow, privately dismayed by her own unease as their time remaining in San Francisco ebbed away.

Sue and Sally were helping address invitations at a desk in the lobby of the consulate, waiting for the other two young women to return. When a middle-aged man with dark hair and a full beard approached Sue, his appearance stirred a vague memory. Sue nodded in greeting. "Do I know you?"

"I'm Wilbur Smythe. I'm quite sure we've never met. Perhaps I remind you of someone else?" He offered his hand. "I wanted to visit with you for a moment because my wife and I have been invited to the banquet Saturday night."

He smiled conspiratorially. "I've been to activities like this before and know how few young people attend. We were wondering if you would like us to bring our own daughter, who is about the same age as this young lady with you. It might make the evening more enjoyable for her if she had someone her own age to talk to."

Sally nodded eagerly and Sue smiled. "We both appreciate your offer. I know Sally has much to learn about San Francisco and would appreciate having a new friend. Thank you for your kind offer."

***

Ted stood between Consular Meriwether and his wife in the receiving line, dividing his attention between arriving guests and Sara and Sue, who stood with Edwina and her father at the end of the line. During a momentary lull, his eyes swept the growing crowd for the rest of the family. Dressed in identical white ruffled shirts, black pants, vests, and ties, their appearance was a distinctive contrast to the rest of the crowd. The three youngest differed from their parents and oldest sister only by the lack of marshals' stars and holstered revolvers.

A discreet elbow in his side drew his attention to Sue's eyes sparkling with amusement at his distraction. "I'd like you to meet Wilbur Smythe and his wife, Anne. They brought their daughter, Nancy, so Sally would have a companion."

He greeted the man before turning to meet mother and daughter. Both were petite and barely reached his shoulder. The two men exchanged pleasantries while Sara and Sue visited with Anne and Nancy. Sue asked Nancy, "Would you like me to introduce you to Sally?"

She nodded, eyes wide, before following Sue into the crowd.

Sally had been keeping tabs on the reception line while listening to the conversation around her. When she saw her mother leaving her place in line, she excused herself.

"Sally, this is Nancy Smythe. I can't stay because I'm needed back in the line, so I'll leave the two of you to get acquainted with one another. Enjoy yourselves." She watched the two girls eye each other for a moment before they drifted toward a more secluded spot.

During another quiet moment, Sue whispered to Ted. "I know I've seen Wilbur Smythe somewhere else before. I just can't remember where."

"I don't ever remember having seen him. Maybe you'll recall where you saw him sometime before the night is over."

CHAPTER 22

The reception was an unqualified success, continuing into the late hours. Sue and Ted had danced often, and now sat at a table, just enjoying the orchestra as it played a multitude of selections for the dancers. She tried not to be obvious whenever she glanced at the seated Smythe family, where Sally was talking animatedly with Nancy. The identity of Mr. Smythe had gnawed at her all evening. She searched her memory, trying to remember where she had seen him in spite of his denial. Momentarily, he turned his head to speak to someone, revealing a different profile. Sue's gasp drew Ted's attention as she whispered triumphantly, "I finally remembered who Mr. Smythe really is! Theodore Preston, Junior."

His eyes widened in astonishment as he recalled, "He saved our lives in Denver when he warned us of the assassin."

The orchestra struck up another number a few minutes later and they moved onto the floor. After they had shared a few numbers, Sue approached Mr. Smythe. Touching his shoulder to get his attention, she asked, "Can I talk to you privately for a few minutes?"

He nodded, eyes suddenly wary.

She led the way to a quiet corner of the second-floor balcony overlooking San Francisco Bay, sparkling in the moonlight. She met his eyes for several seconds before saying softly, "We owe you our lives and the lives of our children. We'll be forever in your debt."

Shock flashed across his face at being recognized after so many years and his eyes hardened at the memory of the night Sue had knocked him out. Subsequently, his father's attempt to murder them had led to the discovery of the body of his mother, murdered years earlier by the senior Preston.

"If you had not warned us, we would have been murdered in our sleep." She was silent while he stared at her, his unease obvious. "Neither of us will ever reveal your secret. Does your wife know who you really are?"

His expression was stony, his voice flat and expressionless. "Anne knows but Nancy doesn't." His eyes shifted to a point behind her shoulder.

She turned to see Anne, who slipped past her to join her husband, her hand anxiously gripping his. Sue waited until Anne turned fearfully toward her and whispered in a voice too soft to be heard more than a few feet away, "I just told your husband my entire family owes him our lives. You can be very proud of him."

A few minutes later Ted joined them next to the railing as they gazed out over the city and the bay. "Edwina's father isn't feeling well because of the excitement and his consumption. I'll take the boys and Sally with me and escort him back to his hotel. You and Sara can escort Edwina back whenever this party is over."

Sue glanced at him sharply. His bland expression would have given no clue to anyone else but spoke volumes to her. *Beware!*

"We'll be careful. If anyone is lurking to attack her, they'll try when we walk to the hotel." She saw his evident concern and repeated, "We'll be careful."

***

The hour was past midnight before they left the ballroom, heading back to the *San Franciscan*. Sue and Sara walked on either side, guarding her, but Edwina was so keyed up she felt as though she was floating inches above the sidewalk. Bubbling with giddiness that bordered on euphoria, she hurried down the gas-lamp-lit street while soft night breezes flowed inshore from the huge bay, cooling her overheated face. Only faintly aware of her silent companions on either side, her mind was in turmoil, reviewing the gala reception and ball.

She was so excited she simply depended on her companions to return her safely to her hotel. A twin row of gas lights stretched into the distance on either side of the street, rising and falling with the steep hills surrounding San Francisco Bay. Neighboring build-ings were a mix of business and residences, mostly two-story, separated from the brick-paved street by a wide sidewalk. They passed an occasional vacant lot, empty except for small amounts of debris. Earlier, the Smythes had explained that many building lots had yet to be fully cleared and rebuilt following the dev-astating earthquake which had virtually leveled San Francisco only a few years before.

The street and sidewalk were almost empty of any other traffic. Other than two carriages in the dis-tance, there were only three pedestrians out. Two were meandering on the other side of the street and a block ahead. The third was steadily approaching a short dis-tance ahead.

The tension grew as the well-dressed stranger closed the gap. Sara's attention was fixated on him. Sue's attention was divided between the man and possible sites for an ambusher to hide. Both relaxed slightly when his hand rose to tip his hat in greeting. They froze an instant later when his hand reappeared from the shadow formed by his bowler, a revolver pointed at them from only a few paces distant.

His sinister voice was low, "Not a sound! Don't try anything fancy or she'll be the first to die!" The deathly silence was broken by the faint whisper of shoes as two more figures holding guns joined the man, who stared hungrily at Edwina. He snarled, "She's going with me. If you try something stupid, she'll be the first to die. But you won't know anything about it because you'll be dead."

Edwina trembled and shrank back as a squeak of fear escaped her lips. The thug snorted with contempt, glaring at her before grabbing her arm. At his touch, shame, anger, and self-disgust overwhelmed her fear and she kicked upward with every ounce of strength she possessed. Her flowing ball gown and soft-toed high-heeled shoes offered no protection for her foot but the thug suffered by far the greater injury when her foot met his unprotected groin. He gasped in agony, dropped his revolver, and doubled over. Overbalanced, Edwina lost her footing and tumbled in a heap.

Sara bitterly cursed herself for being such a fool while he mocked them. Edwina's sudden switch from shocked terror to attack distracted the other men and gave Sara and her mother what was going to be their only chance. They drew and fired as one. Sara's Colt spit fire a fraction of a second faster than her mother's. Keeping subconscious count, she triggered two rounds into the thug standing directly in front of her before shifting her aim slightly, firing twice more.

Both thugs were hurled backward by the impact of the bullets, gunfire echoing back from the surrounding buildings. Half-deafened, Sara asked anxiously without turning from the crumpled figures on the sidewalk, "Ma! Are you okay? How 'bout Edwina?"

"We're both fine. You?"

She gasped a sigh of relief. "I'm fine! I'll keep 'em covered while you reload."

The echoes had scarcely died in the distance before the shrill sound of police whistles filled the night in every direction. The rattle and bang of windows being fully flung open in upstairs residences all along the street added to the noise and confusion.

Sue bent to help Edwina get to her feet, who spotted her attacker's revolver partially hidden under her dress and gathered it in with one hand. Leaning on Sue's arm, she turned to thank Sara for saving her once again. Seeing the bloody bodies sprawled on the walk, her face turned white but she managed to turn far enough to throw up in the gutter instead of on the sidewalk.

Sue holstered her revolver to free her hands and held Edwina closely.

Sara kept the gasping thug covered while pounding feet approached rapidly from several directions. When the first policeman came in view, she holstered her own revolver and held her hands high, waiting a few seconds before shouting, "We're United States marshals! Don't shoot!"

The running policeman stumbled in astonishment at the sound of a female voice. Sergeant Stanley Black had read of the Marshals Storm visiting San Francisco but had never expected to encounter them. He slowed his head-long pace and was the first on the scene. Taking charge as other officers arrived, he assigned some to the downed thugs and others to gather evidence. Two converged on Edwina's victim, who was alive but still writhing in agony.

With the officers on the scene, Sara had time to take in her surroundings, her stomach knotting at the blood and gore on the sidewalk from the two bodies, both badly torn from the impact of four bullets.

A sizeable crowd of spectators had arrived, eavesdropping silently, when Sergeant Black asked, "For the record, do you mind telling me what happened here?"

Before they could reply, a woman on the fringe of the crowd broke in, "I couldn't sleep and was sitting at my window. These ladies were just walking down the street when they were accosted by the man on the ground. He greeted them and pulled a gun hidden in his hat. Then the other two joined him with guns drawn. When the lady in the dress kicked the first one, the other two ladies drew their guns and shot them."

***

San Francisco was agog at the story of the shoot-out, newspapers shouting the news under lurid headlines such as *SAN FRANCISCO'S OWN OK CORRAL*. Each paper tried to outdo its competitors in sensationalism,

hiding most of the facts deep in hyperbole. Little attention was paid by anyone to the motive for the crime,
except for one sentence buried deeply and overlooked
by most readers. *Killer admits he was hired by the British
Ambassador to the United States.*

PART 2

SALLY

CHAPTER 1

The familiar office was empty when Sally entered. She called into the silence, "Squire! Are you here?"

A muffled voice responded from deeper in the building, "Sally, I'm in the library. Come on back."

She hurried to the library, where she found her gray-haired friend sitting in his wooden swivel chair, staring absently at the shelves crowded with law books. He greeted her, his eyes sparkling with good humor, "It's good to see you home again. Did you have a good time in San Francisco?"

"The best!" Sally explained hurriedly, "Edwina found her father. Sara and Ma captured the killers who were after her. And she came back with us!" She laughed. "It's too long a story to tell you everything today. We won't be in town very long and the rest of the family is getting ready to ride right now."

Squire Brown smiled fondly at the young woman who towered almost a foot taller than he. He rummaged in a corner of the library until he found a bulging saddlebag. "I have your first set of textbooks from the University. They promised me the other books that you need, will be here before you get snowed in. Be sure to check with me whenever you're in town."

He was forced to wait until the rumble of a heavy wagon on the street outside faded, to continue. His expression sober, he said, "You have a lot of ground to cover if you're going to take the bar exam next spring.

I know you can do it, but it's going to be a lot of hard work. Especially because you've never been to college."

Sally's own expression matched his. "I know. Not the least because you had to hide the fact I'm a woman."

Squire's eyes crinkled with humor. "I've hidden nothing. I just haven't volunteered certain information. Your application as S. A. Storm was filled out and signed exactly the same as the men who use their initials."

He grimaced. "Unfortunately, you will undoubtedly confront lawyers who will fight you tooth and nail to keep you from practicing law, simply because you *are* a woman."

Her eyes held his for a moment. "Then I'll just have to be the better lawyer."

She abruptly switched topics. "Sara and Andy are getting married in the near future. She took Edwina safely to her father as she promised. Edwina is staying in Denver for a week to get her father settled. That's part of the story I don't have to time to tell. He has consumption and the doctors think it's possible the dry air may cure him. He told Edwina he would not move to Wilford because he didn't want to meddle in her life. This way they'll still be close enough to stay in touch."

Squire said, "You've told me in the past that Edwina's sweet on Mark. I wouldn't be surprised to see another wedding in the near future."

Sally grinned broadly at her friend and mentor. "I'd love to have her as a sister, even if only by marriage."

Smiling in turn, he handed her the saddlebag. "Only time will tell where Cupid's arrows will strike. I'd suggest you take one wedding at a time. The next time you're in town, you can undo my state of confusion."

Sally laughed and hugged him before hustling from his office. He followed her out, watching while she strode rapidly toward the livery. He chuckled when her father's voice carried clearly, "I *told* you she was going to school!"

He watched her strap the saddle bag to her horse, waving as she followed her family out of town, thinking. He and Emma had raised three daughters, all just a few years older than Sue Storm. He now had numerous grandchildren, but they all lived at a distance that precluded frequent visits. Sally had crept into his heart as another grandchild, especially when she showed her interest in the law at an early age.

Gender be damned. He was going to encourage her to strive for her law license in spite of any and all male opposition.

***

The week flew by as Sally helped her sister and mother prepare for the wedding. She stood with Sara as maid-of-honor, choking back tears. After the ceremony, she and the family and friends, waved good-bye as the newly-weds rode off for an abbreviated honeymoon.

The remaining guests all departed soon after, since most were ranch families and had evening chores waiting. Edwina, her father and several other guests from Wilford left in a group, hurrying to beat the approaching sunset. When the last of their guests were out of sight, Sally changed from the dress she seldom wore and donned her rider's clothes. She joined her brothers and headed for the barn, leaving her parents alone with each other.

Ted waited until the house was quiet, with Sue wrapped in his arms. Her eyes were bright with unshed tears as he kissed her gently. "We didn't lose a daughter. We gained a son. They'll always be only a short ride away."

Sue's smile was tremulous. "I know in my head but not in my heart. I can't believe the years have gone so fast. Sometimes it seems only yesterday she was a little girl. I know she's not, especially after our trip to San Francisco and what she went through."

He held her close. "You didn't have a mother to worry about you or to look up to when you were her age. It's okay for you to do it now, for both of you."

***

Everyone was at the breakfast table a few days later when they heard someone ride in. Tom left the table, returning a few minutes later with Marshal Ward Keaton following.

Ted greeted him warmly, saying what was on everyone's mind, "What's happening in Denver that you're here this early?"

"I hate to do this, but I have subpoenas for you, Sue, and Sara," said Keaton.

Ted smiled and replied, "And D. A. Wayne is going

to follow the law to the letter. He doesn't want to lose this case by overlooking something."

The tension on Marshal Keaton's face lessened at the reasonable tone. "Judge Lawson has moved the trial to Cheyenne. He's already dented a few heads to insure a fair trial. When the preliminary hearing first convened, a fancy-pants lawyer from Chicago started spouting off. Court had hardly been gaveled into session when he accused the judge of rigging a kangaroo court. "The judge informed him arrangements had already been made to move the trial to Cheyenne on a change of venue. Since he couldn't keep a civil tongue, the judge was finding him in contempt of court."

He laughed and said, "He gave the lawyer, a Mr. Dixon, ten days. Solitary confinement. Bread and water. The hearing went as smooth as silk from then on. He'll be out in time to make it to the trial in Cheyenne."

"Sit down and have a bite," Sue said. "Sara's married now and has moved to the Franklin's B-bar-F. I'm sure you'd like something to eat before you head over there to serve her subpoena."

He shrugged in good-natured resignation. "I should have expected a few changes. This was too easy. Thank you, I will."

CHAPTER 2

Sally begged for permission to accompany her parents and sister to Cheyenne so she could attend an actual trial. She thought as they waited, *Well, not too hard. I only had to ask once.* She and Andy were seated immediately behind the prosecutor's table. The defendants and their panel of lawyers were seated at their own table across the aisle. Thomas Hollingsworth and Wilson Rahlings were both visibly tense as they conferred with their defense team, discussing last-second strategy. The charge of attempted murder of Marshal Sara Storm Mason hung over their heads as the trial was gaveled to order.

Sally watched, fascinated by her first exposure to an actual trial. She noted how it unfolded one deliberate step at a time. The jury was already selected, with eleven men and one woman seated in the jury box. She thought, *I'd forgotten. Wyoming was the first state in the nation to allow women to vote and serve on juries, way back in 1869. Colorado was a late-comer giving us the vote in 1893, but we still can't serve on juries.* The woman wore a long tan dress with a white blouse, her black hair tied up in a bun. The eleven men were a mixed bag, ranging from one with a somewhat scruffy appearance, to another in a suit and tie, looking like a sober undertaker.

The chief prosecutor rose to address the jury, dispassionately enumerating the facts of the case. He concluded with, "Lady and gentlemen of the jury. The young woman who was the intended victim of this murder plot does not deny she may have unknowingly provoked the defendants. *However,* the response is far out of proportion to the offense and deserves a judgment of guilty of attempted murder."

Sally scanned the other viewers while the defense team held a whispered conference before taking their turn to address the jury. She noticed one woman who was seated across the aisle, dressed in high fashion with her hair piled high. When they made eye contact, she shivered at the blazing hatred in the woman's gaze.

Winifred Hollingsworth was nursing thoughts of murder and revenge. During the few short weeks of her husband's absence, their empire and its riches had vanished. She was now almost destitute, and hatred and dreams of vengeance were her only solace.

The defense's opening statement became a thundering indictment of the Federal Court of Colorado and its officers, charging that they had manufactured a conspiracy of officialdom against two innocent men for reasons unknown. The chief counsel concluded his remarks with arrogance and confidence. "We will prove the young woman is nothing but a shill, and the supposed confession of my innocent clients nothing but a fabrication."

Sally met Andy's eyes in disbelief, unable to believe the audacity of the charge. He grinned and whispered, "If that's the best defense they can come up with, the trial will be over in an hour."

Sara was the first witness called to testify and whispers scurried through the courtroom. Women who wore men's clothes were not unheard of in either Wyoming or Colorado, but a female wearing a gun and a marshal's star was an entirely different matter.

District Attorney Richard Lowman, who served the Federal District of Wyoming, began laying the foundation of his case by asking Sara to describe her encounter with Mrs. Hollingsworth, the resulting humiliation which had infuriated her husband. He asked, "Have you ever met either Mr. Hollingsworth or Congressman Rahlings before today?"

"Not really. The only time I had contact with Mr. Hollingsworth before today was when I arrested him in Chicago. I did meet Mr. Rahlings once, but we were never introduced. He was drunk when I threw him off the train for verbally attacking a young mother. I've never even seen him under any other circumstances."

"Thank you." He turned to the judge. "I have no further questions for this witness at this time."

The judge made a notation on a notepad before turning to the defense table. "Mr. Dixon, your witness."

Sally could see her sister's face tighten as the lawyer raked her with his eyes. He rose to his feet, his smile patently false as he approached the witness stand. "Miss Storm--"

"I'm now Mrs. Sara Franklin. I was recently married."

The lawyer scowled, waving his hand in careless dismissal. "No matter."

The courtroom was silent, waiting for him to spring whatever surprise he might have. "You're pretty cocky, parading around wearing a marshal's star." His smile turned oily. "Why didn't you take charge of the alleged assassin my clients are accused of hiring when he was supposedly about to attack your home? If you were a real marshal, why would you have allowed your father, a civilian, to take charge and extort a false confession from Mr. Scalize!"

Sara's alto was unshaken, "I was obeying a far older law. One of the Ten Commandments, *Honor thy father and mother*. When my father ordered me and my siblings to leave, I obeyed."

Mr. Dixon scowled, about to continue, when Sara made a grave error saying, "Another reason was because at the time, both of my parents were inactive United States marshals, as they have been for almost twenty years."

Dixon's eyes lit up as he turned to the judge. "I demand an immediate mistrial and dismissal of all charges against my clients! They obviously cannot receive a fair trial when the court is stacked against them like this! The law protects the law!"

Sara turned pale as the enormity of her gaffe hit her. Sally's heart sank as the audience erupted.

Judge Walker pounded his gavel until order was restored. "Mr. Lowman."

The DA stood up behind the prosecutor's table. "Your Honor. I insist the motion be denied. I had never heard of a female marshal from Colorado until this case was waived to this court. I personally do not know any personnel from the Colorado office. I have only talked to the Storms, who are on the list of witnesses called by my counterpart in Colorado, to gather facts. I have spoken privately to Mrs. Franklin only to gain knowledge of her testimony to be presented here in open court."

D.A. Lowman's face was suffused by anger. "I

have sworn to seek justice and will never allow favoritism for or against any defendant or witness. Only testimony presented in open court will influence any case I may bring before the bench!"

The judge's own eyes were cold. "Mr. Dixon! The law in this courtroom is impartial. Any further attack on the integrity of my court will find you in contempt." He banged his gavel angrily. "Motion denied!"

Sally's flagging spirits rose as she watched color slowly return to her sister's face. When whispers continued to buzz in the air like flies, the judge banged his gavel for order.

Dixon's eyes were cold as he waited for the courtroom to quiet. "Why did you attack Mrs. Hollingsworth in the Chicago terminal?"

"I did not attack her," Sara stated calmly, while fire flashed in her eyes. "I only blocked her attempt to break into the line for the ladies' powder room because she seemed to think she was some kind of royalty. And then she had the audacity to fake a swoon."

Sara described the scene at the LaSalle Street Station. "I've never liked fakers," she concluded. "You can't depend on them to carry through, because doing something that stupid could get you killed in the mountains. That's what really made me mad."

Mr. Dixon scowled and turned to one of his co-councilors. "Your witness, Mr. Gray."

Nathan Gray, born and raised in Cheyenne, had been appointed by the judge to assist the out-of-state defense. "Why would Mr. Rahlings hold a grudge against you?"

"I would guess because I gave him a bloody nose," Sara sighed. "I undoubtedly humiliated him, but only after he threatened and humiliated a young woman with two toddlers." She recounted her only meeting with the congressman. "I never thought it would be enough motive for any normal person to plan to kill me."

"No further questions."

"The witness is excused at this time," said the judge.

Sally's pulse slowed when Sara left the courtroom through a side door before the next witness was led to the witness stand.

Alfonzo Scalize was sworn in by the prosecution as a hostile witness. He ignored the prosecutor as his eyes swept the defendants and moved to the spectators.

Sally shivered when his cold eyes met hers for a fleeting moment, apparently recalling the sight of her rifle aimed at him. Silence settled heavily in the courtroom.

The prosecutor approached, holding several sheets of paper. "I have here your signed confession. Do you have any comment?" Alfonzo remained silent, staring at the floor.

Mr. Lowman began to read, his voice clear in the deafening silence. The reading took only a few minutes. In the confession, Scalize described what the two defendants had ordered which had taken him to Wilford and the Storm ranch. When the prosecutor finished reading, he waited for several moments, eyeing the witness steadily, before asking sharply, "Do you deny any part of this confession?"

Alfonzo's eyes shifted jerkily to the two defendants, his face paling. He slumped in his chair while the courtroom waited, the only sounds from traffic and birds coming in the open windows.

"Yes or no?" pressed the lawyer. "Is this a true document?"

The witness straightened in his chair, color and hate ablaze on his face. "What the hell, I'm dead anyway! Yes, it's the truth. Both of those bastards were in on the planning when they sent me to kill her."

The defendants jumped to their feet, shouting in protest until they were gagged by the bailiffs. A babble of noise erupted from the spectators as they turned to their neighbors, incredulous at what they had just heard.

Mr. Lowman asked, "What do you mean? *I'm dead anyway.*"

Alfonzo shrugged. "Nobody in a Chicago gang rats. If they do, they're hunted down. If someone even thinks you're going to rat, you wind up in the river tied to a rock." His smile was a ghastly imitation of one. "If they're going to kill me anyway, I'm going to take the bastards with me! I'll tell you everything I know."

His testimony, interrupted by constant objections, made Sally nauseous as he calmly listed a litany of beatings, maiming, knifings and shootings ordered by the defendants. Her face was not the only pale one when he fell silent.

Mr. Lowman asked gently, "Do you swear

everything you have told us is the truth?"

"Yeah! It's all true."

"Mr. Dixon. Your witness."

The lawyer approached the witness, his brow furrowed and his lips tight. "That's quite a story you've hatched. What reason would my clients have to do such things?"

Alfonzo spat back, hatred twisting his face, his voice nearly a shout, "You should know! You were there when they were planning other killings!"

The courtroom became deathly still as the lawyer paled, gasping as though he had been punched in the stomach.

Judge Walker addressed the witness sternly, "Mr. Scalize. Are you saying defense council was a knowing participant in the crimes you have described to this court?"

"Yeah. He was there for some and knew about many others."

The judge's face turned to stone. "Mr. Dixon. You are barred from further participation in this trial. Bailiff. Place this man under arrest for suspicion of murder and remove him from this courtroom. Mr. Gray. You are now chief counsel for the defense. Do you wish additional counsel?"

"No, your Honor."

CHAPTER 3

Sally watched along with the other observers and the press while the defense viciously attacked Alfonzo's confession and testimony. Unable to comprehend the cold-bloodedness of the admitted killer, her skin crawled with frequent shivers. Both defendants, when called for their testimony, delivered vitriolic diatribes in their own defense. The jury proved to be unimpressed by their denials, returning guilty verdicts on all counts against both men after only a few minutes of deliberation.

Neither of her parents had been called as witnesses, due to the explosive testimony of the hostile witness. After court adjourned, Sally and the rest of her family clustered with other attendees on the courthouse steps. She hugged her sister tightly. "I'm delighted they were found guilty. I was afraid the judge was going to throw the case out when Dixon made his accusation."

Sara grimaced. "So was I!"

Sally relinquished her sister to Andy's waiting arms and stepped back to give them room, watching the surrounding crowd. Someone stormed past, almost knocking her off her feet. Irritated, she turned to see the cold-eyed woman who had been sitting across the aisle.

One hand rose to her piled hair. Sunlight gleamed from something metallic she had pulled from within its folds. She changed direction abruptly, striding purposefully toward Sara's defenseless back.

"Sara! Look out!"

At Sally's scream, Sara shoved Andy away and spun on one heel, drawing her Colt. The descending spear just missed her back and she chopped hard with the barrel of her revolver. The attacker screamed when her wrist broke, the inches-long hat pin, which could have pierced a spine or a heart, falling from her hand. Demented fury blazed in her eyes as she went berserk, attacking with her uninjured hand.

It took the combined efforts of four men from the crowd to subdue her and pull her away from Sara. Muttering incoherently and shaking violently, she was led away by two bailiffs.

Sara's face was bruised and bleeding from many scratches as her arms enveloped her sister, joined a moment later by Andy's. "Thanks, Sis! I owe you my life."

***

Winter arrived even earlier than usual in the high mountains, with frequent heavy snows and high winds. Cattle and horses drifted before the winter blasts, requiring the efforts of the entire family to find and care for them. Everyone took a turn, usually riding two days out of three as they tried to move the livestock into the shelter of canyons and meadows. They often were forced to stay out overnight, seeking shelter in a line shack or cave stocked with food and fuel during the summer months. The third day in the rotation was usually spent caring for the animals at the ranch, where chores were endless. Nightfall always found everyone exhausted and ready for an early bed.

The usual midwinter thaw arrived one night

shortly after the beginning of the new year. It was a lucky rare day when everyone was safely at the ranch. Edwina's spirits rose with the thermometer and she asked Sue, "Do you think Mark will be able to visit tomorrow?"

She was answered by broad grin. "You've never seen this much snow melt, have you?"

Edwina shook her head in resignation, suspecting the worst.

"No one will travel in these conditions unless they absolutely have to. A horse would sink to its belly with every step. The only way a man could travel would be on snowshoes." She grinned again. "I would suggest you do what I'm planning to do, sleep for about a week. We won't be able to do much else, even here at the ranch."

Edwina found the rest of the family planned to follow Sue's suggestion. Shortly after the breakfast dishes had been washed, the ranch house was silent except for an occasional snore drifting down the hall.

Sally woke in midafternoon to find herself the first to stir. She tip-toed to the parlor and stoked the Franklin stove before selecting one of her textbooks. She curled up in her father's favorite rocking chair. Immersed in the dry rhetoric of the legal profession, she studied until it was time to help with the chores. After the supper dishes were done she returned to her studies.

***

The thaw lasted for almost a week before bitter cold and clear skies returned during the night. Edwina woke to hear Sally calling through her door. "It froze last night, so we can travel today. If you want to go to Wilford, the rest of us are leaving as soon as everyone has something to eat."

Edwina rolled out of bed and grabbed her clothes. "I'll be there in five minutes."

She was at the breakfast table in less than that to see it was still total predawn darkness outside. When she learned the chores were already done, she protested. "You should have called me earlier. I would have been glad to help."

Ted smiled at her. "I woke up when the wind shifted. I knew it'd get colder fast, so I got up and did the chores. This weather will hold long enough for us to make a quick trip to town. We'll have a few days before the weather changes for the worse again."

***

Sally went to the post office, located in Horwick's General Store, to pick up the family's mail as soon as they arrived in town. A few of her neighbors who had been snowbound as well were already there, waiting their turn. She joined the line, grinning broadly at the good-natured complaining of the busy clerk. She was surprised by the size of the bundle of mail he handed her. Finding an out-of-the-way corner, she rapidly sorted through the pile and was astonished to find several letters addressed to her, from Nancy Smythe, postmarked *San Francisco*. She checked the cancellations and opened the most recent. Skimming it, she slowed to carefully read the last paragraph.

She headed for Squire Brown's with her mind in a whirl. After reviewing the material about which she had questions, she borrowed a pen and some paper. Dashing off a quick letter to Nancy, she explained how the family had been snowbound for months and she had not received anything until the present date. She promised to write a longer letter and mail it as soon as possible, but cautioned it might be months and dependent on the weather.

Squire's pride in his star pupil was plain as he gathered more textbooks that he had received. "You'll be more than ready for the bar exam this spring. I'm confident you'll pass it on your first attempt and a lot of men don't. You're doing so well, even if you're snowed in for the rest of the winter, you'll be ready for the exam the first week of May."

"I'll be here and ready for the test even if I have to snowshoe to town," Sally replied with a smile. "I'd love to stay but I can't. We took a chance on the weather holding long enough for us to make a quick trip to town. Pa doesn't want to linger."

She hugged Squire and scooped up her saddle

bag, stuffed with the bundle of mail in one side and her text books in the other. Folding the bag over one arm, she waved a last goodbye, and closed the door tightly against the bitter cold.

Sally rejoined Edwina and her parents at Horwick's General Store, where they were stacking goods to load.

"The boys have gone to get the horses." Her father asked, "Did we have any mail?"

"Only half a saddlebag full. I got a bunch of letters from Nancy Smythe but only took time to read part of one. Everyone else got letters, too."

The sun had set long before they reached the ranch in winter blackness, the only light from a sliver of moon and the stars. Travel had been relatively easy only because of the contrast between white snow and the black shadows of trees and stone. In spite of the pace, everyone was miserably cold long before their horses climbed the last ridge above the ranch house. Sally knew she was not the only one anticipating the comfort of a warm fire as soon as possible. When her father reached the crest and reined in his horse, he called loudly enough for everyone to hear, "Looks like we have company."

Sally was as curious as everyone else. When she cleared the ridge, she could see several of the lamps in the ranch house were lit, while rising columns of smoke from the chimneys promised a warm welcome.

The column of horses was almost at the front porch when the door opened and three bundled figures emerged. Sara hugged her mother and sister, while Mark and Andy helped unload the heavily-laden pack horses before leading them to the barns.

"Ben and Cathy offered to take care of the chores so we could visit you. We got here about mid-afternoon. When there was no one here, we guessed you made a quick trip to town. We were sure you'd be home early, so the men did chores while I fixed supper," said Sara.

When everyone was seated around the table, the plates of food were passed from hand to hand, conversation lively even as hunger was satisfied. During a lull, Sara addressed her mother. "You're going to be a grandmother next summer." The table erupted in joyous celebration while her mother hugged her tightly.

***

The visitors rode off early the next morning into the ever-deepening cold. Ted and Tim accompanied them for the first few miles before they split off to check on the cattle sheltering in canyons and meadows. Meanwhile, everyone scattered to their own tasks. Tom and Sally were responsible for the outdoor chores. Despite the body heat generated by the animals in the barns, they were thoroughly chilled before they returned to the ranch house.

Sally had shed her heavy layers of clothing and was warming herself next to the stove when Edwina said, "My father's letter asked me to wish you good luck in your studies. He said he'll have need of a barrister in the future and you'll be the first one he'll contact."

Sally laughed along with Edwina. "He might not be able to afford the travel charges."

Still grinning, she settled deeper into the rocker before the fire, and opened the oldest of her letters. It was two months old, mostly Nancy chatting about the happenings in her life and the city of San Francisco.

The next two were of a similar nature but the fourth grabbed her attention.

I remember you said at the dance you had never attended school but had been taught at home by your mother. You also said you were planning to take the bar exam next spring. I don't remember you saying anything about going to college. We don't live far from the University and I'm planning to attend next fall. I visited them and asked some questions. I don't know if you'd be interested, but it's possible to earn credits needed for a degree by passing an end-of-course test. If you could pass the bar exam without going to college, who knows what credits you could earn without having to take the actual classes. You might be able to earn a degree in much less time.

Sue was working at the desk and glanced up occasionally to watch her daughter pore over the stack of letters. Her curiosity rose when Sally reread one letter several times.

"Would you read this and tell me what you think?"

Sue scanned the letter, and then read it more carefully. "I didn't know you could pass college classes by just taking a test. I'll discuss it with Pa, but I'm sure we could work something out if you want to go." She sighed theatrically, "Even if it is in San Francisco."

CHAPTER 4

The first week of May opened with a torrent of rapidly melting snow caused by a mild wind from the south. Sally, as nervous as a young colt, tried to concentrate while laying out the items she would need to pack for her extended stay in Wilford.

Her mother stood in the open door and said, "Is there something I can help with?"

"I'm so nervous, I can't think. Can you think of anything else I need?"

Sue laid a comforting hand on her daughter's shoulder as her eyes skimmed the items spread out on the bed. "I can't think of anything else. You won't need a lot, staying with the Browns."

Sally clasped the hand on her shoulder for a moment before draping the packed saddlebags over her shoulder. Setting her Stetson on her flowing red hair, she kissed her mother on the cheek. "Thanks, Ma. I'll pass the tests and make you proud."

Tears misted Sue's eyes. "You already have. We'll always be proud of you."

A few minutes later Sally was astride a horse as skittish as she was. Tom, who would be riding with her for greater safety along the still snow-covered trails, was far more composed. She gave a last look at her family gathered on the porch to see her off. "I'll be home in a week." She thumped her horse with her heels and raised her hand in a final salute. She waved a last goodbye from the top of the slope above the ranch, with her father and mother still watching.

***

Sally was half-frozen and shivering violently in spite of the spring-like warmth when they rode into Wilford to halt in front of Squire Brown's law office. Many times on the trail her horse had to force its way through melting banks of snow, and the slush had soaked her legs. She was so cold she was doubly grateful Tom had accompanied her.

When they walked into Squire's office, he was appalled by the tremors of cold that were shaking both their bodies. Squire was adamant, "Sally! You get over to the house. Emma's waiting for you. She'll get you warmed up and dried out before you catch your death of cold. I'll take your horses to the livery." He had always treated them as he treated his own grandchildren, with love, tenderness, and no hesitation in providing guidance and wisdom. Sometimes, like today, he disregarded any gentleness in issuing orders or advice.

He switched his attention to Tom. "Doc said he'd put you up until you're ready to go home, because Sally and I will be studying late tonight. He volunteered that he has the room, and would like your company. You get over to his place, because you're as sopping wet as she is."

"Th-Th-Thanks," Sally replied with chattering teeth. "I won't argue with you." She stripped the saddlebags from her horse and slung them over her shoulder before heading for his home.

Tom did the same, heading for Doc's, already anticipating an evening of lively discussion.

Emma Brown met her at the door. In short order, she was toweled dry, wrapped in a warm robe, and sitting in front of a crackling fire. Both hands were wrapped around a hot cup of coffee as she inhaled the warm vapor in satisfaction, sporting a smile. "I'm beginning feel half-way human. You sure know how to get a body warmed up."

"I'm glad you're more comfortable. We definitely don't want you to come down sick and miss your chance to take the bar exam."

When Squire returned from the office, Sally was sitting by the fireplace, warm and comfortable in her now-dry rider's garb. He greeted her affectionately, "I see Emma's taken good care of you."

"She sure has. I never thought I could get so cold on a day like today. It seemed warm enough when we started, but the slush was an ice-water bath. I was half-frozen when we got here."

The evening meal was waiting and they talked animatedly throughout. Having eaten her fill, Sally started to clear the table.

"Not tonight," said Squire. "You need to spend the evening in class."

She gave him a questioning glance.

"We'll hit the books hard tonight. Let's discover if there's anything we need to concentrate on."

They were soon seated at the large table in the parlor with piles of text books close at hand. The hours sped by as she rattled off answers or searched for them. Both were startled when Emma interrupted them by the simple expedient of extinguishing the lamp on the wall. "It's almost midnight. You can't cover the whole bar exam in one night."

They stared guiltily at one another in the spill of dim light from the kitchen as the clock in the hall began to strike the hour of midnight. Sally slid her chair back and stretched. "I didn't realize time could go so fast. Thanks for bringing us back to earth."

***

They spent almost every minute of the next two days in Squire's office, reviewing vast quantities of material in preparation for the bar exam. Sally was mentally and physically exhausted when they sat down for the evening meal.

"There will be no studying for you tonight," Squire said sternly. "If you don't know the material now, you won't know it at test time tomorrow. Go to bed and get a good night's sleep. Don't fret over what you think you don't know. You'll do enough of that on the train tomorrow."

She was up before the sun to catch an early train for the short ride to the county seat of Agate. She rented a room in a small boarding house not far from the station. Checking her reflection in the mirror, she made a minute correction to her hair before nervously checking her purse for her letter of admission to the bar exam.

After a recheck in the mirror for one last time, she walked to the courthouse, a short distance away. She was glad for the boardwalks bordering the street, which made them resistant to the scourge of most western towns: mud. Crushed rock, a by-product of the local mines and their tailings piles, blanketed the town's streets.

Agate was not unaccustomed to unusual visitors but many of the morning pedestrians stopped or turned to stare. She ignored the gawkers, her six-foot four-inch stature towering over everyone else on the street. Men and women alike watched a slim, lithe figure wearing a deep green dress billowing with the motion of her stride, contrasting sharply with her collar-length red hair shining in the bright sun.

The courthouse was built of stone, rectangular in shape. Each corner was capped by a small spire. Carved statues embedded in the walls adorned every facet of the building, overlooking tall windows. A clock and bell tower rose high over the surrounding businesses. The vaulted interior was much dimmer than the exterior. Sally took a moment to let her eyes adjust before she could examine her surroundings. The ceiling rose high above an open foyer, lined with offices opening onto each of the three levels surrounding the central dome. She walked toward the stairs.

A male voice asked, "Can I help you?" A young man stared at her.

"I'm to report to the law library by nine o'clock."

His eyes widened. "You're taking the bar exam?"

"I sure am!"

He stumbled over his words as they headed for the stairs. "I'm Raymond Wolf, from here in Agate. I just graduated from law school last week. This will be my first attempt to pass the bar."

Sally nodded politely and replied, "I'm Sally Storm, from Wilford. Squire Brown was my teacher. This'll be my first try, too."

He gaped, "You didn't go to law school?"

"No. I studied at home, using the law books Squire selected for me."

He was silent for the remainder of the climb up the stairs. When he held the law library door open for her, he said, "Good luck."

"Good luck to you, too."

The library was quiet, crowded with several small tables. Three young men were already seated, facing a heavy wooden desk. The proctor, a local lawyer, looked up, his face showing his surprise at her appearance. Ignoring his expression, she placed her letter of admission on his desk and stepped back to allow Raymond to do the same. The seated men all stared at her.

The proctor sputtered, "You're a woman!"

"Yes! I am! Is that a problem? There's nothing on this application that says I have to be a male. I only have to pass the bar to be a licensed attorney."

Abe Winkler goggled at her unexpected presence as she stared back, face calm, eyes cold and steely. He weighed the implications of the sandbag she had dropped on him, until a tenuous smile twitched on his lips. "*Miss S. A. Storm*. Squire Brown has presented me with quite a surprise. Please take a seat. Since you and Mr. Wolfe are the last of the applicants, we can get started immediately."

The test was spread over two days that were among the longest and hardest Sally had ever endured. Working against a clock rather than the sun, she knew she had to be right the first time, otherwise, she would have to wait another year, which added the very real possibility of having a far more hostile proctor.

Sally and the others had a quick meal at noon in an eatery across the street from the courthouse. Before they had finished, Sally could hear the whispers which would quickly spread through Agate. *'Ted and Sue Storm's* daughter *thinks she's going to be a lawyer!'*

With the end of testing on the second day, the other candidates looked as tired and drained as Sally felt. When she turned in her final test along with the others, she watched as each was placed in an individual envelope marked with their names. Stretching her back to relieve the knot in her shoulder muscles, she groaned, "This is harder work than working."

Raymond agreed, "You won't get any argument from me."

When Mr. Winkler finished sealing the test envelopes, he announced, "Your bar exam is now complete. It will be graded and you will each receive written notice of pass or fail in about six weeks." His gaze swept each in turn, stopping on Sally. He smiled, "Good luck to all of you."

CHAPTER 5

Sally was delighted when she returned to Wilford the next day. Stepping down from the train, she almost collided with Edwina, whose face was radiant with joy.

"Mark and I going to Denver. He asked me to marry him and I said YES! He's going to ask Father for my hand and his blessing."

Sally hugged her almost-sister tightly, congratulating both. More restrained with Mark, she simply shook hands with him. "You'll have to tell me all about it when you get back."

Edwina called back over her shoulder as she boarded, "I will."

She watched the train disappear down the track before walking the short distance to Squire Brown's office, where she was enveloped in the arms of her sister. Sara's body was swollen by her advanced pregnancy but she managed to hug her *little* sister. "Did you see Edwina at the station? Andy and I brought them in to catch the train."

"Yes. I saw her for about a minute. I'm as happy for them as you are."

A few minutes later Squire emerged from his office with a client. After the client left, he eyed Sally with raised eyebrows rose and a smile playing on his lips. "Well, did you pass?"

"You know I won't have the results for several weeks. Having said that, I'm confident I passed. You're such a good teacher, everything on the test was material we discussed in one form or another."

"I know you passed. You've made me proud to have been your teacher." His pride showed in his fierce grin and he cleared his throat gruffly to hide his emotion. "I saw your parents in town. Why don't you find them and tell them, too. Just leave your things here and pick them up when you leave." *And I'm as proud of you as if you were my very own grandchild.*

Sally's throat was tight as she bade him goodbye, her eyes shining. She held him for a moment before following her sister out the door. They found an empty bench on the porch in front of the general store. Sara promptly claimed it, observing ruefully, "I'll be glad when the baby arrives. I'm uncomfortable all of the time and it's hard to walk or ride." She asked, "Did you have a chance to talk to Edwina before they left?"

"Not really. We didn't have time for much more than hi and bye. She told me they were going to Denver to ask her father for his blessing."

Sara was uncharacteristically somber, staring sightlessly at the flow of pedestrians and traffic on Wilford's main street. "They're going to do more. Carl and Mary asked Mark if he'd like to go into business with them at their millwork. They're so busy they can hardly keep up now, and are afraid it's going to get even more hectic.

"Mark's heart just isn't in ranching. He'd like for them to move to Denver after they get married, which they're planning for the middle of July or early August."

Sally took her sister's hand. "You want them to be happy, but you hate to think of them leaving."

"Yes." Sara's eyes were moist. "I feel the same way about you leaving."

"I'm anxious to go, but I'm scared, too. I just wish I'd hear from 'Frisco. I'd like to know what it would take to test out of courses."

***

It was an early morning a few days later when Sue heard the drumming of distant hoof beats and hurried to the porch, greeting Mark, who had galloped into the ranch yard.

"Sara started having labor pains this morning. I headed right out to let you know."

Her face tightened as she took the Stetson Edwina handed her. "I'm on my way. Don't expect me back 'til you see me."

Ted was already headed for the house, leading a saddled horse, before she could descend the steps.

He handed her the reins. "I'll be along shortly."

Ben was watching when Sue and Mark topped the rise overlooking the ranch yard at the B-bar-F. He waved to reassure them, waiting on the porch until they rode up.

"Sara's comfortable. Andy and Cathy are with her. You go on in. I'll take care of the horses."

When Sue entered the bedroom, Sara was propped up on a pillow, her forehead covered with a damp cloth. Cathy was holding her left hand. She turned her head to smile at her mother but gasped and grimaced with pain, holding her body rigid until the contraction passed. Perspiration trickled down her face which Sue gently wiped away.

She smiled tremulously. "Thanks, Ma." After several deep breaths she gasped, "I'm glad you're here."

"I wouldn't miss seeing my first grandchild being born for any reason."

Andy had been holding her other hand and Cathy ordered him out, "Make sure we have plenty of hot water on the stove. Bring a full pail because we're going to need it before long."

His anxiety was obvious as he obeyed, returning in a few minutes with a full pail.

"There's only room for two of us. We'll call you if we need you." His mother's glare froze his protest and he nodded, bending to kiss Sara before he left the room, pulling the door closed behind him.

Edwina and the Storms rode in less than an hour later to find the rest of the Franklins sitting anxiously on the porch. Lacking chairs, most of the arrivals elected to sprawl or squat on the wide porch. Edwina snuggled next to Mark, enjoying his presence.

The morning crept past, the tension rising as the sun neared its zenith. Heads suddenly swiveled toward the sound of a baby's cry. Andy jumped to his feet and rushed through the door, to be back a few moments later, his face showing pride, joy and anxiety. "We have one little girl but there's another baby on the way. It's twins."

Another hour passed before visitors were allowed into the bedroom, where Sara was propped up by pillows, exhausted by the delivery, her face aglow with happiness. Andy held her hand, beaming at Sue and Cathy, who were each cradling a bundled infant in her arms.

Exhausted, Sara whispered, "Ma. We've decided to name our first-born after your mother, June." Sue's eyes glistened with tears. "We're going to name her sister Dawn."

***

Squire Brown was seated at the oak wood roll-top desk from which he conducted most of his business when a loud knock sounded. He looked up at the open doorway and rose to greet an old friend. "Sam! It's good to see you." His face was wreathed in a smile as they shook hands. "I've been anxious to see you ever since you wrote you wanted to come to Wilford to meet my protégé."

Sam Wallingford, Dean of the Colorado School of Law, smiled at his former classmate. "I'm always glad to see you. No offence, but this time I'd rather meet the young man you sent to take the bar exam. He must be rather extraordinary!" When Squire grinned, he waved him off. "No. I'm not going to tell you because the young man deserves to hear the news first."

Squire smiled, mischief dancing in his eyes as he waved his friend toward the door. "I passed your message on, but the Storms are all attending a wedding at the moment. The newlyweds will be taking the train to Denver this afternoon. Let's go get something to eat while we wait. The youngster you want to meet will come here after the ceremony."

When they returned to the office, they selected

comfortable chairs and chatted about mutual acquaintances each had dealt with over the years. When he heard footsteps, Squire went to the door and beckoned the new arrival to enter. Professor Wallingford rose to his feet and turned to the door, where he found himself facing a very tall, red-haired young woman dressed in a flowing, deep green skirt and blouse.

"Sally Storm. I'd like you to meet Professor Wallingford, Dean of the College of Law."

She smiled, offering her hand. "I'm glad to meet you, Professor."

The professor shook her hand as his face flushed.

Squire could not stifle his laughter as his eyes twinkled. "Sally is also known as S. A. *Storm*."

"You really set me up this time, Squire." Sally was trying hard not to laugh when he turned to her. "Miss Storm, I wanted to meet you in person to deliver the law license you have so ably earned. You've also earned renown for having attained the highest score ever recorded for the bar exam in this state. You were only one point short of a perfect score. May you learn to be as good a practicing lawyer."

Sally turned to Squire. "I owe you this. I could never have done it without your guidance." She hugged him tightly. "Thanks, old friend!"

CHAPTER 6

Sally was nervous and too uncomfortable to sit still. Days of travel by train had left her long legs tired and cramped, her body aching and sore. In spite of the discomfort, she was eagerly anticipating new experiences when the Oakland rail station hove into view.

She waited for a break in the stream of passengers before unfolding her long, jeans-clad legs and booted feet. Carrying her traveling bag, she followed the slow-moving line out of the car onto the platform and glanced around. She heard an excited voice call above the crowd noise. "Sally! Over here!"

Turning to her left, she could see Nancy waving enthusiastically over the heads of the crowd. When the crowd shifted, Sally saw she was standing atop one of the many benches scattered throughout the station. When she reached Nancy she was enveloped in a hug as the smaller woman gushed, "I'm so glad to see you! Mother and Father are waiting near the baggage car. They decided they didn't need to fight the crowd here at the train."

"I'm glad to finally get here. I've been looking forward to seeing all of you again."

Nancy teased, "It's easy to spot you in a crowd. Wearing a Stetson and being a foot taller than anyone else makes you hard to miss." Sally laughed, unembarrassed. Nancy led the way to the baggage car where Wilbur and Anne welcomed her, talking animatedly until her luggage was unloaded.

***

Monday morning Sally sat facing Abraham Wood, the Dean of the College of Law. He examined her in silence for several moments, his drumming fingers showing that he was less than delighted by her presence. "When I received a letter from my old friend, Doctor Wallingford, I was very intrigued. I could not imagine why he would ask me to be an advisor to a newly-licensed lawyer. We usually find lawyers achieve their Bachelor degree first, before getting their law degree. But, after I read his letter several times, your situation began to make sense. Miss Storm, I have scheduled several tests for you. Your first one is at nine this morning, with more this afternoon and tomorrow. The tests you take will be graded each evening. *If* you pass each level, you will be allowed to take additional tests on Wednesday and Thursday."

"Thank you for your help, sir." Sally was nervous.

"I doubt someone who came so close to a perfect score on the bar exam will disappoint anyone." Standing, he extended his hand. "Good luck."

***

"Time's up! Turn in your tests." The brusque command broke the silence. Sighing thankfully, Sally picked up the test folder and as the only female in the room, joined the short line at the proctor's desk, adding her last test of the day to the growing pile.

From behind her someone asked, "Are you as glad to be done as I am?"

"You can't be half as glad as I am." She returned his chuckle. "Right now I'm just numb except where I ache." She tried to unobtrusively stretch.

"Hi, I'm Bob. Want to share a cup of coffee?"

"Sally Storm. Sure." She extended her hand to shake his. "Is there a good coffee house on campus?"

"None on campus, but several across the street. You can take your pick from about a dozen good ones."

***

When Sally bade him goodbye much later, a thoroughly bemused Bob watched until she vanished. Shaking his head, he ordered another coffee as a friend slid into the just-vacated seat.

"Has Cupid strummed your heart strings again?"

Bob laughed, "No, but I've never met a woman quite like the young lady who just walked out of here."

Eyes widened as Craig waited for an explanation.

"She's not even a freshman. She's never spent a day in a school house or a college class. In spite of that, she almost aced the bar exam in Colorado. She didn't tell me that, though. I'd heard it elsewhere but didn't put much stock in it at the time."

His respect was obvious. "She took the same pass-out tests I did today. I'm not sure if I passed any of them. She's confident she did. Confident, but not cocky. She's smart enough there's no reason for her to expect any other result." His own bemused expression mirrored his friend's. "I think she's probably the youngest student on campus. I wouldn't be surprised if she is also the smartest."

Bob asked, "Do you remember reading in the papers a year or so ago about the two female marshals who had a shoot-out with the hired killers?"

Craig nodded, mystified as to where this conversation was going.

"They're her mother and sister."

Craig was goggle-eyed. "No wonder you didn't try any moves on her! She could probably break either one of us in half."

Bob glared at his friend for a moment before laughing in rueful agreement. "I'm sure she knows how."

***

Sally was seated in Dean Wood's office Friday afternoon, where instead of almost-hostility, respect showed in his eyes. "Miss Storm. You have done remarkably well in your tests. The faculty has agreed to admit you for this semester as a probationary senior student. If you do as well in your classes as your initial testing indicates, it might be possible for you to graduate with a full Bachelor of Arts degree next spring. That would be an outstanding accomplishment for someone as young as you are."

Sally gawked at him in disbelief, trying to collect her wits. "I never thought I could do so well. I'd have been happy to test out of a small part of my first year."

Dean Wood laughed gently before continuing in a more serious vein, "Doctor Wallingford also indicated you'd like to work part time to help pay for your

222

education. I know many lawyers in the area. I'm sure I could find an office where you could be employed, if you'd like me to do so?"

"I'd appreciate it. Working for someone here would give me a different view of the law than what I got from Squire Brown."

"I'll see what I can find for you. I almost wish you hadn't already passed the bar, because I'd like to observe your classroom work." He offered his hand. "Good luck, Miss Storm. If I can be of help, please let me know."

***

Sally's first week of college was daunting as she attended formal classes for the very first time. She had anticipated the first weeks would be hard, but was still overwhelmed by the initial challenges. Since she was the sole female in almost all her classes, her uncharacteristic struggles made her profoundly grateful for the stability offered by the evenings she spent with Nancy and her parents.

She was thankful when the last class of the week dismissed, anticipating the freedom of the upcoming weekend. Nancy was waiting for her so they could walk home together. "One of the fraternities on campus invited us to a party tonight. Would you like to go?"

There was no mistaking the eagerness in her friend's eyes. Sally felt she couldn't disappoint Nancy this early in the school year and accepted with feigned enthusiasm, "Sure. I'd like to go."

***

Sally finished dressing while Nancy chattered at her through the partially open door into the hallway. After giving a final stroke of a brush to her red hair, she slipped into her boots and eyed her image in the mirror on the back of the door, smiling slightly. The new boots she was wearing, touted as the height of San Francisco fashion, were almost identical to her cherished riding boots.

When she stepped into the hall, she could see Nancy was wearing a bright red dress falling just below her knees. Sally said, "This dress may mark me as a country girl from Colorado, but I wouldn't be comfortable wearing a dress like yours. Just don't give up on me, I might wear one like yours by the end of the year."

Nancy was suddenly anxious. "I don't want you to feel out of place. I didn't realize until now that no matter what you wear, you're going to be the tallest person there, man or woman."

Sally shrugged. "I'm so used to it I don't think about it."

CHAPTER 7

The young man doing duty as a greeter gave Sally an incredulous stare when they arrived at the fraternity house. Her hackles rose when he leered. He asked Nancy brusquely, "Who's your friend?"

Her voice was shrill with tension, "Eldon, I'd like you to meet Sally Storm."

His breath was reeking of alcohol as he offered his hand with exaggerated care. "Pleased to meet you, I'm sure."

Sally gave the clammy hand a perfunctory shake. Suppressing an instinctive desire to wipe her hand, she followed Nancy inside. The large front room of the fraternity house was crowded wall-to-wall with partiers and a matching noise level. The evening passed more quickly than Sally had anticipated. Her irritation level rose steadily with her internal alarm keeping pace. She made no comment when most of the male attendees made repeated visits to a makeshift bar in the kitchen, resulting in their demeanor shifting from jovial and charming to loud and obnoxious. Some of them tried to force their new-found charm on the young women in attendance.

Nancy found Sally clustered with a small group of young women, who were warily watching as the party grew rowdier. She giggled, holding up a glass of punch. "Have you had any of this?" Sally shook her head. Nancy's response was slurred. "It sure tastes good."

Sally took the glass and tried a small sip, grimacing. "This's been spiked with something strongly alcoholic." The others ears perked up as she asked. "How many glasses have you had?"

Nancy mumbled, "Four. I think. I don't know. I didn't know it was spiked."

Sally was bitterly sarcastic, "Our generous hosts are trying to get all of us drunk. I don't think they're doing it out of the goodness of their hearts and it's definitely not for our own good."

Belle suggested softly. "I think we should pass the word to the rest of the girls before anyone else leaves with someone."

The group quietly began passing the warning, resulting in a slow exodus of young women. Sally was the youngest woman in attendance, but the torch of leadership was passed to her as most of the distaff guests began noticeably drifting from the party.

Several of the young men turned surly when they realized their female guests were leaving early and alone. Other than their small group, only two remained when Sally whispered, "We can't protect someone who doesn't want to be protected. Let's leave."

As they neared the door, they were confronted by one of the fraternity men. His face was a thundercloud as he challenged Sally, "Who gave you the right to ruin our party?"

Sally kept eye contact but didn't reply, smiling slightly as his face turned even darker. He cursed and grabbed for her arm. She caught his wrist and spun on her heel, dragging his arm over her shoulder. Aided by his momentum, she heaved and flipped him over her shoulder to land on his back with a crash. She eyed the limp form for a few seconds in the dead silence before she said, "It's time for us to leave."

Nancy was unable to resist a last dig at the stunned fraternity brothers. "Sally's been roping steers for years. Your hero wasn't much of a challenge for her." Her chance remark bestowed the nickname of *Roper* on Sally, which lasted for the duration of her college career.

The attitude of many of the male students in her classes was decidedly cool the following week. In contrast, most of the female students on campus were openly admiring. She tried to ignore the hostility but enjoyed the discomfort of the fraternity brothers who glowered when other students gleefully addressed her with her new nickname.

She had expected the first week of study to be the hardest, and it was. Having established a routine, she found to her surprise her favorite class was Philosophy. Her teacher, Professor Freeman, proved to be an expert at making his students think by throwing a concept at a student before tearing apart their reasoning and exposing any flaws.

She listened with great interest to some feeble efforts in response to Professor Freeman's technique and was unsurprised when he turned his attention to her. "Now that we've exposed the limited reasoning ability of most of the males in this class, let's see if the sole member of the gentle gender can do any better." He eyed her silently, ignoring a chorus of muffled snickers. "Miss Storm, please explain to the rest of us the adage 'turn the other cheek.'"

Her unwavering eyes met his for several seconds while she collected her thoughts. "First of all, it's an ideal very hard to achieve in practice. I know it's often quoted from the Bible, and there are many times when following it would be the best path. However, there are times when you must fight back."

Professor Freeman pounced eagerly. "Explain!" The class waited expectantly, eagerly anticipating the impending shredding of the uppity female's argument, whatever it might be.

"The most obvious example is waging war for national interest and survival. My strongest reason is personal. I wouldn't be here if my parents hadn't defended themselves."

This turn of the discussion took Professor Freeman by surprise, tempering his approach, somewhat, "Explain."

"The day my mother and father first met, they were both wounded in a gun battle with an outlaw gang." She shrugged while the room buzzed. "If they hadn't fought back and survived, my siblings and I would never have been born." She added dryly. "There's a lot to be said for fighting back when personal survival is at stake."

The professor met her eyes thoughtfully for a moment before smiling. "I cannot argue with your example. Please continue."

***

The first snows of winter were approaching as Sue sprawled in her favorite chair next to the stove. She was vicariously enjoying the college experiences

Sally shared in one of her frequent letters, stopping often to chuckle over some humorous passage. She finished the letter, before passing it to Ted, half-asleep in his rocker. She selected another letter, which had the return address of Mrs. Wilbur Smythe and began enjoying the long-distance companionship of a new friend.

I'm so glad our daughters met when you came to San Francisco and are now best friends.

Wilbur and I have always known our Nancy was a bit flighty in spite of our best efforts. Sally has been a very positive influence on her and we see more maturity in Nancy's attitude and actions. We feel it is largely due to her being friends with such a fine role model, even though Sally is the younger.

Nancy and her friends and classmates at the University have never had to work as hard as Sally and it shows. I must tell you when Sally started classes here, the other students, especially the girls, didn't know what to make of her. They have since discovered her wonderful talent of never bragging or belittling and having a clear head in a crisis.

My Nancy has told me Sally is one of the true leaders on campus in spite of being the youngest woman on campus.

We are grateful to you and Ted, and especially to Sally, for providing such a shining example for our daughter Nancy. God Bless you.

Anne Smythe

Sue held the letter for several moments, thinking of her youngest daughter and her adventures. She handed Ted the letter, watching fondly while he read it.

He reached for her hand. "We have two fine daughters following in their mother's footsteps."

"And two fine young men who take after their father." Her eyes swept their sons, half-asleep in their chairs by the stove.

CHAPTER 8

During the third week of school, Sally received a message from Dean Wood, asking her to come to his office. "I won't keep you long, Miss Storm. I received a response from the State Prosecutor's office concerning my inquiry regarding employment for you. They would like you to interview with them for a position. Do you think you can handle the extra work this early in the semester?"

Sally brightened. "I appreciate your help. Yes, I'd like to talk to them," she said soberly. "I believe I can handle both school and work, now that I've had a couple weeks of classes and know what to expect."

"Just don't forget it would be no crime to drop either a class or work if your studies suffer."

"I won't forget. Thank you again."

***

When winter arrived, or at least what passed for local winter, Sally's reaction to the mildness of the change of seasons caused vast amusement among her friends. She protested. "Last winter at this time we'd already been snowbound for two weeks! It was another two months before we had a break in the weather and dared to ride to town for mail and supplies."

"It's just you know so much about so many things." Mary Beth laughed at her embarrassment. "Then you're so surprised at something the rest of us take for granted.

"This weekend is a holiday and you obviously know a lot about horses. Would you and Nancy like to go to a polo match with me and my parents on Saturday?"

"I'd love to, but I know nothing about polo." Sally mused, "I'm sure I can talk Nancy into going."

"Be sure to bring your riding clothes. I'm sure Father would let you ride one of our horses between matches."

***

Sally, Nancy, and Mary Beth arrived at the polo field on a warm and sunny Saturday morning, joining several other young men and women. After a friendly round of verbal sparring, two of their male companions left to prepare their horses before joining opposing teams.

Sally watched with a critical eye while the riders raced all over the field in pursuit of the ball. She deduced the rules before the end of the first period, after which she devoted her attention to the quality of the horses and their riders. When one of the winning young men strutted back to the group of young women at the end of the match, he observed rudely to Sally, "I doubt any of your Colorado riders could handle a horse as well as we do."

"You're right." She smiled sweetly when he puffed up with pride. "We'd be laughed out of any roundup if we rode like what I saw today. It's the difference between playing and working with a horse."

She could hear her friends gasp in the background.

Warden Burns' face flamed. "I suppose you think you could do better?"

"I could sure handle a horse better than any I saw out there. I don't know about using the mallet, because I've never touched one."

He flushed even darker.

She snorted disdainfully. "Get me a horse. I'll change to my riding clothes and ride against you right now."

Indignant, he snapped, "You change and come down to the horses! I'll make sure you can choose any you want except my own!" Furious, he stomped off.

Her circle of friends stared at her in shock as someone protested, "You don't know what you're doing! He's one of the best."

She frowned and said, "If he's one of the best, it doesn't say much for the rest. What I saw was not great horsemanship." Her friends gawked, trailing after her in shocked silence when she headed for the tent reserved for ladies.

Word of the grudge match spread quickly. When Sally emerged a few minutes later, dressed in rider's garb and wearing her Stetson, a crowd had gathered in anticipation of seeing her trounced. Some, mostly women, anticipated that she would make a good showing but would certainly wind up losing. All of the men fully expected her to lose and were looking forward to it.

Mary Beth was waiting to escort her to the horses. She gulped, "I never intended for you to get in a polo match. I hope you don't get beaten too badly."

"I can handle the horse with no problem. I just hope I can hit the ball."

Warden Burns and the rest of the male riders were waiting near the horses when the group of young women arrived. "The bay, number nine, is my horse," he snapped. "You can choose any of the others."

She nodded and started to walk among the other mounts. Eyeing each one, she kept up a running commentary directed at Mary Beth as she listed the strengths and weaknesses of each horse. Her challenger's face was beet red as the other men exchanged incredulous glances, painfully aware this young woman knew as much or more about horseflesh than they did.

Sally made her selection and caressed the horse gently. It eyed her with suspicion but quickly warmed to her presence. She checked the fit and tightness of the girth, adjusted the stirrups to her long legs, then climbed smoothly into the saddle. One of the watching horsemen handed her his mallet. She grasped it, taking several tentative swings before nodding in satisfaction. "I'm ready whenever you are."

Warden was suddenly apprehensive. He had issued the challenge in the heat of anger, cocksure of his superior skill. After watching her appraisal of the line-up of horses, he realized this woman would be no pushover. Nervous, he flicked the reins and guided his horse to the playing field.

They faced each other in the middle of the field for a moment before she saluted.

Startled, he returned her salute, and after a

moment's hesitation the match began. Sally swung her mallet at the ball whenever the opportunity arose but seldom made solid contact. The few times she hit the ball it was never square and it shot off in all directions.

The match was scoreless through two periods as they raced from one end of the field to the other. Sally was learning how to hit the ball but still could not get the ball to go where she wanted. In compensation, her skill at getting everything possible from her horse kept her between her opponent and the goal, denying him any opportunity to score.

When time ran out both horses were tiring. The crowd cheered wildly for both players when Sally and Warden met in midfield and she extended her hand. "How about calling this match a draw? If this were my own horse, I'd be willing to ride for another period but I don't want to ride a borrowed horse into the ground."

He returned her handshake respectfully. "Miss Storm, if you knew how to handle a mallet properly, you would be an even more formidable foe. If you could handle one as well as you do a horse, you would be extremely difficult to beat."

"Thank you." She raised her hand in salute before making several slow laps around the field to allow her mount to cool down. The crowd cheered when she dismounted and handed the reins to its owner. "You have a champion in this horse. If you have a towel and a curry comb handy, I'll work him down."

Awed by her ability, he said, "That's not necessary. I'll take care of him."

"Thank you." She tipped her Stetson in salute and walked toward the changing tent accompanied by a crowd of young women who closed ranks around her.

Mary Beth wondered aloud, "I never thought a woman could outride a man like you did. How're you going to get a man interested in you if you keep beating them like that?"

"Why shouldn't I try to beat them?" Sally said bluntly. "If they can't take getting beat, that's their problem, not mine! My mother told me having no husband is better than having a bad one. I'm not going to settle for one who can't accept me as I am."

When her circle of young friends stared at her as though she had uttered a blasphemy she laughed.

CHAPTER 9

The school year became a whirlwind of activity for Sally as she juggled a heavy load of classes with social events and regular employment at the Prosecutor's office. She became a leader among the female students in spite of being regarded as a loose cannon by many of the male students, who expected women to be shy and submissive. A few regarded her with tolerant amusement, while the more reactionary males could scarcely conceal their hostility. Male and female students alike agreed she was a force to be reckoned with.

Spring arrived with such a mild change from one season to another it was hardly noticeable to Sally. A few weeks later, graduation arrived as well. At the ceremony she was by far the youngest of the graduates awarded their degrees by the Dean of Liberal Arts.

"Ladies and Gentlemen. It is my great pleasure to award this diploma to Miss Sally Storm. I would also note she is the recipient of this year's title of Honor Graduate, which I believe has never been presented to a more-deserving student. Congratulations, Miss Storm."

***

After graduation, Sally spent a few days exploring the Bay area before starting fulltime at the Prosecutor's office, where she had worked during the school year. Having spent most of her time doing research for many cases, she was surprised on her first day to be directed to the daily staff meeting.

She had been in the large conference room on only a few occasions to deliver materials she had researched. This morning's early arrival gave her a few minutes to examine her surroundings in detail. The high ceiling was decorated with a large mural depicting Justice and her scales. Following the blindfolded gaze of the painted figure, she eyed the luxurious, dark, and heavy carvings adorning the walls and furniture.

She remained standing when the senior lawyers began to file in, waiting respectfully. When they were seated, she selected an empty chair near the foot of the table, taking notes as pending cases were discussed. After reviewing several cases, the chief prosecutor, Mr. Hayward, introduced a new case in which charges had not yet been filed. The discussion continued for some time and when it ground to a halt, he growled, "I know he's guilty. You know he's guilty. What can we prove that will stick and put him away for a while?"

The silence dragged on until Sally asked hesitantly, "Would a federal charge be easier to get a conviction? I remember seeing a similar case while I was doing research earlier. United States versus Hollowford Bank, if I remember correctly. I could find the case file in a few minutes."

Mr. Hayward considered her idea for a moment, then said, "If you think you know of a precedent we can use to file charges successfully in another jurisdiction, we'll go on to another case while you're searching."

Some of the older members suddenly found cause to shuffle papers or fidget at the positive response. Two began to whisper as Sally rose and quickly left the conference room. After the door closed one of the older lawyers groused, "Cocky young thing, isn't she?"

Mr. Hayward snapped, "It would seem no one else has a better idea. She's done very good work as an intern. We'll wait to see what she can find."

Sally returned a few minutes later and placed the open casebook in front of Mr. Hayward. "I skimmed it to make sure this was the case I remembered. If I correctly understood the earlier discussion, it should be possible to file charges in federal court and win a conviction."

She returned to her chair and waited, remaining calm and composed despite the barely-concealed hostility from the lawyer who had complained. The room was silent for a few minutes while Hayward skimmed the brief. Handing the volume to the lawyer on his left, he said, "Amos, I know this is your case, but I agree with Miss Storm. The facts are very similar. I believe the Fed's would have a better chance to make it stick than we would.

"Miss Storm. Our primary concern should be justice, not whose jurisdiction or who gets to pursue the case. Unfortunately, that ideal is not always followed. Any time you have information in the search for truth, please don't hesitate to bring it to our attention."

***

The arrival of fall was only a few weeks away when Mr. Hayward called Sally into his office and waved her to a chair. "Miss Storm, you have proved yourself to be a very good lawyer in spite of being both young and inexperienced. Despite that, I've decided to assign you as the lead prosecutor for a major case going to trial in just two weeks."

Sally had learned to appreciate his penchant to be blunt but now she was uncharacteristically flustered, and she gasped and stared at him. Her mind raced as she considered the possible ramification. "What's the catch?"

"The defendant is a rather well-known local businessman, Robert Hunsaker. He's best known publicly for his business acumen. Privately, he is known for his temper and brutality." His voice was cold, filled with loathing, "The charge is the first-degree murder of his wife, Mary. We have a solid case. Unfortunately, it's only circumstantial evidence. I want you to lead, because as a female you would have greater empathy for the victim than a male would." He slapped the desk for emphasis. "This is a case where justice demands a conviction!"

She stared at him for several seconds in uncertainty before asking in a husky voice, "Do you really think I can get a conviction?"

A smile warmed his craggy face, "Yes. I believe you can. Remember, you're one member of a team. You'll be the leader, but you have the entire staff to call on for help. You won't have to do it all by yourself."

His voice softened and he used her first name for the first time without either of them realizing it. "Sally. You are a far better lawyer than I was when I first started. You are better than you think." He handed her a thick file. "This is the case. I've scheduled a strategy session for tomorrow morning at nine. After that it will be primarily your responsibility. Don't forget, everyone on the staff will be available to help if you need it."

She took a deep breath and picked up the heavy file. "I won't let you down, Sir."

***

Sally spent the next few days reading the voluminous report, making notes as she went. Next, she interviewed the investigating officers and witnesses who might be called to testify. During the final staff meeting on the morning of the Friday before the trial was scheduled to convene, she reviewed the facts as established, answering questions as best she could.

"We know he's guilty. Unfortunately, proving it is going to have to rely only on strong circumstantial evidence. I'd like to take Fred with me to the victim's home so I can get a better feel for her. I've reviewed the original search warrant. It has no expiration date, so anything we find today would still be admissible."

Mr. Hayward had been repeatedly impressed by the capability of someone so young and inexperienced, and most of the Neanderthals on his staff were beginning to agree. "Go ahead. I agree we need any scrap of evidence we can find."

Sally and Fred searched from room to room throughout the huge house, carefully examining every object they could open or move, hoping to find something the investigating officers might have overlooked. Several hours had passed before they were back at the front entrance, frustrated and disappointed by their failure to find anything significant.

She shook her head in disappointment and

sighed. "I'm afraid we struck out this time. We'll just have to go with what we have."

Fred nodded in dejected agreement.

Turning to leave, she took a last look around, her eyes sweeping the arched doorway into the grand staircase, halting so suddenly Fred bumped into her. "Do you see anything odd about the Bible on the stand over there?" Excitement colored her question.

Fred's eyes also swept the unremarkable scene. He was mystified, "No. I don't. What am I missing?"

She hurried to the displayed Bible, which was now spotlighted by sunlight streaming through a window. "The reports we have state Mr. Hunsaker lays claims to being a pious, God-fearing churchgoer!" She snorted in distain. "The dust on this Bible is so thick it can't have been touched for many months, long before he was jailed. Maybe he's not as pious as he claims."

Fred watched while she opened the Bible and began to turn the pages, skimming the flyleaf which showed the usual family history, written in a neat hand. She skimmed several more pages before she discovered several folded sheets of paper.

Her heart was pounding in anticipation as she unfolded them and began to read, shocking Fred with an unheard-of burst of profanity. "We've got the murdering son-of-a-bitch now!"

He skimmed the papers as well, reading over her shoulder. "We sure do!"

CHAPTER 10

The opening day of the trial proved to be the prelude to a three-ring circus when an army of reporters and spectators tried to gain entry to the court room. A tawdry but unremarkable murder trial had become center stage, simply because of the gender of the lead prosecutor. Lurid headlines brandished the news of the first female to ever prosecute a criminal case in the San Francisco area, if not the entire state. The headlines became even more sensational when a reporter researched her background and was astounded to discover there were three U. S. marshals in her family, two of them female.

Sally was repeatedly shoved and jostled as she worked her way through the crowd toward the courthouse door, ignoring shouted entreaties for comment on the case or her family. One especially persistent and obnoxious reporter tried to block her way at the door. He suddenly screamed and glared at Sally but she smiled innocently. Limping badly, his eyes fell to the high-heeled rider's boots showing below the hem of her dress. The indentation in the leather of his shoe matched the shape of her heel, applied with her full weight.

***

Sally's pulse was hammering so loudly she was sure Fred Hughes could hear it from his seat beside her. The jury had been seated and several motions to dismiss had been denied. She was holding a deep breath to settle her nerves when the bailiff announced, "All rise. Court is now in session, the Honorable Hector Wall presiding."

After gaveling the court to order, the judge addressed her, "Is the State ready to present its case?"

The waiting was over! She could feel the tension drain from her body as she faced the bench. "The State is ready, Your Honor."

"Then please proceed."

Sally stood, towering over everyone else in the courtroom while her eyes slowly met those of each juror in turn. She knew without looking that Nancy Smythe and her parents, as well as several former classmates, were in the gallery, thanks to the pass system the court had been forced to adopt for this trial.

She had learned enough showmanship to let the suspense build for several moments before she began in a deliberate tone. She concluded her presentation of the State's case. "Gentlemen of the jury, we will prove, beyond the shadow of a doubt, the defendant did, deliberately and with malice aforethought, murder his wife."

Sally tried to maintain a deliberate pace as the trial progressed. Testimony of the few witnesses was often emotional, but the coroner's was especially so. "Doctor White, what was the cause of death of the victim, Mary Hunsaker?"

His face was drawn and grim. "The cause of death was a severe and brutal beating. When found, the body was in very poor condition and it was impossible to determine the exact cause of death. However, it was one of two possibilities, both related. She had been beaten so badly in the chest area that all of her ribs were fractured. The victim died either because the broken ribs punctured her lungs and she drowned in her own blood, or because of the broken ribs she could not draw breath and she suffocated. Either would have been a particularly cruel and painful way to die." Several jurors were noticeably pale when he concluded.

It was late in the afternoon the next day when the judge asked, "Miss Storm, does the State have another witness?"

Sally's hand dropped to a parcel wrapped in plain brown paper lying on the table in front of her. "We do, Your Honor."

She peeled off the covering to reveal a thick Bible which she picked up and carried to the bench. "Your Honor. Our final witness is the written testimony of the victim herself."

The judge's scowl muted the buzz growing in the courtroom.

With great difficulty Sally kept her voice calm and neutral. "The State would like to introduce into evidence two items, this Bible and the letter concealed within it."

The sound of whispers and the creak of chairs scurried through the room as Sally handed the two items to the judge. "Your Honor, you will note the family entries on the flyleaf and the letter were written by the same hand, the hand of Mary Hunsaker, the victim. These two items were found on display in the vestibule of the house shared by the victim and the defendant."

The judge closely examined the two items of evidence as the room quieted. "So ordered."

Sally left the Bible lying on the bar. "The State would like to read the letter to the jury."

The judge nodded and returned the letter to her. When she turned to the jury, making eye contact with one after another, their attention was riveted on her, as was every eye in the courtroom.

She began softly, her soprano carrying clearly to the far corners of the courtroom as she explained, "We found the Bible displayed prominently in the front hall of the defendant's home. I'm sure there are witnesses who will vouch for his piety and devotion to his church, but contradicting his public reputation, the dust was so thick on the Bible it was obvious it had not been touched for many weeks. We find this very suspicious for someone so religious, and believe this to be an indication of a lack of truthfulness." *I really mean he's a damn liar!* she thought to herself.

She turned slowly away from the jury, indicating the defendant with a dismissive wave of her hand. "The letter I am about to read to you will clearly explain that strange discrepancy and make clear why it was never found and destroyed by the defendant."

She stared at him for a moment, her face hard. Facing the jury, she began to read. "*To whom it may concern: if you are reading this letter, then I am already dead, murdered by my husband, Robert Hunsaker.*"

A tide of shocked gasps filled the room and the defense sprang to his feet to protest. The motion was denied before the judge angrily pounded his gavel to restore order. When it was silent again, she resumed reading.

"The only place I can hide this so he will not find it is in my Bible, a book he has never read. He attends church and spouts piety but he is evil and cruel, the Devil Incarnate."

Sally's voice wavered and she swallowed hard, momentarily unable to continue, even though she had read this many times. *"You may ask why I have never left him. He has warned me if I were to ever leave him he will find me and kill me slowly. I do not doubt him, because he once kicked me in the belly, killing my unborn child, who was stillborn a short time later.*

"I know he will kill me soon, but if I run I will die alone with no one to bury me. If I stay, the few friends he allows me for show will bury me in sacred ground. Pray for my soul in Heaven because I have spent my time in Hell here on earth."

The defendant's bellow interrupted her, "It's a lie! I never killed her! It's a lie!" His ranting continued until he was handcuffed and gagged by the bailiffs.

When silence had been restored, she met the eyes of the jury, tears glistening in her own eyes, "This letter was signed by Mary Hunsaker."

She took the Bible from the bar and handed it and the letter to the jury foreman. "When you compare the handwriting, you can see for yourself they are written in the same hand."

The courtroom remained deathly silent while the jury examined both pieces of evidence. When they were done, she turned to face the judge. "Your Honor. The State has no more witnesses."

The judge's gavel echoed in the still-silent and stunned courtroom. "Court is adjourned until nine o'clock tomorrow morning."

CHAPTER 11

Sally gave her summation shortly after the recess, smoothly marshaling the facts she had presented. "You must find this man guilty. He is a coward, a bully, and a vicious murderer. He has admitted here in open court that they fought and he beat her. His claim, *she made me do it*, is preposterous!'"

Unable to contain her contempt, her words were hard and ringing in the packed courtroom. "He outweighed her by over a hundred-twenty-five pounds and *she made him do it!*" She paused and let the silence stretch on for emphasis for a full minute. "Your Honor. The State rests."

The defense was dispirited and perfunctory throughout the attorney's closing argument. Every time Sally glanced at the defendant he was glaring at her.

When the jury had been dismissed for their deliberations, Sally, Fred, and the other members of the Prosecutor's Office who had been observing the trial, crowded into a small conference room a short distance from the courtroom. Sally's cheeks warmed when Mr. Hayward praised her conduct of the case. "You've done a magnificent job! I watched the jurors' faces while you were reading the letter. They're convinced of his guilt. They believed every word she wrote and they'll convict."

She waited until the heat had fled from her face before sipping at a glass of water to ease her throat. Someone knocked on the door and announced. "The jury is coming back!"

Mr. Hayward grunted in surprise. Reaching the door first, he held it open for Sally. "Has to be a guilty plea. No other verdict would be returned so quickly."

When Court had reconvened the judge ordered the defendant to stand. "Mr. Foreman, have you reached a verdict?"

"We have, Your Honor."

The already-quiet courtroom waited in suspense. "What say ye?"

"We find in unanimous verdict, guilty of murder in the first degree."

Sally was watching the defendant, rather than the jury, and saw madness in his eyes. "Uh-oh!" she said.

Mystified, Fred turned toward her at her exclamation as the killer twisted, grabbing at the bailiff standing behind him.

Sally back-handed Fred out of his chair and kicked her chair out of the way, diving for the floor as gunfire erupted in the courtroom. Sheltered by the dubious protection of the wooden table, she grabbed the .38 revolver which had replaced her Colt and was small enough to fit in her handbag. She rolled as the killer's gun belched flame, and returned fire with five rounds that blended into one continuous roll of thunder.

She sprang to her feet amid the eruption of terrified bedlam and bellowed at the top of her lungs, her still-smoking .38 in her hand. "QUIET!"

Shocked, the onlookers obeyed as she pointed at a man in the back row. "You! Go for help at the Sheriff's office down the hall!" She pointed again. "You! Find a doctor! Anyone who knows anything about first aid come up here. The rest of you stay in your seats and keep quiet."

The gunfire had been heard throughout the court house. Sally's orders were heard clearly on the floors above and below. One shaken reporter who witnessed the carnage later headlined his column, *A Magnificent Valkyrie!*

The silent room watched as Sally stepped to the defense table, where the killer was lying on his back, dead with five bullets clustered in the center of his chest. Her face was gray when she checked the bailiff, badly wounded with a bullet in the chest but still alive. She gagged when she saw the defense lawyer dead with a bullet in the head.

Doors began to slam open as uniformed deputies rushed into the courtroom. She ignored them, kneeling beside the fallen man protected by the ornately carved wood of the bar. When Judge Wall tried to sit up, she was overwhelmed with relief. He was pale but snapped, "I was hit but it's just a flesh wound. I was hurt worse in the war. Take care of the others first!"

Chaos reigned in the hallway outside when a crowd began to gather, drawn by the sound of the gunshots. Deputies began to interview each spectator before escorting them out as doctors arrived, pushing through the crowd to attend to the wounded. The crush of reporters protested bitterly when they were also ejected after having made their own statements to the deputies, furiously demanding to interview

Sally and the rest of the court staff.

Sally, Fred, and Mr. Hayward stood together, watching the evidence being collected. Fred's face was already turning black and blue from the blow she gave him when she knocked him from his chair to the safety of the floor.

The sheriff worked his way to them through the blood and gore and asked Sally, "The Press is screaming to see you. Do you want to talk to them?"

Sally looked to Mr. Hayward, who shook his head and said, "Tell them there'll be a press conference in my office at ten tomorrow morning. Inform them I'll hang anyone who tries to pry the story out of Sally or any of my staff before then."

"Can I quote you on that?"

He said dryly, "You may."

Night was falling before the evidence had been collected, the bodies removed, and the cleaning staff given permission to begin their gruesome task. Sally was unsteady on her feet from exhaustion and reaction when Mr. Hayward clasped her shoulder. "It's over now. Let's get you out of here."

He escorted her from the courtroom and down the hall. "I'm not letting you go home alone to your rooming house. Nancy Smythe has been waiting for you all afternoon. You'll be going home with her tonight. I'll drive both of you home and pick you up in the morning in time to be at the office for the press conference."

Sally mumbled a thank-you as Nancy stepped

forward to greet her with a fierce hug. They followed him outside to stand beside a waiting horseless carriage, the first she had ever seen up close. Haywood helped her into the rear seat next to Nancy. She was totally exhausted, but her curiosity roused her and she watched, unsure of what to expect when a policeman stooped in front of the vehicle. The machine suddenly roared and vibrated. After a fit of bucking it quieted and they began to move away from the curb.

CHAPTER 12

The next morning was bright and sunny, a stark contrast to Sally's mood. Nancy and Anne shared breakfast with her, though she just picked at her food. After they finished eating, they stood with her in silent support while she waited at a front window of the mansion, listlessly watching the street. The sun was almost directly in her eyes, but she saw a horseless carriage come chugging up the hill. She shared an embrace with mother and daughter before stumbling sluggishly out to meet it.

Mr. Hayward was not surprised to see Sally with red eyes surrounded with dark circles, obviously exhausted, with slumped shoulders and no spring in her step. His voice was unusually gentle. "You look like you had a bad night."

Sally sank into the seat beside him, morosely silent for several minutes. When she did speak, her voice was flat and lifeless. "Let's just say I didn't have a good night. I couldn't sleep at all for most of the night. It was very late when I finally got up and tried reading, without much success, until Mr. Smythe suggested a glass of wine to relax me."

She glanced at him. "I'd never had more than a few sips before. It must've helped, because I was finally able to get a little sleep."

Mr. Hayward manipulated a lever on the steering column and the machine began to pull away.

Sally stared sightlessly out the window for

several minutes before she spoke. "I'm going to have to resign after what happened yesterday."

"Why do you say that?"

"If I were to continue to practice as a prosecutor in this area, I could never be sure of giving a defendant a fair trial. There'd always be the thought in the back of some defense lawyer's mind the judge might show favoritism to me because I saved another judge's life. Even if there were no bias, any court I served in would be a circus even worse than this one."

She sighed. "That'd be unfair to anyone accused of a crime, especially if they were convicted unjustly."

He easily followed her line of reasoning, which heightened his respect for her. "As I've said several times, though you are a very young woman, you are a very good lawyer. You have again proved how out-standing you truly are. You're more concerned with justice than your own career. I will not let you resign immediately, because it could very well confirm the biases of a lot of narrow-minded clods who believe no woman is capable of being a lawyer." He was adamant. "When the time comes, I want it to be known it's your desire for justice driving your decision, not some mis-placed guilt."

He negotiated a sharp curve in the street before adding, "I hate to admit it, but I've had some of the same doubts you expressed. I have to agree with your reasoning."

He spent several minutes planning a course of action. "We'll wait a bit before I announce your res-ignation. When I do, I'll make it very plain why I wouldn't let you resign immediately, and what my reasons were."

She was relieved by his attitude. Less than nine-teen years old and having been thrown into a storm of publicity, she was no longer alone. The crushing tension of the day and night began to ease. "Thank you!" His eyes met hers for a moment before returning to his driving. "I never thought about how it might appear if I were to resign immediately."

When they turned the last corner to the office, he commented sourly, "You'd better get your armor on. I can see members of the press already waiting on the front steps."

She could see the mob of reporters crowding the front door and groaned. Faced with a direct physical challenge, she sat more erect, her tension lessening.

Mr. Hayward nodded his approval and was rewarded with a wan smile.

He drove to the rear of the office and parked the horseless carriage. Using his key for the private entrance, they entered and walked unhurriedly down the hall to his office. The rest of the staff was already at work and called greetings to Sally as she passed. They halted at his office long enough to leave his brief case before continuing on to a large conference room.

"You might as well let the wolves in before they start to howl," he informed the secretary. "It's almost ten. We'll just make them madder by having them wait." Moments later a rising tide of voices filled the hall as the mob descended on them.

***

Wilbur was relaxing in the comfort of his chair in the parlor. A small fire crackled in the fireplace to keep the evening chill at bay while he scrutinized the day's news. Anne was sitting close by and glanced up when he abruptly sat straighter in his rocking chair, minutely examining a page.

When he finished he looked up with a grin. "The whole paper's devoted to Sally today, but the best part's in the editorials." He handed her the paper.

This writer has seldom witnessed true selflessness in any person serving in the public domain. Today was one of those very rare exceptions, the more noteworthy because of the extreme youth of that person: eighteen-year-old Miss Sally Storm.

Miss Storm confirmed her resignation from the county Prosecutor's Office at a raucous press conference, after it had been announced by Mister Robert Hayward.

Miss Storm's resignation was a gesture of unselfishness. After yesterday's dramatic shootout in court, she believed her presence in any courtroom in the Bay area would be prejudicial to a fair trial for any suspect.

This observer, who witnessed both the shootout and the press conference, must unhappily agree. I quote Mr. Hayward. 'I had first suggested to Miss Storm it would be best to delay her resignation, the better to avoid any misperceptions following yesterday's gun battle at the courthouse. I must stress to you of the Press, Miss Storm is truly more concerned with the true concept of justice than any desire for personal achievement. Every member of my staff has the utmost respect for her integrity!'

They smiled at each other when Anne finished reading. "We've been blessed to have Sally as a second daughter for as long as we have. She's certainly been a positive influence on Nancy." She laid the paper on the table between them and snuggled into his lap.

He whispered, "The Storms have had a great influence on more than our daughter's life."

***

Sally stared in wonderment at the mansion, set back some distance from the brick-paved street. Looking up and down the street lined with similar homes, she asked the driver. "You're sure this is where Mark Franklin lives?"

"That's it, alright." He grinned. "Quite a house, isn't it?"

She nodded absently, digging for coins in her purse to pay the fare. "If you say so, I must be at the right place. Thanks for the ride."

She climbed down from the closed carriage and walked slowly toward the house at the end of the bricked walkway carrying her travel bag. Tall pillars guarded either side of elegant double doors of carved oak. One end of the mansion was graced by a bricked drive curving under a pillared overhang to protect arriving guests from the elements. She eyed the roof, covered with red ceramic tile to protect the house from the ravages of wind and weather. At the intricately carved front door, she found a hinged knocker made of heavy brass. She let it drop, rewarded by a mellow clang she could hear echo inside. Her heart beat furiously as she heard approaching footsteps.

Edwina exclaimed in astonishment, "Sally!" She threw her arms around the much taller woman, hugging her tightly. "It's so good to see you! Are you coming back to Colorado to stay?"

Sally returned the embrace. "Yes. I'm on the way home, but it's a long story."

"Then we can let it wait 'til later." She laughed delightedly. "You looked so stunned when I opened the door, and I know why. I knew long before Mark asked me to marry him he didn't want me to think he was marrying me for my money. I waited until after we were married to tell him I had inherited a fortune from my mother, and now it's ours."

She smiled in fond remembrance. "He found it much easier to accept after Hiram was born. Our son is such a dear little thing. Let's see if he's awake."

They crossed the open entry to a sweeping curved staircase and started upstairs. "Mark didn't know his own skills, but he's turned out to be a born businessman. The millwork has expanded greatly since his sister Mary and her husband Carl invited him to join the firm."

She smiled ruefully. "He's independent and stubborn enough I had a very hard time persuading him to use some of my inheritance to invest in the millwork.

The partnership has already paid off handsomely, and the business is the largest supplier of building material in the Denver area."

Her voice softened as they neared an open door at the end of the hall. She peered in silently before leading Sally to the cradle. In it, the sleeping infant wore a frown only a baby could muster. They admired the infant in silence for several minutes, until Edwina picked up the cradle and led the way downstairs, walking silently to the veranda on the back of the house. Edwina placed the cradle gently on the floor beside a small table.

Her face was aglow as she announced, "We're expecting another baby in the spring. If it's a girl, we're going to name her Melissa Sara in honor of my mother and your sister. I literally owe my life and my happiness to Sara. I've been blessed beyond belief to have both of you as sisters, even if only by marriage."

They took facing chairs so they could silently appreciate the view. The Platte River meandered slowly southward in the foreground, in front of the Rockies towering to the sky in the distance. They talked the afternoon away, watching the shadows of the mountains creep eastward, retreating from the setting sun.

The evening meal was a festive affair for everyone and Sally was delighted to reunite with Mark's sister Mary and her husband, Carl, neither of whom she had seen since she attended their wedding as a little girl. The conversation was animated as they caught up on the events of the intervening years. Edwina's father joined them later and she was impressed with the improvement in his appearance

He smiled at her, shaking her hand. "I'm delighted by the positive effect Denver's climate has had on
my consumption. I've grown to love this city and I've
found a position which makes good use of my experience. Better, I live in an apartment over the carriage
house, close enough to spoil my grandchild."

They all joined in the laughter, which was interrupted by the tinkle of a bell announcing supper was
ready. The table was crowded with plates and serving
dishes, letting Sally enjoy a delicious meal and friendly banter extending late into the night.

CHAPTER 13

Squire Brown was startled by a sharp knock on the door and looked up to see a very tall and slim woman dressed in man's clothes and wearing a Stetson. He thought for a few seconds it was Sara, until the red hair registered. "Sally! It's good to see you! Welcome back!" He frowned then and said, "No one told me you were coming home."

"I didn't know it myself until recently. When I wrote to tell Ma and Pa I was coming home, I asked them not to tell you. I wanted to be the one to tell you what happened."

His sharp ears caught the hesitancy in her voice as he beckoned her to be seated. "Why don't you tell me about it, whatever it might be."

She slumped into the chair beside his desk, staring at him for a few seconds before sighing and relating the chain of events which had led to her decision to leave San Francisco. He listened sympathetically, asking an occasional question or offering an observation, until she finished and slumped in her chair, her eyes downcast.

He said gently, "Sally." She raised her eyes to meet his. "There was nothing else you could have done. Unless you let him keep shooting, but I can't see you doing that."

Some life returned to her eyes. "You're right. I couldn't have sat there and done nothing to stop it."

After a comfortable silence, when some of the

tension had left her body, he asked softly, "What are your plans now you're back?"

She avoided his eyes. "The first thing I want to do is talk to Ma and Pa. I don't know what I want to do, but I know for sure I don't want to work as a prosecutor again. That much I do know! I don't want to work with criminal cases all my life."

He smiled playfully. "I'll answer the question you want to ask, but are afraid to. Would you like to go to work with me?"

Her face lit up as hope returned to her eyes and she smiled sheepishly. "Am I that transparent?"

"Yes. You are. It helps I've known you all your life." He laughed. "Emma and I have discussed having a young lawyer join me to share the practice. We're not young anymore and we'd like more time to visit our grandchildren."

"It would be an honor to work with you!" She couldn't conceal her joy. "Thank you! Thank you! Thank you!"

Squire was embarrassed by her intensity.

She didn't notice his discomfiture and continued, "I did discover in 'Frisco I'd like to work in a general practice, like you have all these years. Especially here in Wilford."

Squire extended his hand. "We'd love to have you stay with us, room and board as part of the deal. There aren't any rooms in town suitable for a single young lady."

"Only if you and Emma let me help around the

house! I won't stay if someone else has to do all of the work."

"Done! We can work out the details later."

***

Sally carried most of her luggage to the Brown's home and discussed details with Emma for a bit before taking the short walk to the livery. A few minutes later she was riding out of town on a rented horse, taking the familiar trail for home.

The ranch house and the corrals were empty when she rode in. Stripping the gear from her horse, she turned it loose in the corral before walking to the house. Embers of a dying fire were still glowing in the kitchen stove. Stoking them with kindling and several pieces of wood, she brought a flame to life. Waiting for the fire to grow, she went to the pantry, selected cans of vegetables and several potatoes, and set them on the table. After a quick stop at the ice box, she added several cuts of meat to the collection.

The stove was hot and the skillet and pans were waiting when she heard the sound of horses. She waited on the porch and waved. When her mother saw her, she swerved toward the ranch house. Her father and brothers called greetings.

Sue wrapped Sally in her arms, her eyes glistening with tears of joy as she hugged her tightly. "Welcome home!'

Sally was overwhelmed by the welcome and the cold knot in her middle began to unravel as tears glistened in her own eyes. She was still sniffling when her brothers joined them, having taken care of all the horses. Her eyes widened, tracking from one brother to the other. "Tommy! You've really grown. You're even taller than Tim."

Her oldest brother laughed good-naturedly. "Yeah. The runt is no longer *the runt*." He playfully punched his brother. "He's grown about five inches while you were away."

"Well, we don't want either of you to starve. Supper is on the stove. It'll be ready shortly."

Sally finished preparing the meal while the others cleaned up. While they ate, they bombarded her with questions about her experiences, both in college and the city of San Francisco. She was the last to finish eating, thankful no one had asked about the raw emotion resulting from the shootout in the courtroom.

When Sally finished her father said, "It'd be a good idea for you and your Ma to take a walk." He indicated her brothers with a wave. "We'll take care of the dishes."

"Thanks, Pa." Her eyes met her mother's as they rose from the table.

Tom stared after his departing sister, mystified. "What's that all about?"

"They need a mother-daughter chat without any men around." He grinned. "No man will fully understand. I don't, but it would be best if you were to remember it exists." He handed over the dish cloth. "You get to wash."

***

Sally leaned on her mother's shoulder in their

265

secret hideaway, reverting to a little girl as she dragged the moments of pain and horror from her memory. She told her mother how the trial and the pain of the victim had torn her up and about the explosion of violence at its conclusion. Her voice was tremulous, her throat dry. "The sheriff told us there were two bullet gouges in the table top and two bullet holes in the wall. They calculated the trajectory and told us if Fred and I had been in our chairs, we would have each taken a bullet in the chest."

She inhaled a long, shuddering breath. "All the evidence makes me know the shooting was self-defense. Emotionally, I still can't make myself believe it." She shivered. "I've had a lot of nightmares ever since the shoot out."

Sue embraced her gently. "I'm not surprised. I still have an occasional nightmare and it's been twenty years for me." Her voice lightened. "When I was recovering after the shootout, a very wise man gave me some good advice. He said he would have been more worried about my stability if it hadn't bothered me. That man was your father. He's proved to be right about many things over the years. I think that is what has helped me the most."

***

Sally awakened slowly. On several previous attempts, she had lapsed back into deep sleep after momentary awakenings. Her mind was sluggish as she recalled staggering back to the house with her mother's help, drunk with fatigue from many nights of sleeplessness. The catharsis of sharing her fears had broken the barriers to sleep and she barely managed to make it to her bed before she collapsed fully dressed into dreamless sleep.

She tried to sit up, muscles protesting from being in one position for too long. She shook her head and rolled onto her side, struggling to a sitting position. Suddenly dizzy, she held herself rigid until it passed. She struggled to her feet, using one hand braced on the headboard to steady herself.

Scanning the room, the shadows told her the sun was far to the west. Too sluggish for amazement, she realized she had slept for almost a full day. Upon reaching the kitchen, she took two slices from the bread box before opening the ice box. A thick slice of cold roast beef completed her sandwich, while several cups of cold water from the tap quenched her thirst.

The food and drink settled her stomach and cleared her mind before she went outside. Standing on the porch, she listened for any activity, but it was quiet except for the sound of a hammer from one of the more distant outbuildings.

She found Tim staring dejectedly at some sort of construction housed in one of the empty hay sheds, a pitch fork and a pail of newly dug potatoes lying nearby. After a moment's confusion she recognized a flying machine. "Where are the others? What do you have here?"

"They're counting cattle at Irish Canyon," he said sourly. "And what I have here is a total failure." He waved his hand in disgust at the winged machine. "I thought I copied everything exactly right, but it just will not fly!"

"I don't have a clue what you're talking about. Why don't you tell me the whole story?"

"Last fall when we were in Denver, I saw a magazine with an article on flying machines. It included a story about how others had built full- and half-scale copies of this machine all over the States. They all flew."

He grimaced. "I had to try, so I ordered the material and spent all winter cutting out pieces for a half-scale model. Everyone, even Ma, helped. She was very cool to the idea at first, but finally came around. I started assembling everything when spring finally arrived and finished it a couple of weeks ago."

Dejected, Tim's shoulders slumped. "I've tried everything I can think of but it will absolutely not get off the ground! Will you look at my drawings and calculations? Maybe someone with a fresh perspective can find something I've overlooked."

"I'd be glad to, but I don't know anything at all about flying machines, other than I saw one at a distance when I was in San Francisco." His eyes lit up. "But you mentioned something which could be important. Where did the other gliders fly?"

He stared at her, baffled. "What difference would that make?"

"It might be critical. What was the elevation?"

Excitedly, he named several locations, bursting out when realization dawned. "They were all near sea level!"

"And the air here is much thinner. After living for a year at sea level, I was winded just walking from the station to Squire's. We're even higher here."

Tim was so excited about a possible solution to his problem he tried to drag his much taller sister toward the ranch house. "Come on! One of the books has a formula for lift versus altitude. Maybe you can tell me if all my work has been for nothing!"

Sally laughed at his enthusiasm, teasing, "Slow down, will you? A few minutes more or less won't make any difference."

A few minutes later she was swamped with an avalanche of books and magazines Tim had collected. She waited while he selected drawings, diagrams and charts, placing them in front of her. He first selected the blueprint for the glider, then his calculations and enlarged drawings.

When he tried to explain how he had arrived at his figures, she interrupted gently, "First, you have to let me read at least some of the theory you used. I don't understand a word you said."

Tim reined in his excitement as best he could. "Okay. While you're doing that, I'll finish the chores and bring in the potatoes I dug and forgot about." He grinned mischievously. "Then I'll start supper because the others will be riding in before either of us is done."

She remembered the unwritten family rule: whoever stayed at the ranch during the day was responsible for the evening meal. She remembered some of the more memorable disasters served to the family before the siblings had learned to be even passable cooks.

CHAPTER 14

Sally could almost feel the intensity of Tim's gaze while she worked through the formulas he had shown her. After a final check of her calculations, she looked up. "I'm sorry, but your machine will never fly as-is. The lift-to-weight ratio at our elevation will never let it get off the ground."

His face fell.

"When you scaled down the size, your materials weren't scaled down proportionately. Now it's too heavy. Unless you can figure out how to lighten it, it just won't fly." She showed him the formulas and calculations she had used, waiting while he scanned them.

"Well, now I see where I made my mistake. Unless I can remove material and keep the strength, I have to start over?"

"I'm afraid you're right." Sally was proud of his reaction to his disappointment, limited to a sigh.

The rest of the family gathered around while they discussed the problem. Tom asked. "How much could you lighten it by carving out the middle of the spars, or do you have to have the whole thing for strength?"

Ted chimed in, "If you went to the full-size spacing and spar thickness, instead of half-size, you'd still have plenty of strength and half the weight."

Tim watched, holding his breath while Sally

redid her calculations using the proposed changes.

"Just by changing the spacing, I'd say it should fly with about a ten percent margin. If you can reduce the weight by removing every bit of excess, it might even take you with it."

Tim heaved a sigh of relief. "Thanks, everybody!" He hugged his sister before backing away from the table. "Now I can get started again."

"Not tonight," his mother said severely. "Now you can deal the cards." The others laughed. "We'll see if Sally can figure the odds in cards as well as she can figure on paper."

***

Sally rode into Wilford three days later, her rented horse trailing at the end of its lead rope. She was riding her own favorite horse, the dappled gray mare named Dolly that she had trained at the same time her mother had trained her. She savored the memory, as well as the memory of her last night at home. The family had used dried beans for chips while playing poker, but even with no actual money at stake it had turned cut-throat. Her father had finally won the entire pot, but only by drawing to an unheard-of four aces.

She left the next morning, stopping at the Franklin ranch to visit for two nights with Sara and her family. The twins, June and Dawn, would soon be joined by another sibling and the house would be expanded to meet their growing needs.

In town, Sally stopped at the livery to return their mount and arrange for the long-term care of Dolly. She stripped the saddle from her mare before turning her into the corral. Lugging the saddle and blanket to the tack room, she racked it, with the rest of the tack going on pegs. She drew her Winchester from the saddle scabbard with one hand and grabbed her satchel with the other.

Carrying her burdens, she headed for Squire's (and now her) office. She halted, startled, gawking at the new shingle hanging in front of the office. In large letters it proclaimed BROWN AND STORM. Smaller letters on another line added ATTORNEYS AT LAW.

Lyndon Hanes, a neighboring rancher who had known her all her life, laughed at her expression from the open doorway. "I've known you since you were a toddler, but I've never seen you so startled."

She blushed and said, "I had no idea Squire would do anything like this."

He laughed as he shook her hand. "Congratulations!"

She waited for the flush to fade before entering the office, only to halt in astonishment. The familiar office had been transformed by a wall splitting the old office in half. Centered in the wall was a door with a frosted glass window emblazoned with her name in black letters.

Squire welcomed her discomfiture with a smile. "You are a lawyer and entitled to some privacy for yourself and your clients. Most regard confidentiality as the most important precept of our profession." He paused before adding, "Actually, it's a toss-up between that and justice, which is somewhat like quicksand."

He waved her into her new office. A desk, a chair on wheels with a slatted back, a wooden file cabinet, and two straight-back chairs almost filled the room. She stared in wonder for a moment before her eyes were drawn to a folded newspaper lying on her new desk.

The headline screamed:

SALLY STORM RETURNS TO WILFORD

Saves many in shootout

She glared at him. "Why? I'm no heroine."

He was unrepentant. "Two reasons, actually. Some nasty rumors were starting to circulate since you came home so suddenly. I wanted to defuse them. Dean Wood sent me one of the 'Frisco papers after the shoot-out. I gave it to *The Messenger* to reprint. I thought it would be the best way to squelch the rumors."

"And the second?"

His face lightened and he said, "Purely selfish. I'm proud of you."

She flushed.

"Why don't you take your things to the house before we start your initiation?"

She headed out the back door of the office, walking across the yard, past the wood shed, the garden, and the privy. Emma was watching, waiting on the back porch of the house.

She gave Sally a welcoming hug. "I'm glad you decided to partner with Squire because he's no spring chicken any more. Not to brag, but for a small-town lawyer, he has a lot of clients." Emma hugged her again. "Now I'll show you your room."

Sally and Squire spent the rest of the day doing a general review of client files. She was amazed by both the quantity and the variety. Some were as simple as a single transaction for the sale of a building lot, others covered multiple jurisdictions.

It was growing dark when Squire leaned back in his chair. "The way I envision things, I'd like you to be the traveling partner because I'm getting too old for a lot of travel. You'd do the legwork, visiting clients outside of town, researching cases at the courthouse in Agate. Or wherever."

He was obviously delighted to have added her as a partner. "Some of these cases are going to necessitate going to Denver, either because there's no adequate local law library, or because they involve the Federal court. Your eidetic memory for details will be invaluable for research, no matter the location."

She spent the next several days working at her desk, a notepad in constant attendance. Working from Squire's list, she first reviewed case files having deadlines of some sort in the near future. Whenever she found something she did not understand or might do differently, she added notes of her own. After separating the files requiring immediate or long-range action, she began on the former, again taking notes.

The week was almost done before Sally completed her task, uttering a sigh of relief Squire could hear from his own office. "Why don't we wait until next week to start on your questions? You need a break. I suggest you go home, relax a bit, and plan on going to the dance tonight."

"I'd vote for that!"

He smiled at her instant acceptance.

Sally had never attended a dance in Wilford, although she had at several neighboring ranches closer to home. Kerosene lanterns were alight on posts and porches surrounding the town bandstand on the school lawn, giving a festive air to the evening. A band consisting of four local men was tuning up, two fiddlers, a drummer, and an ex-army bugler. Most of Wilford's population was in attendance, as were many families living within an hour's ride of town.

Young couples congregated together at the bandstand, while older adults and children mingled at a distance. Sally was wearing one of her favorite dresses, a simply cut, deep green one emphasizing her full figure and flaming red hair. It had been the height of fashion in San Francisco only a few weeks before. Women of all ages sought her out during the evening, eager to view it, eying her with envy and admiration. A crowd of young men, townies, cowboys, and miners, clustered together, talking among themselves, admiring their girlfriends or potential dance partners. The atmosphere was merry as the band finished tuning their instruments. Their first number was a lively one, putting most of the crowd in motion.

Sally chose a friend since childhood, Adam Westman, for the first dance. She joined the crowd of square dancers, exchanging partners as the squares mixed and separated.

She danced every dance except when she was visiting the tables covered with food and drink. During one of the breaks, she chatted with another childhood friend, Janice Tschantz, who asked, "Have you heard about Mary Fennell?"

"No. About what?" Mary was a townie, a close friend for as long as Sally could remember. She had brightened many a Saturday trip to Wilford.

"She died a month ago, giving birth to her third daughter." Sally was shocked and saddened by the tragedy, an all too frequent occurrence, even in the new Twentieth Century.

Her voice was husky when she replied, "Mary was even younger than I am. What happened to her daughters?"

"The baby survived and her mother took in all three girls. Her husband was from Agate and he left town the day after her funeral. I heard he went to Denver because he couldn't face the empty house." Janice scowled bitterly, "I also heard gossip that he didn't want another daughter, even if Mary had lived."

The two women raised a glass to toast their departed friend.

***

Sally attended Sunday services the next morning with the Browns, after which she fixed a large meal while Emma and Squire watched. When they finished eating, Squire went to the parlor while the two women cleaned up. When Sally finished washing dishes she said, "It might have been my imagination, but last night it seemed as though every man I danced with was wary of me."

Devilment danced in Emma's eyes. "As sharp as you are, you mean you haven't figured it out yet?"

Sally stared at her in bafflement. "Whatever do you mean?"

"You scare men. You're smarter than they are. You've used a gun and killed a man in self-defense. They're probably not only scared, but terrified. They don't know what to make of you because you sure don't fit their image of the *gentle gender.*"

Emma added gently, "Whatever you do, don't change. Be true to yourself."

Squire echoed from the other room, "Amen!"

CHAPTER 15

Sally's first trip as Squire's partner was to the court house in Agate, where she received a friendly reception. Everyone knew her parents and she had established her own reputation by becoming the very first female lawyer in the county, and one of only three in the state. The male staff was helpful, but she suspected some of them harbored reservations about allowing a woman, particularly as young as she was, to join the hallowed halls of the legal profession. When it became necessary for her to go to Denver for the first time, to do research and file papers at both the State and Federal Courthouses, she spent hours planning her strategy with Squire.

Disgruntled, Squire forwent his usual manners, "To be blunt, the head librarian of the State law library is an ass! He didn't get his position by being capable when he was appointed ten years ago, and he hasn't learned anything since. All he knows is cutthroat and knife-'em-in-the-back dirty politics. Worst of all, the word *woman* is a profanity in his vocabulary. I have no idea why. Hopefully, when you meet him, you'll give him apoplexy and it'll kill him. That would be one way to get rid of him."

Sally was shocked at his uncharacteristic bitterness.

"Anyway, the best defense is a good offense, so we're going to prepare you with malice aforethought. Your mother and sister have impressed the world while wearing men's clothes. We'll plan our opening barrage the same way."

His lips twitched. "Seriously, when you go into his domain wearing pants and a gun, it's going to be a lot harder for him or his staff to ignore you. Or attack you.

"Just remember, in any situation the people in power with the most to lose are those who never earned it in the first place. They'll fight viciously to keep that power, so don't ever underestimate them!" He paused, then said, "Especially this one."

***

Sally had breakfast the next morning in the Drovers' House dining room, where butterflies in her stomach warred with her appetite. She forced herself to eat as she exchanged pleasantries with other diners, finally giving up breakfast as a lost cause.

When she left the dining room, she stopped in the lobby to place her new white Stetson atop her flaming red hair that fell to her shoulders. Checking her image in a handy mirror, she nodded with satisfaction. The stark contrast between her red hair and the black and white of her man's clothing was striking. Squaring her shoulders, she strode briskly out the door with her brief case in her hand.

An extended walk brought her to the Capitol entrance with its broad steps. Reaching the doors at the top of the stairway, she turned for a quick scan of the view. After a moment's nervous hesitation, she entered through massive wood and brass doors. When her eyes adjusted to the dim interior, she checked the directory hanging on the wall, confirming the instructions Squire had given her.

She paid no attention to the mass of people

streaming in and out. Unknown to her, one of the mass was a newspaper reporter on assignment. Always on the outlook for news, he first noted her red hair and white Stetson, then her unusual attire and attractive figure. Intrigued, he altered course to follow her.

At a closed door with the placard LAW LIBRARY, she straightened her spine and took a deep breath. The high-ceilinged room was enormous with tall shelves filled with books crowded in neat rows, light from arched windows throwing shadows on the floor. A massive desk was centered a short distance from the door. A bored clerk sat behind it with an open over-sized ledger facing him. Small tables were clustered at the intersections of the shelves, but only a few had anyone seated at them, all of whom were male.

The clerk stared at her in astonishment as she tucked her Stetson under one arm and picked up the pen lying next to the ledger. She handed him the list of references she had prepared. "I'd like these brought from the shelves." Her soprano was at a conversation-al level but carried clearly, causing heads to turn. She was unaware that the others who had seen her en-ter, and a growing group of observers behind her, lis-tened expectantly. The head librarian's reputation was well-known for being difficult even with men and im-possible with women, few of whom ever entered his domain.

The clerk gaped at her like a landed fish while she scanned the open pages of the ledger and frowned. There were only a few signatures, none dated with-in the past two weeks, which eliminated any of the males sitting at the occupied tables. Why should *she* sign? She laid the pen down.

The gaping clerk stammered. "No. I won't. You have no right to use the library."

Sally glared coldly and he retreated from the menace in her eyes. Leaning over the desk at less than arm's length, her tone was dangerous. "I'm a licensed attorney in the State of Colorado and an active member of the bar. I have the right to use this facility." She did not raise her voice, but he flinched anyway.

He gulped and looked down at the desk. "Yes, Ma'am. I'll get them."

She suddenly felt the pressure of eyes on her back. A quick glance toward the door startled her at the number of onlookers. The clerk was back in a few minutes, so rattled he almost dropped the books he carried. After nervously handing them to her, he scooted away. Part way to one corner, she found an unoccupied table. She placed her Stetson atop the stack of books, and sat facing the door, curious about the still-waiting crowd. Opening her brief case, she laid out a pad and pencil.

A few minutes later she could see a scarecrow-like figure advancing toward her, stiff-legged with anger, his face dark as a thundercloud. She watched warily from the corner of her eye. When he was close enough, she gave him a courteous nod.

He ignored her courtesy. "Get out!" His voice was shrill and grating, echoing through the room, assaulting the ears of the witnesses. "You don't belong here!"

She kept her tone civil, repeating, "I'm a licensed attorney of the State of Colorado and a member of the bar, giving me the right to use this facility."

"I don't care!' He was fairly frothing at the mouth. "GET OUT!"

"I won't leave unless you give me a written reason citing the section of the state code giving you the right to evict me."

His scream was heard clearly in the hallway. "You uppity bitch! GET OUT!"

Sally rose so fast her chair went flying. The scarecrow jerked back in sudden fear, his face drained of color. She towered over him, face red, eyes boring into his from inches away. "Mister, you have ten seconds to apologize." Her voice was frigid and cutting. "The Great State of Colorado has never seen fit to abolish the archaic practice of dueling. If I don't hear an apology this instant, I will see you on the field of honor at dawn tomorrow!" Her right hand dropped to the butt of the revolver in the holster on her hip.

He wanted to flee, but retreated as quickly as he dared, trying to keep his dignity when he realized the significance of her action and words.

Sally followed him, matching his pace, step for step.

Terror and shame held him in its grip. He had used his power to abuse so many times over the years he expected every victim to cave instantly. The shock of her defiance was so total he didn't know how to deal with it and the threat of a duel completed his collapse. His apology was scarcely a whisper, "I'm sorry."

"LOUDER!" she snarled. "You didn't hesitate to attack when you thought you could get away with it!" She nodded at the crowd at the door. "I want everyone to hear just what a tin-horn dictator you are."

She admitted to herself later that she might have gone too far but excused herself. *I'm only nineteen. I can always claim inexperience.* As did her mother and sister, she did not suffer fools gladly.

His hate was great but fear was the greater. "I'm sorry." He managed to get the words out loudly enough to be heard at the desk and the doorway.

"Get out of here!" Her tone was frigid, spitting her words as she leaned even closer.

He fled.

She watched his flight, her hand resting on her gun butt until he disappeared from sight. She glanced warily at the astounded crowd watching from the door. Satisfied, she turned slightly, her eyes meeting those of the two men at the nearest table. They grinned back, giving her the universal sign of approval, a firm thumbs-up. She relaxed minutely before trying to concentrate on her research.

She had read several pages of the first volume when she became aware of someone standing at the edge of her vision. When she looked up, he asked, "Would your last name happen to be Storm?"

She started. "Yes. Sally Storm. How did you guess?"

"I'm Wayne Hancock, reporter for *The Denver Post*. I've covered stories featuring your mother and sister in the past." He chuckled. "You have the same look. And the same subtle touch." He grinned as she flushed. "Mind if I sit down?"

She glared at him coldly, a tactic which accomplished exactly nothing, before acquiescing. "You might as well. From what Ma told me, there's no way to avoid your type."

He laughed heartily as he drew back a chair.

CHAPTER 16

The librarian cursed steadily as he paced the length of the room. When he hurled the newspaper to the floor, the headline stared up at him like an unblinking eye.

IT IS TIME FOR WESTMAN TO GO

Both the legal profession and the public at large have suffered the despotic rule of State Law Librarian Amos Westman for far too long. It is long past time for the State Executive Committee to replace Mr. Westman. The final straw was yesterday's incident, reported elsewhere in this paper, only one of the many which necessitate his removal.

His unprovoked attack on a young female lawyer is far outside the bounds of decency, much less any reading of the law, especially when it is founded only in the Librarian's own arbitrary and autocratic rules.

Many citizens, including this reporter from THE DENVER POST, witnessed the incident and applauded its sudden turn. Sally Storm, as have her mother Sue and sister Sara before her, refused to be intimidated by an obnoxious member of the male gender.

After verbally attacking her, Mister Westman discovered to his dismay he had tangled with a tigress and wound up being justifiably mauled.

The Editorial Board of the POST unanimously endorses the propriety of Miss Storm's actions and the urgent removal of Mr. Westman from his present position.

His fury ebbed and morphed into fear. *The Denver Post* was highly respected, and had a commensurate level of power. *They hate me because I refuse to kowtow to little minds. They think ANYONE should be allowed to use MY library. If you let just anyone in it'll soon be overrun by scum. Just like that bitch!* His ranting increased in pitch as he sat at his desk and took a long pull from the neck of the whiskey bottle.

***

Sally was exhausted when she returned to the Drovers' House late in the afternoon. Two days of exhaustive research at both State and Federal law libraries had made her tired from sitting on hard chairs and reading fine print in sometimes poor lighting.

She waved at the clerk on duty, turning aside when he beckoned. "Miss Storm. There's a lady been waiting for you, right over…" He frowned. "Well, she was there a few minutes ago. She's been waiting quite a while for you. Maybe she'll be back." He shrugged helplessly. "That's all I can tell you. She wouldn't leave her name or a message. Said she had to talk to you personally."

Sally was mystified. "I don't know any women in Denver who wouldn't leave a message. It doesn't make sense. Oh, well. Maybe she'll come back. Thanks anyway."

She trudged up the stairs, her mind already attacking other problems. The hallway was empty when she reached for the lock and a voice spoke from down the hall. "Miss Storm?"

Her head snapped up and her hand dropped to the gun on her hip.

A woman emerged from an alcove, and said, "I didn't mean to startle you. I need to talk to you and I can't do it in public. They might see me."

At Sally's gentle wave, the woman moved closer, into the late-afternoon sunlight shining through a window. "Who might see you?"

"I can't tell you standing here in the hall. I really need a lawyer. Can we go into your room and get out of sight?"

Sally made a quick appraisal as the woman neared. She looked to be in her early thirties, average height and dressed in clean, neat apparel. Her visitor did not seem threatening, but was watchful. "Sure."

Sally held the door for her unexpected guest, and then locked it behind them. She indicated the single chair in the corner. "You take that. I'll sit on the bed. Who might you be?"

When she sat down, her back was so rigid it never touched the chair. "Wanda Benson."

"Wanda. I'm Sally, and I'm curious. You say you need a lawyer but 'they' might see you. This sounds like something out of a mystery novel."

Her guest flushed. "I don't doubt it does to you, but it's true. I've been watched often since I tried to bring him to court to get back my father's estate. I couldn't take the chance of meeting you in public."

"And who is him?"

"Sydney Ulysses Underwood. He's a swine and supposedly owns the second richest gold mine in Colorado. He was once one of my father's partners, before he died."

Sally's eyebrows rose. She knew only a little of miners and even less of mining, but she had heard about the man. "You'd better tell me the whole story."

***

Twenty years earlier, Wanda's father was one of three partners who found and worked many claims throughout the West. Most proved to be worthless or nearly so, yielding only a hardscrabble living for the three, until they struck pay dirt with the *Sunset Mine*. The mine proved to be the richest they had ever seen. It took only a few days of unrelenting labor to confirm its potential. Underwood left for Millville to register their claim, while Wanda's father Harold and the third partner, Amos Wanderman, stayed behind, one working while the other stood guard.

"Underwood should have been able to make the round trip in about a day and a half. Three days after he left, the ceiling of the mine collapsed on Amos, crushing his leg. Dad ran in to rescue him, but another fall caught both of them. It killed Amos and badly injured my father. He was nearly dead when Underwood returned (he thought only an hour or two after the fall but was never sure) and dug him out.

"Dad was badly injured but made it to the doctor in Millville, who patched him up enough to make it first to Denver and then home to us. It was almost two years before Dad could walk. In all that time he never heard a word from Underwood.

"When my father was finally able to walk, he went back to the mine to find their claim was now the *Sunrise Mine.* Underwood flatly refused to meet him and always claimed he discovered the claim by himself. Dad tried to fight him in court for years but it was always in vain. The doctors said his injuries killed him in the end. I think he died of a broken heart, betrayed by a once-trusted friend.

"My father's death killed my mother," Wanda said bitterly. "She died within the year and I lay the blame squarely on Underwood for both of their deaths."

The room was silent except for street noises filtering in through the open window. Sally held her eyes for several long moments before asking questions about her father's travels. When, where, how long, who with, anything and everything Wanda could recall that might be of help.

"I have letters from my father. I haven't read them for years, but if I remember correctly, he wrote a few times regarding where he was living and about the claims they worked."

Sally was thinking hard. "That information could make it much easier to conduct a search to prove partnership. Mail them to me in Wilford. My partner and I will review them and decide if we can start to gather evidence."

"IF!" Wanda was horrified by the qualifier.

"If. We need to determine if there is any chance at all of winning a lawsuit. If so, we need to start a title search by first checking out the partnership's old claims. Then we can file on the disputed one. Don't expect this to happen overnight. There'll be a lot of travel. With winter coming on we may not have much information until next spring."

Wanda was crushed by disappointment. "I thought you just went ahead and filed a lawsuit."

"No." Sally explained. "If we go ahead with a lawsuit, it will take time. We'll want to file it here in Denver where you live. Get it on friendlier ground - or at least more neutral ground. We don't want to file too early or it might alert him and give evidence more chance to conveniently disappear before we can have a subpoena served."

Wanda buried her face in her hands. "I've lived with it this long. I guess a few more months won't make any difference. It'll give me more time to come up with your fee."

"Why don't you let my partner and me review the case and what evidence we can gather. If it's a good case, we'd probably take it on a contingency basis at no initial cost to you."

They wrapped up the details in a few minutes before Wanda slipped out the door and down the back stairway. Sally scrubbed the dust of the day from her face and combed her hair, her mind busy all the while.

She was in the dining room a few minutes later. She was hungry and the food delicious. She was cleaning her plate when she spied Wayne Hancock. "You might as well sit down. I can't seem to get rid of you."

He didn't smile at her barb. "Have you read today's POST?"

She shook her head, puzzled.

"I thought you'd want to know before tomorrow's edition hits the street. Amos Westman is dead. His butler found his body this morning. He shot himself in the head."

Shocked, Sally asked, "Why?"

"The police think it was today's editorial in the POST calling for his resignation. He had the paper open to the editorial page with an empty bottle of whiskey sitting on his desk. Our editorial cited his treatment of you as the latest of many outbursts, and urged him to retire or be replaced."

He shook his head at her obvious feelings of guilt and horror. "It was NOT your fault! The incident involving you was only one of many cases of unacceptable behavior. He'd never been called on any of them in public before. It was the first one to ever make the editorial pages. He never could take criticism."

Sally's excellent meal had turned to an icy lump in her stomach.

"If I may make a suggestion, there's a Vaudeville production at the Opera House tonight. Even by yourself, it would help keep your mind off of the tragedy."

She shivered, suddenly cold. "Thanks for the suggestion. I'll do that."

CHAPTER 17

Sally returned to Wilford the next day, grateful for the evening of raucous, bawdy, hilarity which had her laughing in spite of herself. The positive mood kept her from brooding all night. Despite the day's events, she'd been able to fall asleep at a reasonable hour. She was up at dawn, walking to the station and her train home.

When Squire welcomed her, he could tell from her body language something was amiss. "Okay, now tell me what's wrong." He waved at the chair next to his desk.

Sally swallowed hard. "Amos Westman is dead."

Shocked, he said, "I was joking when I suggested he fall victim to apoplexy."

"He didn't. He shot himself." She explained about her run-in with the man, resulting in his humiliation and the subsequent editorial. "Wayne Hancock tried to tell me it wasn't my fault. Intellectually, I know he's right, but emotionally it's another matter."

Squire gently placed his hand on hers. "It was absolutely NOT your fault. I know it'll be hard for you to accept, but you are not responsible for someone else's actions."

She shook herself, and began to sort the voluminous paperwork she had gathered in Denver. They discussed the information as they sorted each document into the appropriate file. Only then did she mention her conversation with Wanda Benson.

Squire's eyes hardened at the name Sydney Underwood. When she finished relating the facts she had gathered, he growled, "I'd take this case pro bono if necessary. That man is a right bastard - sorry for the language - and I'd love to hurt him."

She was startled.

"It's been years since I've dealt with him. He's hurt many others, including an old client he shafted by forging paperwork and twisting the law like a pretzel. You're absolutely correct to file in Denver because he has his local law in his back pocket."

A box from Wanda Benson arrived the next day, stuffed with letters her father had sent her mother over the years. Sally pored over the letters one at a time, setting aside any with references to mining claims or where the partners were living at the time.

When she finished the last one, she stretched hard enough for her spine to pop, gathered the pile of relevant letters, and headed to Squire's office. "I have at least a dozen references to both Amos and Sydney in these letters, proving they were partners, at least some of the time. You'll have to help me locate the towns I've never heard of." She grinned mischievously, "Maybe a decrepit old man like you would know of them."

Squire laughed, took the list and skimmed the names. "Most of these are long-gone, ghost towns. Despite that, the claim records should still be at the court house in the present-day county seat. You'll just have to find them."

She sighed, "I was afraid you'd say that." She went to the book shelves, searching for the state atlas.

He thumbed through it, adding notes to her list, highlighting the various locations. When he finished, the dots were bunched in five areas. Only two were on rail lines. All were widely separated, some by as much as a hundred miles or more.

"I'd better get packed. If I have to visit all of them, I might get snowbound if I wait too long."

Squire agreed soberly. "You'll definitely be in a race with winter."

***

Shortly after the noon hour the next day Sally loaded her horse in the cattle car coupled behind the tender. She laid her saddle on the floor in a corner of the car along with her saddlebags and bedroll. Dolly had never been in a rail car. Her eyes were wide and she was skittish.

Sally tied the reins to a slat at the front of the car before urging her horse to lie down as she had been trained. When the whistle wailed, Dolly tried to surge upright. Sally leaned on the neck of her horse, murmured softly in her ear, and stroked her muzzle gently. Dolly relaxed, stiffening again when they began to move.

The sun was setting several hours later when the train stopped at the station in the town appropriately named Dusty. Sally walked Dolly to the livery and arranged for her care.

There was only one boarding house in town. The tiny lobby was empty, dimly illuminated by a single lamp. She set her saddlebags and Winchester on the floor before tapping the bell on the counter. Several

294

minutes elapsed before a large woman lumbered through the doorway from the dining room.

"Yeah?"

"I need a room."

The proprietress gaped at the soprano voice, squinting in the dim light.

Sally took a step into the light, revealing her holstered Colt.

"I'll be damned! I thought I'd seen everything, but you're the first woman I've ever seen packing iron." Her tone was much warmer as she chuckled, "How long?"

"Tonight for sure. Maybe more. I won't know 'til tomorrow."

The woman handed over a key, jerking a thumb over her shoulder. "Supper 'll be served in about five minutes. The dining room is open for a half hour. After that, anybody late is out of luck, unless you want to drink your supper at one of the saloons."

"I like the sound of your menu better."

***

Sally had no trouble finding the courthouse, a ramshackle wooden structure in the middle of town. She explained to the clerk of court she needed to research old claim records to help settle a disputed estate. She joked, "If I can't prove who gets what, there'll be more bodies to bury."

The sour-faced clerk grinned. "Everything we have from that time is back here." He opened the heavy steel door of a small vault and pointed to the left-hand shelving. "Good luck."

Sally considered herself shot through with luck, finding what she was searching for in little more than an hour, a mining claim for Sunset Partners, signed by Sydney Underwood. She stared in wonder for several seconds, afraid it might evaporate in front of her eyes. She searched ten more pages while the curious clerk watched from a distance. Only then did she jot a note on her legal pad. Two hours later she skimmed the last entry in the last ledger, thanked the clerk, and left.

***

Two days of hard riding under threatening skies brought Sally to Castle Rock. She was bitterly disappointed when the clerk explained, "The old courthouse burned ten years ago. They didn't save much. Early claim records weren't in what little they did save. I'm sorry."

Sally was crestfallen but tried to make the best of a bad situation. "Why don't I look at whatever you do have? I've nothing to lose, and I might get lucky with some later record."

"Suit yourself."

Several fruitless hours later she gave up, thanking the sympathetic clerk for his help and the coffee he had provided.

CHAPTER 18

When Sally returned to Wilton after two weeks on the road, she was travel-worn, weary and half-frozen, leading Dolly off the train amidst the first heavy snow of the season. She had ridden most of the day in an unheated boxcar, huddled under a blanket, pressed tight against her horse for warmth.

She led Dolly to the livery, where she stripped off the saddle and saddle bags and gave her a good rubdown and curry. After caring for her horse, she wearily picked up her saddle bags and trudged off through the snow to the Browns.

Emma was shocked by her gauntness and dished a bowl of soup from the pot simmering on the stove. "You go sit in front of the fire and get some of this in you. I'll take care of your things."

"Yes, Ma'am." She smiled weakly. "I won't argue with you."

When Squire arrived, she was seated in a rocker, huddled under a wool blanket near the pot-bellied stove. He eyed her severely. "Abe told me you didn't even have enough sense to ride inside where they had some heat."

She groaned, "I knew someone would tattle. At least they had an enclosed freight car for Dolly instead of an open cattle car. I couldn't tie her to anything to keep her in place, and I wasn't about to leave her alone and take a chance of her breaking a leg." She met his glare. "At least it was tight enough to block the wind."

Squire's scowl vanished. "I'm proud of you. A good shepherd who puts her animal's needs ahead of her own."

He continued, "I see Emma's already given you a bowl of soup. Why don't you eat some more and get thoroughly warmed. We'll wait until tomorrow to hear about your trip."

Emma had overheard everything from the kitchen and brought another steaming bowl of soup. She and Squire retreated to the kitchen for their own meal. When she glanced in a little later, she smiled. "She's out like a light. Hot soup works wonders."

Sally woke the next morning to the muffled sound of someone doing dishes and tantalizing aromas drifting in from the kitchen. She winced, stiff and aching, both from the rigors of her trip and a night asleep in a wooden rocking chair.

Emma heard her stirring and greeted her with a smile and a steaming cup of coffee.

They shared a hot breakfast and lengthy conversation before Sally donned her heavy coat and walked to the office, taking the path Squire had shoveled through the yard. He greeted her cheerfully, grinning unrepentantly when she scolded him for shoveling the path instead of waiting for her. He laughed. "You're feeling better if you can complain."

Sitting in his office, she recounted her travels to seven county seats. "I thought I might as well check the records at every county I went through because they might have had claims Wanda didn't know about.

"I only found claims records in two counties, plus a property transfer in a third. Two counties had their courthouses burn down in the past and the claim records weren't saved. The two not on my list had no records relating to my search.

"I found one sale of a claim where the title was signed by Amos Wanderman, which proves the three were partners for at least some period of time. I never got to Millville, so I can't say if our most critical claim record is still available."

He scowled. "Well, I'm afraid you'll have to find out as soon as possible. I have a feeling about this winter and it's not good."

Sally frowned and sighed in agreement, "Then I'd better plan on leaving Monday."

"I'm afraid so."

***

Sally was apprehensive and halted momentarily at the worn door into the courthouse in Millville. Her briefcase in her left hand, she unconsciously patted the butt of her holstered .45 with her right hand before she grasped the worn brass knob and pulled firmly.

The recorder's office was on the first floor. When she entered, she winced as a blast of heat poured out. Two men were standing beside an over-worked radiator, one of whom suddenly struck it with a large hammer. A loud curse and a louder *CLANG!* echoed in the office as the hammerer pronounced, "That should fix the damn thing."

Neither man heard the door open. When they saw movement and turned to it, both were startled when they realized she was a woman. The other man stumbled over his words. "What can I do for you, Ma'am?"

She explained what records she needed and the general time span involving a disputed claim.

The custodian gathered his tools while the clerk stared at her suspiciously. "Who did you say this estate involved?"

"I didn't. I said I needed to research a disputed claim."

"Well, you can look at our old records, but the ledger covering those years disappeared long before I started working here."

"Thanks." He reddened at the sarcasm in her voice.

She left the recorder's office two hours later, frustrated and angry. As the clerk had said, the records she wanted were not in the vault. He had avoided her the entire time, keeping as far from her as possible in the cramped office, and doing a poor job of hiding a satisfied smirk.

She stopped in the foyer, trying with limited success to control her breathing and temper.

The custodian suddenly emerged from a closet behind her. He bumped into her and mumbled, "Excuse me."

She was about to snap at him, when she suddenly realized he had pressed a folded piece of paper into her free hand. Trying to stay in character, she glared at him. He studiously ignored her and disappeared down the hall. She crumpled the paper in her hand and stalked to the stairs, climbing to the Clerk of Court office on the second floor, where another unfriendly clerk directed her to the door marked *Law Library*.

She set her briefcase on one of the tables and then moved behind a book shelf to read the note: *Meet me at Casey's Café 11:45*

Crumpling the scrap of paper into a very small wad, she put it in her pocket and pondered the possibilities. She considered that it was some sort of a trap, but rejected the idea. All the open hostility she had encountered made it outside the pattern. Whatever the situation, it just didn't seem right.

"Can I help you?"

Startled, she focused on the speaker, and saw a man with cold eyes that shifted away when she caught his gaze. "No. Thank you. I'm searching for a ledger which seems to have been misplaced."

"What's its title? Maybe I can find it for you."

"I don't know the title, but I'm looking for the records of the original mining claims from twenty years ago. I'm trying to settle an estate, but no one in the Recorder's Office knows where it disappeared to."

He sneered. "Yeah. Right! And I'm King Solomon."

She towered over him, her holster coming into his view. "Sally Storm, Attorney at Law in the State of Colorado. Why don't you get lost?"

His face flamed at her obvious contempt and appeared about to ridicule her again when her hand dropped to the butt of the gun on her hip. His fists clenched and he glared at her. Spinning on one heel, he stalked away, slamming the door on his way out.

Shaken by the confrontation but determined not to show it, Sally began a systematic scan of every title on the shelves. An hour later she walked out, head high, ignoring the icy glare directed her way. Reaching the wooden boardwalk, she flipped a mental coin and turned right.

She was in luck. *Casey's Café* was only a few buildings down the street. Two of a half-dozen small tables were occupied, one at either end of the room, with one person at each one. Recognizing the janitor's back, she selected a nearby table at right angles to his.

He was eating steadily, concentrating on his plate. The waitress was approaching when she feigned surprised recognition, "Do you fix everything in the courthouse with a hammer?"

He looked up and nodded at the direct question, grinning fleetingly. "Sometimes. Not always. Those old radiators accumulate rust in the valves. A good whack with a hammer usually takes care of the problem. For a while, at least. You're the visiting lady lawyer, aren't you?"

She nodded. The waitress was waiting and could overhear their conversation. Sally indicated his plate and asked her, "Is that your special for the day?"

"It is. He always has our special, whatever it is."

"Looks good. I'll try the same."

She watched the waitress retreat to the kitchen with her order as he masked his whisper by pretending to chew. To any casual observer his attention was on his plate. "No questions! Someone who works for the State took the records back to Denver. Don't know who or where."

She started, masking her assent with an unladylike grunt.

His lips twitched as he returned his attention to his meal.

***

Sally caught an early-afternoon short-line train to her intermediate stop, where she was forced to lay over for the night, waiting for her train home. Morning dawned with bitter cold and heavy, blowing snow. She and a few other passengers clustered in the rickety depot, shivering in spite of a roaring fire in the pot-bellied stove.

The train was late, and the agent explained, "When it's this cold they have trouble keeping steam up." Her heart sank but she boarded anyway. Shivering with cold, she sat as close as possible to one of the two pot-bellied stoves, whose combined efforts fought a losing battle against the gale leaking around the poorly-fitting windows. She never got comfortably warm, but found if she curled her feet under her long riding coat, keeping them off the floor, she was somewhat less miserable.

They were hours late when the train squealed to a stop in Wilford. The street was deserted as she hurried away from the station, to the Browns'. Halting on the porch, she shook the snow from her coat as she stomped it from her boots.

Squire opened the door as she reached for the knob.

"Welcome home! Do you have to always bring snow with you?"

Emma beamed a welcome from the kitchen.

CHAPTER 19

The skies had cleared and a moderate blanket of snow covered the ground when Sally boarded the train for Denver two days later. Neither she nor Squire were optimistic about the chances of finding the missing records, but both felt she must at least try, no matter what the odds against success.

She was the only woman to board and took the seat closest to a pot-bellied stove and its anemic heat. Bending to shove her briefcase under the seat, she froze for a second. One of the two men who had boarded at the other end of the single car looked strangely familiar for some reason. Her thoughts raced as she tried to recall where she had seen him before.

He boarded the same train when I left Millville! He's following me. He didn't get off the train when I got home, but it wouldn't have taken much detective work to find out where I live. He could've gotten off at an earlier stop before coming on another train the next day so I wouldn't notice him.

Sally spent much of the trip speculating on what the opposition might know while she reviewed the material in her briefcase. The winter weather had drastically reduced ridership so she made sure not to show any unusual interest in the other passengers. An occasional glance sufficed to insure he was still seated with his back to her.

When she arrived in Denver, she carried her burdens to the Drovers' House in the darkness of an early winter evening. After checking in, she slipped a folded note to the familiar clerk as she signed the register. "Would you see this gets delivered as quietly as possible?"

He grinned at the sight of the bill peeking out of the fold. "I'll deliver it myself when I get off."

"Thank you." *I'm in Denver. DO NOT try to contact me in person. I'm being followed. Sally Storm.*

***

The Capitol had opened for business only a few minutes before Sally arrived the next morning. She spent hours moving from one office to another, explaining to various clerks that she was searching for an unnamed but innocently-misplaced record of mining claims. The staff in each office was helpful, at least on the surface. She knew some were wary of her presence, aware of her much-publicized run-in with the late, unlamented, law librarian.

There were many departments in the Capitol and many volumes in the libraries of those offices. Accuracy forced her to work slowly and systematically, checking the spine or title page of every book, notebook, or ledger.

She searched all day, except for a short break at noon, until an apologetic clerk interrupted to warn her the office would closing in a few minutes. She plodded dejectedly back to the Drovers' House, where her spirits rose when Ken greeted her cheerfully. "Mail for you, Miss Sally. Just came today."

"Thanks." She slipped it into her coat pocket, going on to her room before she opened it.

Thanks for keeping me advised.

As far as I know I haven't been

followed for months. I'll wait

to hear from you.

Wanda

"At least something is going right for someone." She shredded the note, making a mental note to dispose of it later.

***

Sally spent much of a second day at the Capitol, going from one department to another, avoiding the Law Library until the last because trepidation tied her stomach in knots. The same desk was still centered in the foyer but occupied by a different clerk. The attendance register was gone. Glancing around quickly, she was surprised to see most of the tables were occupied, unlike her first visit.

The new clerk proved to be friendly, although his eyebrows rose in recognition. "Can I help you?"

"I hope so."

After she explained what she was searching for, he frowned. "I'm afraid I can't help without a title, but you're welcome to look."

"Thanks. I'll do so." The clerk returned to his duties as she selected an unoccupied table where she could leave her briefcase before continuing her methodical search. She spent the afternoon searching without success, and when the clerk announced the library was closing she walked glumly for the door.

The hotel's dining room was warm and inviting, but her disappointment placed a damper on her hunger and she paid no attention to what she was eating. She stumbled wearily to her room and collapsed on the bed, thinking, *I'll just rest a few minutes.*

Accumulated weeks of hard work and nervous tension proved to be her downfall. When she woke the next morning, she discovered she was hours too late to catch the day's train for Wilford. Grumpily changing from her sleep-mussed man's clothing to a dress, she muttered ruefully, "I might as well take a day of vacation. I sure don't have anything else to show for my time here."

Out of nowhere came a thought. *Why not go out to the University? They have engineers. It probably won't help at this late date, but someone could probably confirm my calculations for Tim's flying machine. If they're entirely wrong, I'd at least be able to keep him from wasting all winter on something that'll never work.*

Energized with new purpose she was dressed and headed for the station in a few minutes. After catching a short-line train for Boulder and the University, she was soon only a short walk from the campus.

The Administration building was too prominent to be missed. From there, she was directed to the Engineering building, a stately stone building a short walk away. The directory on a pillar just inside the main door directed her to another floor, where she explained who she was looking for.

The clerk was impressed by her purpose, and her figure, as his eyes kept straying. "Wait here. I'll see if Dean Larson has a few minutes to speak with you."

A few minutes later she was ushered into the Dean's office. After she explained what she was seeking, he was obviously skeptical. "I can check your drawings and the calculations, but they have to be accurate. Did you bring them with you?"

"No, but I can re-create everything in a few minutes if you have some paper."

In spite of his doubts, he handed Sally several sheets of paper and a pencil. Sitting at a small table, she began to sketch quickly, drawing on her perfect memory for the dimensions and formulas.

The dean rose from his desk to watch over her shoulder, checking her calculations as she went, his eyebrows rising at her accuracy. He had almost finished checking her work when she laid down her pencil.

"Young lady. Your skill is fantastic, working just from memory! Unfortunately for your brother, I agree with the conclusions you reached. The original plans will not fly at an elevation over ten thousand feet and would barely fly at sea level. The modifications you showed would probably make the difference, but I'd have to see the actual machine before I could pass final judgment."

"I was actually hoping I was wrong because Tim has put so much work into it." Sally said, "Now I can tell him with some confidence the changes might let it fly."

The dean asked for more details. She was able to answer a few of the questions but her unfamiliarity with the actual science of flight hampered her ability to respond.

"Miss Storm. I'm pleased to have met you. When you talk to your brother, invite him to write me with his questions. I'd like to talk to him about his interest in airplanes."

Sally thanked him profusely as she left. Once again outside, the day had warmed up considerably, and without the already-heavy snow of higher elevations, it proved to be a beautiful day for a walk around the campus. The vast majority of the faculty and students were male and many turned to stare as she passed.

She stopped abruptly when she caught a glimpse of a sign marking one of the buildings SCHOOL OF MINES. Her hopes soared. *What'd be a better place to hide mining claims than in the School of Mines? Hide it right in plain sight. I'd never thought of it if I hadn't seen it!*

A few minutes later she was in the second-floor library, explaining how she was searching for a lost document. "Do you mind if I search your book stacks?"

The librarian stared at her, his doubt obvious. "I can't imagine we'd have it. I can't help you without a title, but it's your time. Go ahead."

Eying the many shelves of books, her hopes waned. After deciding to start at the back and work forward, in two hours she had progressed only to the middle of the top shelf in the second row, her initial euphoria long since evaporated.

She suddenly blinked hard to make sure she was not imagining something, staring intently at a medium-sized black ledger with a plain black spine. Unlike all of the other volumes she had examined, there was nothing visible on its spine about its title or subject. Pulling it out, she brought it to eye level with shaking hands. Opening to the title page, her heart began to race.

Mining Claims, Harrison County, Colorado

The dates on succeeding lines covered the time span she was searching for! Clamping her jaws tightly, she stifled a cheer. Guiltily, she glanced each way down the aisles, but no one was in sight. She closed the volume and slid it back into its place on the shelf.

She continued to mechanically check the rest of the books on the shelves as her mind raced. She was sure she had been shadowed. If she left the ledger where she found it, Underwood's accomplices would certainly remove it before spring. If she took it, it would be theft. Since she wasn't a student, she couldn't check it out on loan, especially not for several months.

Circling slowly back to her target, she was well hidden from the entrance by the massive shelving. Opening the book, she paged through the dates to the period she had been searching for. Scanning slowly, the penciled entry *Sunrise Mine* stood out. She focused on the signature of Sydney Underwood.

Moving furtively to the bright light from the

windows at the end of the shelves, she squinted close-ly at the entry. Flipping to the next page, she stared in-tently at the surface of the paper and stifled a cheer with difficulty.

She closed the book and reluctantly returned it to its hiding place. Half-way down the next row, the solution struck her and she chuckled. Working her way back to her prize, she slipped it from its innocuous hiding place. Continuing to play her part, she checked every book until she was four rows closer to the desk. Stooping quickly, she slid it between two much larger, slightly dusty, volumes on the bottom row.

Sally hummed nervously to herself as she walked back to the table where she'd left her coat. Doubly grateful for the relatively warm weather, she folded her coat into a compact square approximating the size of the claims book. Carrying the 'book' under her arm, she wore a satisfied smile as she strolled to the exit.

CHAPTER 20

Severe winter weather arrived a few days after Sally returned to Wilford. Frequent blizzards accompanied by high winds closed passes everywhere, disrupting rail traffic. On-time trains did not exist. Most days they were cancelled, until the railroad gave up even trying, waiting for the weather to improve.

Business was slow to non-existent for everyone in town, including lawyers. She put Wanda's lawsuit in the back of her mind and with little else to do, she concentrated on helping Emma or anybody else in town needing assistance, often shoveling snow for a good part of the day.

Wilford was totally isolated by the beginning of the year. The town folk often tried to avoid cabin fever by holding periodic dances at the schoolhouse. Card parties and game nights were also scheduled, but most were cancelled by weather too severe to safely venture out.

Many nights when they were shut in, Sally and Emma would sit at the kitchen table talking, while Squire read or napped in the parlor. One night Emma said, "You're looking pensive tonight. Is something wrong?"

"Not really," she sighed. "It's just, at the last dance I realized - again - there aren't very many eligible young men here in town."

"You mean the quality isn't the greatest, don't

you?"

She grimaced. "Well. Yes. I like most of them as friends, but, well, I don't think I'd want to marry any of them."

"Sally, Sally, Sally. I've said this before. You're smarter than any of the young men in this town, whether they would admit it or not. You scare them. I'm afraid if you married one, it would be like putting a race horse and a plow horse in harness together. It might work, but there's potential for disaster as well."

She added in her most grandmotherly manner, "You're not even twenty-one years old! Definitely not an old maid. You have years to meet the right man, but I'm afraid you might have to leave Wilford to find him."

Sally's eyes twinkled. "I know, Granma. I just needed someone to tell me what I already knew."

Emma laughed, her own eyes twinkling at the young woman who reminded her of her mother, so much alike, except for Sally's flaming red hair.

***

Sue Mason was orphaned at sixteen when her father was killed after being thrown from a horse. A few days after his death, the local banker demanded a meeting with Squire, who was instantly suspicious because of the man's reputation and his insistence they meet after dark in Squire's office.

He had discussed the meeting with Emma because of the man's reputation for being greedy and known to push the law to the limit. Her own suspicions were aroused but she didn't tell him of her own plans.

When Squire left the house, she followed a few minutes later with their shotgun cradled in her arms.

Emma listened through the open window to the banker's demand for Squire to force the sale of Sue's ranch, inherited from her father. The mortgage on the property was current except for less than a hundred dollars but that made no difference to the greedy banker. "She's underage and can't legally do anything. I want that land! Do whatever you need to get it for me."

Emma was shocked at what she heard. Squire's face flamed in outrage. "I will not! You have no legal right to force her out, especially since the mortgage isn't overdue!" His face was inches from the banker's. "You greedy bastard! If you aren't out of town by sundown tomorrow, I'll hang you myself!"

The banker jerked back in alarm, his face contorted in rage, his hand dropping to the revolver on his hip. He sneered, "You and who else?"

From the window, Emma's voice was harsh and cold. "I'll help him. I'm sure Doc and Mary will be glad to help as well. You touch that gun and you won't live long enough to hang!" The banker turned pasty white at the sight of a double-barrel shotgun resting on the sill, aimed rock steady at him. He froze in fear as Squire took the gun from his holster.

"Remember, sundown tomorrow."

***

He remembered, Emma reflected. Her thoughts returned to the present to find Sally eying her with obvious curiosity. "I was lost in thought. What were you saying?"

CHAPTER 21

Winter stayed late in Wilford, ending with a blizzard that virtually buried the town. When the wind finally died, Squire had started to shovel a path from the house to the law office but a firm thump on the shoulder got his attention. Sally glared at him, jerking an imperious thumb toward the house. He surrendered the shovel, resigned to her nagging him for his own good. Much later she broke through the last drift to the office and sighed with relief, grateful she had been able to 'persuade' the much older Squire to leave the task to her.

Two days later the wind shifted to the south and the temperature rose dramatically to well above the freezing point. Huge drifts shrank dramatically, resulting in torrents of water which ran everywhere. The soil turned to mud and walking turned to slogging. The stream flowing through town at one end became a raging river, threatening to carry away the bridge.

Another few days passed before the whole town was electrified by the wail of a steam whistle in the distance, the first anyone had heard in many weeks. People gathered all along the tracks, waiting in anticipation for the train to pull in. The train was an unusual one, with two locomotives and their coal tenders head-to-tail. A huge snow blower was mounted on the leading unit which powered it, scarcely visible under mountains of piled snow. The only freight cars were four heaping coal cars.

The relief train stayed in town only long enough to unload the cars of coal in the bunkers located high on the mountainside at the edge of town. The locomotives restocked their tenders with fuel and water before moving out. A few minutes later everyone could hear the roar of the blower attacking the mountainous drifts still covering the rails to the west.

The next day became another celebration as a few ranchers and settlers trickled into town, released from their long winter's confinement. The excitement escalated when another work train pulled in, its crew having repaired the many breaks in the telegraph line between Wilford and Denver, restoring communications with the outside world.

With the arrival of spring, and rail service restored, Sally and Squire completed their review of documents she would need for filing the lawsuit for Wanda Benson. "Since today's Friday, it makes no sense for you to go tomorrow, so plan on catching Monday's train. That'll give you the rest of the week to get everything rolling. After the judge sets the hearing date, we'll know our next deadline."

***

Her trip to Denver was accompanied by a sense of relief, thankful her family had made it to Wilford on Saturday after months of isolation. She hadn't realized how their absence had weighed on her mind, and what a relief it was to see them once again.

Denver had become familiar ground for her. Ken was on duty when she checked in and she gave him another message to deliver.

Wanda was waiting in the dining room when Sally came downstairs the next morning, her eager anticipation apparent. "Today?"

317

"Today. We'll go file as soon as we finish eating." She grinned. "I'm buying."

While they ate, she explained all their preparations, chief of which was the hidden ledger. Her face hardened. "As long as no one else found it, we have this suit locked up."

Wanda was alarmed by the qualifier. "Why didn't you take it last fall?"

"I'm an officer of the court. If I had taken it and produced it after the fact, the judge might very well throw out the suit. Without that claim record we don't have much chance to prevail. I had no choice but to leave it there."

They both ate sparingly, their appetites dampened by tension. It was only a short walk to the county courthouse, where they arrived in the Clerk of Court office shortly after it opened. A slight elevation of a few eyebrows was the only reaction when Sally said she'd like to file a lawsuit. Handing over the documents she had prepared, she was keenly aware of the palpable tension radiating from Wanda.

When the clerk read the name of the defendant, he looked up, his eyes alight. "Miss Storm, would you and your client mind coming with me? The Chief Clerk would like to talk to you."

They stared at him in confusion, then at each other, both mystified. "Why?" asked Sally.

"I can't tell you here in public. It would be well worth your time. Mr. Dirks will explain everything."

They eyed each other, still mystified, before

nodding agreement.

The clerk led them toward the back, where they were ushered into a large office. He handed over the file and left. Mr. Dirks said, as he waved them to waiting chairs, "Miss Storm. What I am going to tell you is privileged information. Does your client fully understand what that entails?"

Wanda shook her head.

"This information cannot be shared with anyone outside this office under penalty of heavy fines and possible imprisonment."

Her eyes widened. "I'll be sure to keep my mouth shut."

"Good!" His expression hardened. "The reason I wanted to talk to you is because the State Attorney General has been looking for a case which would allow him to purge the Harrison County government. Your case would give him cause, which he has been unable to establish previously.

"The AG knows Underwood has subverted every office in Harrison County, but has not had just cause to raid the courthouse and prove it. Your suit, filed in another county, would give him the leverage to do so, because Underwood and his minions would stymie any effort to conduct a trial involving him in any way."

Both women gaped in disbelief. Sally asked, "What do you want us to do?"

"What we are asking is for you to give us seventy-two hours before your suit is officially filed. The paperwork will be placed in a pending file here in my office during that time. The AG will need the time to get a State Police taskforce entrained and transported to Millville. If the courthouse gang were to have any advance warning, they'd destroy evidence, maybe even burn the courthouse. In return for your cooperation, the AG will freeze all of Underwood's bank accounts so there will be assets available if you win your suit."

Sally turned to Wanda, sure her own eyes were as glazed as her client's. When Wanda nodded agreement, she said, "The only thing I need in turn is a subpoena for a claims record ledger hidden in the library of the School of Mines."

"That sounds mysterious, but I don't need to know the details. I'll make arrangements for a deputy to serve the subpoena."

"I'll have to go with him. It's hidden in plain sight, but if you don't know where to look, you could spend many hours searching."

"Done!"

***

Sally walked into the School of Mines library with a deputy beside her, a knot of tension twisting her middle, terrified that someone had discovered her subterfuge and removed the evidence. The deputy handed the subpoena to the startled clerk and turned to her. "It's your turn now, Miss Storm."

She kept her face serene, but the tension ratcheted higher in her middle as she walked slowly down the aisle to where she had hidden the claims book, her knees weak. Bending, her hand sought her target. The deputy grinned at her explosive sigh of relief when she

320

grasped it and handed the volume to him. "Guard it well."

***

Squire could tell from the bounce in her step and the smile on her face she had succeeded. He was astounded when she told him of the planned raid of Harrison County. "I knew Underwood was crooked from personal experience. I never expected the State to try to close down the whole county government."

"I would never have thought of it, either. It has to help us, even if all it does is keep his tame dogs occupied enough to not blind-side us in court. I'm not much worried about the preliminary hearing next month."

"And I have a surprise for you, even if it's not as dramatic as your news."

"And what, pray tell, is that?" She teased with exaggerated patience.

"While you were gone, I was asked to run for the State House from our district. Emma and I discussed it and," he paused and then, "I'll be a candidate this fall."

"Congratulations!" Sally hugged him, lifting him from the floor in her excitement. "I know you'll win." Her face suddenly fell. "I won't be old enough to vote for you, but I'll help campaign."

"Thanks! You're my secret weapon. When we win you'll be going to Denver with me as my aide." Her eyes grew round as she stared at him in disbelief. "No one else can do as good a job for me. You're going with me, so no argument."

321

CHAPTER 22

A flurry of motions and counter-motions were filed in the Denver court during the next three weeks. An old friend of Squire's who lived in Denver, Harry Worth, happily agreed to act in their stead, saving many trips for Sally. They were reviewing his latest report when the local telegraph office delivered a message.

PRELIMINARY CANCELLED STOP

GOING STRAIGHT TO TRIAL STOP

SAME DATE STOP

HARRY

"They're either overconfident, arrogant, or both. Definitely arrogant." Squire's grin would have done a shark proud. "The only change is that we have a trial instead of a hearing next week. They're just trying to spook you. They'll learn soon enough how well-prepared you are."

***

The gallery was jammed with spectators when court was gaveled to order, drawn by the drama of an extremely young female lawyer pitted against a wily opponent with a reputation for ruthlessness. Sally and Squire were seated to Wanda's left, while Harry Worth was seated to her right.

Sitting across the aisle, Underwood was flanked by a bevy of six lawyers.

Harry whispered, "Five are from the highest-priced firm in Denver. The other one is his token lawyer from back home. You have Underwood worried, if he's paying for that much firepower."

Jury selection proved to be a lengthy process because Underwood's lawyers took turns picking at the pool of jurors with hard-edged questions and accusations. In sharp contrast, Sally's questions were non-confrontational, almost friendly. When the opposition recognized its effect, they abruptly changed tactics. Succeeding jurors were treated to a honey-and-butter approach, which did nothing to impress the earlier victims who had already been chosen.

With the jury impaneled, the judge called on Sally for her opening statement. Standing erect to her full height, her calm exterior hid her inner tension as she approached the jury box. Moving slowly from one end of the box to the other she met the eye of every juror in turn, her clear soprano carrying clearly while the jury and the gallery hung on her every word.

***

Sally's team met for supper in one of the better restaurants in Denver, ushered to the most prominent table in the house. Diners at nearby tables made no effort to hide their interest while Sally and Wanda were seated.

Harry was the last to sit, placing a newspaper on the table. "I picked up the evening edition on my way over. There's a lot of coverage of the facts of the trial. However, there's one special item everyone but Sally might be interested in."

He grinned hugely, his eyes dancing. Sally was immediately suspicious because he was enjoying himself too much.

"Today's trial was a vivid study in contrasts. Miss Storm is a very tall, willowy redhead, while her opponents are short, dark and dour. She represented her client with dignity and style, presenting a reasoned and reasonable argument to the jury. This writer finds the contrast between her manner and that of her numerous opponents is the difference between the lilting melody of a songbird and the braying of a chorus of jackasses."

Their table exploded with laughter, as did every table within earshot. Sally turned crimson to the roots of her hair, glaring at her tablemates for their hilarity.

When Squire recovered his dignity, he patted her hand. "A lovely songbird indeed. You truly did give the jury a reasoned argument." His levity vanished. "Tomorrow they'll try to blow us out of the water."

***

Sally called Wanda as her first witness, and led her through a careful review of the history of the three men as partners. Her father's letters documented their movement throughout the region in search of riches. At every point where Wanda's letters showed the men as partners matching her list of filed claims, she introduced the letter into evidence.

After completing her questioning, she returned

to their table and picked up a folder. "Your Honor. I have here a list of claims filed and real estate transactions consummated under the name of the Sunset Mining Company. These transactions occurred in several counties over a period of years, as annotated by volume, page, and paragraph in the records of the appropriate jurisdiction. Three men have signed those legal documents at different times, Sydney Underwood, Harold Benson, and Amos Wanderman. I would like to place this list of documents into evidence as verifying the partnership of Sydney Underwood with the other two men."

The judge took the offered folder and scanned the neat handwriting, while the defense lawyers' postures turned rigid as they sat up straight, tension showing in every line of their bodies, as if they were prepared to protest. He peered over his glasses at them. "Does the defense have any objections?"

Several minutes of vehement argument ensued until the judge raised his hand, cutting them off. "These records can be verified. If it becomes necessary, I will send a bailiff to each county of record to do so." He glared fiercely at both tables. "However, if I am forced to do so for any reason other than compelling legal reasons, the lawyer or lawyers in the wrong will spend ten days in jail for contempt. Do I make myself clear?"

Underwood's lawyers wilted.

Sally replied quietly, "Yes, Your Honor. I have one last document to present to the jury. It is the Harrison County claims ledger which records the mining claim in dispute." She picked up the ledger lying on the table before her.

The defense rose as one to protest that they never had the chance to examine it because Sally had taken it last fall and had kept it from them. The bang of the judge's gavel cut them short.

"Miss Storm. Would you care to explain?"

She met the glares from the defense table squarely. "Your Honor. Three days after we filed suit, I accompanied a deputy sheriff from this court to the library at the School of Mines in Boulder. He served a subpoena for this volume and witnessed my discovery of it, thus recovering it from years of exile from its proper home in Harrison County. It has been in the possession of this court ever since."

She let the suspense build while she made eye contact with the jury before turning to the judge. "I would believe from the protests of the defense that they were fully aware of the original whereabouts of this evidence, which is suspicious." She smiled innocently, knowing in this instance her own youth bolstered her believability against the hardened defense team. "Before the defense accuses me of hiding it in the School of Mines, I must point out I was a mere babe-in-arms when it disappeared from the Harrison County Recorder's vault."

The judge's glare silenced any protests. "Miss Storm. You may continue."

CHAPTER 23

The courtroom was utterly silent, waiting in suspense. Sally opened the ledger to the page she had marked and soberly faced the jury, some of whom showed signs of skepticism. "The disputed claim, as recorded on this page, is listed as the *Sunrise* Mining Company." She admitted as if dejected, "If we are to take the entry at face value, then my client has no case, because the entry was signed only by Sydney Underwood.

"However." she let the word hang in the air while she turned the open volume so the jury could see it. "You will notice the entries are all in pencil by many different writers."

She laid the ledger on the table and turned to the next page. Every eye in the room was glued to her when Squire handed her the salt shaker from the table, which had mystified every viewer. She applied a small quantity of salt to the page, tapped it with her finger, and added another shake.

"Your Honor, with your indulgence, I would like to ask the members of the jury to step out of the box so they may closely examine this page." She explained. "When the original claim was filed, whoever record-ed it wrote rather heavily, indenting the paper on the next page, this page, outlined by the salt."

She let the tension ratchet higher, to an almost palatable presence in the air. "*Sunset* Mining Company! The partnership we have already proved existed!"

The courtroom began to buzz and the defense table turned pale. Her soprano carried clearly, "Someone changed the name on the first page, *after the fact,* to SUNRISE. I believe, and the evidence bears me out, that the only person who stood to gain was the defendant. Sydney Underwood stole the mine from his partners by fraud."

The courtroom erupted, the clamor rising as the judge tried to restore order. He succeeded only after several minutes when he threatened to clear the room. When order had been restored, the jurors slowly filed from the box to examine the evidence. They intently examined the suspect page, using the magnifying glass Squire provided, before they returned to their seats.

"Your Honor. I have no further questions for my client at this time."

The judge said, "Mr. Wheeler, your witness."

Wanda was subjected to intense questioning by the defense as they attempted to regain lost ground. Armored by righteous indignation, and having been coached by Squire on how to retain her composure, she held her ground against the verbal attack. Repeated attacks on her testimony were dispelled, until the defense silently conceded defeat and she was allowed to step down.

Wanda was the only witness on the stand before the court recessed for the noon hour. After a hasty sandwich and much discussion among the team, Sally and the others returned to the courtroom.

"Miss Storm, do you have any further witnesses?"

Her heart was pounding when she faced the judge and the defense. The observers watched, mystified, suddenly to be shocked by her audacity. "Yes, Your Honor. I call Sydney Underwood to the stand as a hostile witness."

He glared at her, flat, almost-black eyes radiating hate and fury. After being sworn, he warily followed Sally's every move.

She knew he was expecting a hostile attack, so she used a moderate, almost friendly approach. Unexpectedly flustered, he stumbled and contradicted himself on several answers while she reviewed his version of those momentous days.

Underwood explained how he discovered the mine by himself before filing the claim in his own name. Sally stared at him, deadpan, her disbelief palatable in the silent courtroom, waiting while her unruffled silence honed the edge of his uneasiness. Her next question caught him totally off guard. "Why did it take three days for you to file the claim for you and your partners?"

"Because I got drunk celebrating."

Sally pounced, "You mean you decided to take it all for yourself and didn't care about your partners! You snuck back and sabotaged the mine so it would collapse.

"Didn't you?"

He turned white, gasping.

"*Didn't you?*"

His lawyers jumped to their feet, objecting

vociferously while she waited for his answer, impaling him with her eyes.

"Objection sustained. The jury will disregard the question."

Underwood sat shaken and shrunken in the chair.

Her voice was filled with contempt when she said, "I have no further questions for this witness." She turned from the witness stand with dignity and returned to her own chair in the utter silence.

He remained sitting, too shocked to move until the bailiff led him away, his eyes shifting away in terror, rather than meet hers.

The case went to the jury late in the afternoon after detailed instructions from the judge. The court adjourned for the day, with deliberations to begin the next morning.

Sally slept very poorly, meeting the team the next morning for breakfast in the hotel dining room where she was too nervous to do much but pick at her meal, finally giving up.

The proceedings reopened with the jurors being dismissed to the jury room. Sally's team moved to the room assigned to them down the hall. Faced with nothing to do but wait, Wanda volunteered to pour coffee for everyone. Sally sank into a chair, her head in her hands, as she tried to stop the whirl of thoughts. She soon fell asleep, startling awake when the door scraped open, setting excitement astir in the room.

"Jury's coming back."

When Court had been gaveled to order, the judge asked, "Mr. Foreman, have you reached a verdict?"

"We have, Your Honor." He inhaled deeply. "We find for the plaintiff, Wanda Benson, and any heirs of Amos Wanderman."

Underwood screamed curses as he started for Wanda, bulling his way through his lawyers, brushing aside the bailiff. He was white with fury, eyes ablaze as he followed when Wanda retreated. Sally stood her ground as he reached for her throat, unleashing a right uppercut that started near her knees. The blow lifted him off his feet and sent him crashing in a shapeless heap on the floor. She glared at his prostrate form, shaking her right hand to ease the pain resulting from the blow.

When an unconscious Underwood had been carried out and order restored, the judge read the decision of the jury to the court. Wanda and any heirs of Amos Wanderman were awarded three-quarters of all his assets, far more than she had sued for, amounting to hundreds of thousands of dollars. All of his accounts were frozen until such time as settlement had been reached. Only then would his lawyers and other debts be paid from his remaining share.

Most devastating to a man with his monstrous ego were the loss of his reputation and the influence he thrived on. Even worse for him, his personal kingdom of Harrison County had collapsed with the takeover by the State of Colorado.

Squire exuded undisguised satisfaction. "The only thing positive for him is he can't be prosecuted for theft by fraud because of the statute of limitations."

It would be weeks before Wanda received any of the settlement but Harry kept them informed at each stage. When the final settlement had been made, Wanda came to Wilford in person.

Sally whistled silently when she read the amount of the check Wanda handed her. She had added a hefty bonus to the total they had agreed on.

"I can never thank you enough." She grinned devilishly. "I won't lie and tell you it was only for the principle, but it was heavenly to prove to the entire world he's a liar and a thief." She hugged them both. "Thank you! Thank you! Thank you!"

CHAPTER 24

Sally took several days off and went home to the ranch for a short vacation. Her eyes grew damp at her mother's loving embrace, and danced with humor when her brothers teased her about her one-round knockout, as reported in the *MESSENGER*. She rumpled Tom's hair, teasing him about being the runt, just because he was the youngest, though he was only a fraction of an inch shorter than she, and a head taller than Tim.

"Remind me never to get in a fight with you." Tim laughed. "You'd send me flying."

"Speaking of flying. Have you had any luck with your glider?"

His eyes shone. He practically danced in excitement. "It works! Whenever you want, I'll be glad to show you."

Her mother laughed before Sally could respond. "Go ahead. He has a right to be proud of it, even if it does scare me half to death."

The family trooped off to the overlook above the corrals with Tim leading, pulling his craft on a wheeled trailer. With their help, he shifted it to a single wooden rail mounted on posts, centered on two skids. He hooked a loop of rope to a small hook fastened to the front of the undercarriage. The rope ran the length of the rail, through a series of pulleys, to a large weight at the top of another post off to one side of the rail.

Sally watched, mystified, while the rest of the

family scurried around doing different tasks. Tim readied himself, stretching out in the body of the flimsy craft. Satisfied with the preparations, he called, "Launch!"

Tom pulled a lever on the upright post which dropped the heavy weight. The glider shot forward, launched out into empty air.

Sally's heart was in her throat because the glider bobbled before stabilizing and gliding several hundred feet to a dusty landing near the corrals. She cheered loudly enough for Tim to hear as he unfolded himself from his machine. He acknowledged her with a wave of his hand.

The glider was a topic of lively discussion at the supper table while he and Sally debated a letter he had received from Dean Larson. "I'm glad you got it to me before we were snowed in because it was the last time we were in Wilford until the spring thaw. It gave me plenty of time over the winter to make the changes he suggested. I think the letter was what made it all work."

Sue interjected, "Let's finish the dishes and then we can continue this over cards." She made a face at Ted, remembering the night he drew four aces. "I'm feeling lucky."

***

Election Day was approaching as fall advanced with winter close behind. Sally had tried to visit every town and hamlet in the county to publicize Squire's candidacy. She talked to as many potential voters as she could, and left campaign posters at every stop. She pushed hard, quitting the campaign trail only after nearly getting caught by an early snowstorm while crossing a high mountain pass.

When she stumbled into the office after her last trip, wet and bedraggled, Squire glared at her with manifest disapproval. She nodded, chastened. "That's enough winter riding for one year. I'm sticking close to home unless it's absolutely necessary."

"I'm glad to hear that. I'm sure Dolly will appreciate it, too." His expression softened. "You had me worried." He waved at the pot-bellied stove radiating heat in all directions. "Pull up a chair and thaw out."

***

Election Day dawned clear and cold, with a light dusting of snow in Wilford and heavy blankets of snow visible on higher elevations in all directions. When they met in the office after he returned from casting his own ballot, she complained good-naturedly. "I wish I was old enough to vote for you. You decided to run just a few months too early for me to help with my vote." She thought ruefully, *At least I can't vote because of my age, not my sex.*

"You've helped tremendously. I don't think I would've have had much of a chance without you out there campaigning for me. Now all we can do is wait for the results to trickle in to Agate. I'm hoping they'll have a final tally by the end of the week."

Sally was on edge for days in spite of knowing the election results would take time to reach Agate. She began looking up in anticipation every time someone came to the door, hoping for the telegraph runner. Even Squire was beginning to show signs of angst.

They were getting on each other's nerves when Emma joined them at the boarding house for dinner. The runner found them there and handed over a yellow envelope. "This just came in. Smitty thought you'd like to see it."

The room waited in silent anticipation as Squire unfolded the yellow sheet. He beamed and exclaimed, "We won!"

***

Several weeks flew by with Sally solely responsible for dealing with their clients' needs. Squire made trips to Denver for legislative meetings and party caucuses and was gone for several days each trip. Returning from his first trip, he reiterated his plan for her to be his aide. "No one else could possibly do as good a job as you do. I'm not just saying it to make you feel good. After talking to some other aides, I know you know more about what it takes to make things work than any of them. And even more than some of the other House members." He grinned smugly. "I'm counting on you going with me."

"I will."

***

Sally made sure her long coat was securely buttoned as she pulled it tightly around herself. Wrapping her scarf snugly around her throat, she looked at Squire. "I guess I'm ready."

He opened the lobby door of her rooming house and followed her outside, where the sudden onslaught of frigid winter wind took their breath away. He closed the door and they set off into the night. The walk to the hotel took less than fifteen minutes at a brisk pace but she was thoroughly chilled before they arrived.

The bright lights, plus the warmth of the lobby began to dissipate the chill as she sidled up to a steam radiator radiating mightily, grateful for the heat.

Squire chuckled when she complained sourly, "I never got this cold riding line on the ranch. It must have been because I dressed for warmth instead of fashion."

The caucus was held in rented rooms near the back of the hotel. When they entered, Squire took a quick look and pushed through the crowd, introducing her to the Speaker of the House.

"Sally Storm. I'd like you to meet Brooks Tyndall." His pride was obvious. "Brooks, you'll be seeing a lot of Sally because she's my aide for the session."

The Speaker looked up at the much taller Sally. "I've seen you from a distance several times here in the Capitol and read about you in the papers. Would you be related to Ted and Sue Storm?"

"They're my parents."

"Then I know you're of fine stock." He extended his hand. "Welcome to the House."

Sally was the sole woman in attendance at the get-acquainted party, limited to legislators and their aides. The crowd soon gravitated into legislators and aides, separating into groups on either side of the ballroom. Mingling with the aides, as a very junior member she spent most of her time listening, absorbing everything she could about the upcoming session.

When hunger made its presence known, she excused herself, and went to the refreshment table. She made several selections before looking for an empty chair. She settled into one across the table from a young man sitting slightly askew.

"I'm Sally Storm. I don't believe we've met before."

His head was at an odd angle but his eyes were bright. "Pleased to meet you. I'm Ed Mason."

Sally started and his eyes widened. "Did I say something wrong?"

She shook her head, embarrassed. "No. I was just startled. My grandfather's name was Mason, but I've never met anyone else with your surname."

He chuckled at her flush. "I took the bar exam last fall. Are you the lady who almost aced the exam a couple of years ago without going to law school?"

Ears all along the table perked up, waiting for her reply.

"Yes."

He smiled while others turned to stare. "I thought you must be, because there are only a handful of women lawyers in the state. I'd like to congratulate you. When I was in law school, our professors held you up as the standard to which we could aspire with dedication and determination."

Sally blushed, uttering a strangled, "Thank you."

The evening turned out to be an extended affair as Sally mixed with the aides standing and talking, or the ones seated at tables. She enjoyed taking refreshments several times, and if the seat across from Ed Mason was empty, she took it for herself. Fascinated by the brilliance of his mind, she wondered why he never stirred from his own chair.

The hour was late when Squire found her seated in what had become her usual spot, deep in conversation. From a distance, he enjoyed watching the animation on her face and moved closer until she became aware of his presence. "This old man needs some sleep before the session starts in the morning. Are you ready for me to escort you home?"

She excused herself as her new-found friend struggled to his feet, bracing himself with a set of crutches hidden under the table. Her breath caught for a second as she saw the twisted torso and withered legs supporting his brilliant mind.

His eyes were wary but softened when she extended her hand without hesitation. "I'll see you in morning. I'm looking forward to working with you this session."

He offered his hand, caressing hers lightly before clasping it in a firm grip. His smile was bright. "I know I'm going to enjoy working with you as well."

CHAPTER 25

The legislative session opened the next morning with great pomp and ceremony. Sally and the other aides crowded the balcony with many other spectators to watch the ceremonies. When they were completed, she was immersed in a flood of activity as Squire led her from one meeting to another. She sat in the background with other aides, learning the duties and procedures necessary for her to assist her mentor.

She saw Ed Mason in passing on several occasions, but neither had time to stop and talk. Nearing midday, he stopped her and invited her to lunch in the capitol cafeteria.

"I'll meet you about noon," she said with a smile. "Just be aware I'm hungry."

His infectious grin was a mirror of hers. "I am too. I'll see you then."

They met at a small table, surrounded by a multitude, making the most of their few minutes of leisure. The background noise level was loud enough to make talking difficult but his physical handicaps in no way hindered his mind. She could see the intelligence shining in his eyes while she tried to keep pace with his wit and wicked sense of humor. Sally felt an unfamiliar sense of companionship. They ate quickly before going their separate ways.

****

Several weeks of the session passed in activity, sometimes frantic, but more often dull, a routine of committee meetings and floor debate. Her routine was shattered when she arrived at their office early one morning, startled to find Squire was not already at work. She hurried through her own duties, her concern increasing while she waited because he was always punctual, usually at the office before she was, and had never been this late before.

After an increasingly anxious hour, she locked the office and headed for his apartment, a short walk from the Capitol. When she arrived, she found the door locked with no sound of activity inside. She banged loudly enough that a neighbor heard and opened her door across the hall.

Sally asked, "Have you seen Squire this morning? He didn't show up at the office and he doesn't answer the door. That's not like him!"

"I haven't seen or heard him." The neighbor offered, "If you want to check his room, I have a skeleton key that might let us in." She disappeared for a moment, reappearing with the key in her hand.

The lock was a simple one. Sally's heart was in her throat as she pushed it ajar with a sense of foreboding. "Squire! It's Sally! Are you all right?"

There was no answer. They pushed the door wide and entered. The sitting room was empty, the pot-bellied stove cold and forlorn in the middle of the small room. Sally led the way to the closed bedroom door, her stomach knotted and her throat tight. She knocked again but there was no response so she pushed the door open. Bright sunlight poured through the window, highlighting the sleeping figure in the bed, a smile on his lips, the blanket pulled up to his chin.

Sally's feet and heart were leaden as she extended her hand to touch his forehead, already knowing the truth. Her eyes were streaming tears when she touched the face of her dear friend, his skin cold and no longer soft.

The neighbor hugged her in sympathy. "I'm sorry. He died in his sleep."

Sally choked on her flood of tears, hiccupping. "I always thought I'd have one last chance to say goodbye."

***

Sally stumbled back to the Capitol to find Brooks Tyndall in his office. One look at her face and he knew what had happened. He consoled her for several minutes, offering to take care of the necessary details to return Squire's body to Wilford and notify the necessary people.

Sally said with a quaver in her voice, "I have to be the one to let Emma know. If someone else needs to know, I'll let you do so. I know who to contact to deliver the bad news in person, 'cause I'll not just hit her with a telegram!"

Tyndall said, "I'll let you take care of that. You're welcome to use the Capitol's telegraph office. You don't have to go downtown to send it."

"Thank you so much. I'll take care of it right now," she snuffled.

"I'll walk with you. I have messages to send as well."

A flurry of messages spread from the Capitol, the

first of which was Sally's plea to Parson to tell Emma of Squire's death. Brooks sent several messages to people in Denver to arrange for the transfer of Squire's body. A later one was to the county commissioners in Agate to inform them of the death of their representative.

It took two days of endless labor in Denver to complete the preparations of shipping Squire's body home. Sally slept poorly each night, before an early morning found her aboard the train headed home to Wilford, escorting the flag-draped casket containing the body of her friend and mentor. Several other passengers, who were regular travelers and knew both Squire and Sally, sat quiet and somber in respect for a man widely-known and well-liked.

Marie Hoekstra slipped into the empty seat beside Sally, putting a comforting arm around the much younger woman. She whispered, "We'll all miss him, Sally."

Sally leaned on the comforting shoulder while tears trickled down her cheeks, choking helplessly. "He was my best friend."

Marie held Sally silently, feeling the suppressed sobs shaking the slim figure.

***

The county commissioners met in emergency session that morning at the courthouse in Agate, the sole agenda item being to decide whether to appoint someone to fill the remainder of the term of the late Squire Brown, or hold a special election. Spirited debate ensued as each commissioner pressed for his preferred candidate.

After one especially acrimonious round, some-one observed sourly, "None of us wants to give up on our own favorite. Why don't we just appoint somebody neutral?"

Another commissioner said sarcastically, "Better yet, why don't we just appoint Squire's aide, Sally Storm? She's been there for the entire session and knows *everything*, which is more than anyone else we could appoint."

Despite the sarcasm, incredulous stares greeted the suggestion. Someone snorted in disbelief. "A woman?" They were silent, stunned at the thought. "She's Ted and Sue Storm's daughter, meaning there's no better recommendation. She's extremely young, but has proven herself to be a brilliant trial lawyer. I know she's well-regarded by everyone here in the courthouse." He shook his head at his own temerity. "I move to nominate Sally Storm."

CHAPTER 26

Emma wrapped Sally in her arms while the flag-draped coffin was unloaded from the train, sharing her grief and love. "You've always been a granddaughter to both of us. I want you to be with us in this time of sorrow." Her waiting family closed around them as the coffin was escorted to the church, already filled to overflowing with friends and family. Many additional mourners stood outside, listening through an open window. The sermon was brief but eulogies were many, an outpouring of respect from family, friends and neighbors

The committal ceremony at the cemetery was brief. When it was over, Sally joined her parents, trudging back toward the church carrying her burden of grief. They had just reached the main street when they were approached by a man in funeral black. Sally didn't recognize him, but he shook hands with her parents with the enthusiasm of an old friend.

"I'm glad to see both of you, but I need to talk to Sally."

She waited numbly, only mildly curious.

"Sally, I know we've never met. I'm Oscar West, chairman of the county commissioners. Squire's untimely death will force us to appoint a successor to fill out his unexpired term."

He glanced at Ted and Sue for a moment before returning his attention to Sally. "I have a question for you. How old are you?"

Some of her grief was replaced by curiosity. "I turned twenty-one three weeks ago."

His face relaxed somewhat as he smiled at her. "We as commissioners have voted to appoint you to fill the rest of Squire's term, subject to your being both old enough and willing to serve."

Sue and Ted were astonished. Flabbergasted, Sally stared, speechless for several seconds before gasping, "You're kidding!" He met her eyes, his face sober.

"You're not kidding," she said.

"I'm not kidding. If you're willing to take the position, it's yours." He smiled. "We've already taken action to make the appointment official. The only reservations the commission had were if you were of legal age and would be willing to serve."

She stared, trying to fix in her own mind what she had been offered. She turned to her parents, who were beaming at her with pride and confidence. She turned back to meet his eyes. "Squire Brown was one of the finest men in this state," she declared as her spirits lifted to meet the challenge. "I just hope I can live up to his standards." Proudly, she said firmly, "I'll take it."

Oscar shook her hand before giving her an envelope. "This is the written appointment from the board. When you get back to Denver, give it to the Speaker. He'll make the arrangements to have you sworn in and seated in the House."

***

Sally was nervous and anxious, waiting in the wings of the House chamber as the day's opening ceremonies neared. Glancing at the visitor's gallery in the balcony, she caught her mother's eye. Her parents were seated in the front row, leaning forward to better see the chamber. Her mother gave her a discreet wave just as she felt a gentle hand on her arm.

Ed Mason's usually smiling face was somber. "I'm sorry I wasn't here last week for you. I know how much Squire meant to you."

His sympathy warmed her heart. Before she could speak, the Speaker called the House to order. "We have two items to address this morning before we move to the agenda. The first is a short memorial service for our late colleague, Squire Brown." He continued soberly, "I have also received the appointment of his successor, who will be sworn in this morning."

The memorial service was short and dignified. After the closing prayer, the Speaker addressed a judge seated next to the podium. "Your Honor, if you would."

The chamber buzzed. There had been no announcement regarding the name of the newest member and speculation was rife. The judge took his place with a smile on his face. Placing his Bible on the podium, he waited for the murmurs to die away.

"Miss Sally Storm. Please come forward and be sworn in."

A gasp of astonishment was followed by absolute silence in the chamber. Sally worked her way through the crowd of stunned aides to the dais, where the judge extended the Bible, invoking the time-honored ritual upon the chamber's newest member.

Ted and Sue watched from the gallery, bursting with pride in their daughter as she raised her right hand and repeated the oath of office, and became the first female and the youngest member to have ever served in the House.

At the conclusion of the oath, the chamber remained deathly silent until the Speaker announced, "Representative Storm. You may take your seat."

Applause, some of it grudging, built as she took the seat left vacant by the death of her friend and mentor.

Upon completion of the opening ceremonies, the representatives and aides began streaming from the chamber, heading for the committee meetings which would determine much of what would become law. Many of them stopped to congratulate Sally as they streamed past.

The last to congratulate he was her former fellow aide, Ed Mason. His smile filled his face as he shook her hand, joking, "You really outrank me now. Congratulations. I know you'll be a fine representative."

Her smile matched his as her parents waited and watched nearby. "Ma, Pa, I'd like you to meet my good friend, Ed Mason. He's an aide to one of the other members. We've worked together a lot."

***

The remainder of Sally's first day as a representative was largely ceremonial; her second day was not. Rather than reshuffle the memberships of the committees in the middle of the session, the Speaker had simply decreed Sally would assume Squire's positions.

This created no open hostility until she arrived at her first mine-safety meeting where she was greeted with frosty silence and an empty Chairman's chair.

She ignored the uncomfortable silence, her eyes meeting those of the committee. "Gentlemen. I realize as well as you do, if not more so, that I am not qualified to chair this committee. I will do everything I can to serve my constituents, but the best service I can render them is to yield to one of you as chair. Each of you has far more experience than I have and would be a better choice."

Startled glances swept around the table and the atmosphere warmed noticeably when she moved to an empty chair farther down the table.

When the meeting ended, she returned to her office, exhausted and suffering from a pounding headache induced by a heavy cloud of cigar smoke. She was digging in her purse for her key when the door opened. She froze in bewilderment when a smiling older woman beckoned her to enter.

"You have to be Sally Storm. I'm your new secretary, Mary Anne O'Brian."

"I never hired you," she protested. "How can you be my secretary? How did you get in?"

"Your last question first, one of the cleaning crew I know let me in." Mary Anne waved a bewildered Sally to a waiting chair. "I read in last night's newspaper you're the first woman ever to be sworn in as a representative. If your predecessor had any staff other than you, it was male, and no man would stick around to work for a woman, especially one as young as you are. I need a job, you need help. I know enough about where the bodies are buried around this building to deflect at least some of the garbage sure to come your way."

A smile danced on her lips as Sally eyed her new secretary, a woman a full head shorter than herself, her hair beginning to show a touch of gray. Her clothes were clean and neat, though not of the very latest fashion. Clear and honest, twinkling eyes met hers above a wide smile.

"You should be the captain of a pirate ship, Mary Anne. You're right. I need someone who knows the ins and outs of this place. Tell me what we need to do to get started."

They shook hands and both erupted in relieved laughter.

CHAPTER 27

Word of Sally's refusal to accept a chairmanship for which she knew she was unqualified spread quietly through both houses of the legislature. Some members derided her naivety behind her back, contemptuous of her lack of desire for power. Offsetting those few, her stature rose among the majority of members who had also sought election to *serve* their constituents. As the session advanced, additional members of the House accorded her respect for her hard work, albeit sometimes grudgingly.

She knew she was the most junior of junior members and willingly showed proper deference, considering carefully both sides of issues raised. Some of her beliefs she would not compromise on, but would bow to the will of the majority, not sulking if on the minority side of a vote. She garnered respect when addressing the chamber in debate, her clear soprano raising points of view very few, if any, male members had ever considered.

Sally was working at her desk during one of the rare moments when she was not in a committee meeting or reading mail from her voters, when Mary Anne knocked on her door. "You have a visitor who'd like a few minutes of your time."

She stretched to ease the stiffness in her back. "Send him in."

"It's not a him. It's a her."

The woman who entered was dressed in the

height of fashion, old enough to be her mother. Sally stood to meet her guest, and indicated a chair in front of her desk. "I'm Sally Storm, and you would be...?"

Her unexpected visitor smiled warmly. "I'm Mollie Brown, from Leadville. I don't live in your district. I just want to offer my congratulations and best wishes."

Sally searched her orderly memory, trying to remember why the name was so familiar. Finally she gasped, awe-stricken, "You're the *Unsinkable Molly Brown*, from the Titanic."

"I am, but enough about me." She took the chair, settling comfortably into the deep cushions. "I've been following everything about you in the newspapers. I want you to know, what you're doing takes far more courage than commanding a lifeboat.

"I did what I needed to do to survive, though much of what you may have read was greatly exaggerated. You, on the other hand, had the option of refusing this job. In my opinion, you're showing true courage. I have sources who tell me very few of the House members are going out of their way to make things easier for you, and when they do, it's grudging."

She grinned smugly when Sally reddened. "I'm old enough I pay no attention to either condemnation or praise. Nothing much bothers me, as it probably would someone as young as you."

She laughed delightedly as Sally's blush deepened. "You'll have many years to learn to accept praise."

When Molly got ready to leave much later, she took Sally's hand in her own and bestowed a motherly hug. "I'll be on the sidelines cheering you on. May you have the best in the future."

***

The pace of the legislative session accelerated as the date of adjournment loomed. Sally spent almost every daylight hour, plus many in the evening, at the Capitol. Bills that should be passed, or correspondence Mary Anne had prepared for her, consumed her time. Lunch was usually a quick one, shared with Ed Mason, amidst conversation and jokes.

They often met in the evening as well, in the dining room of his rooming house, arguing points of law until late. After one especially trying day, she collapsed into her chair, a long sigh escaping her lips.

Deep concern darkened his eyes. "Was today that bad?"

"It was long and tiring!" She gulped most of a glass of water in one long swallow. "Today was one of the many times I've asked why I ever accepted this job. Ignorance is not bliss."

Her hand was cuddling the glass on the table when he reached out and pushed it aside.

"You need someone to share your life and help carry the load." He swallowed, concealing something in his free hand. "Would you marry me?"

The glow in her eyes matched his. "YES!

His face was alight when he opened the small box in his free hand, gently slipping the ring on her finger. A burst of cheers and applause startled them.

Most of the other diners were also regulars and had been watching hopefully, and one viewer commented, "We've been wondering when you'd finally decide to tie the knot!"

***

The closing day of the session dawned clear and warm in springtime Denver. Seated at her desk on the floor of the chamber, Sally scanned the packed gallery during the final moments before the Speaker was to gavel the meeting to order. She waved at her mother, crowded together with her father and siblings, as well as Edwina and Mark Franklin.

Her eyes met Ed's, who sat with his widowed mother and siblings. Together both families almost filled the front row of the balcony.

The bang of the Speaker's gavel startled her and forced her attention to the front of the chamber. The closing ceremonies seem to crawl until the Speaker finally banged his gavel again. "This session stands adjourned." The room remained silent. There was none of the usual shuffling and chair scraping. "However, it is my pleasure to perform one unofficial duty today. Miss Sally Storm, please come forward."

Her knees were weak and her stomach aflutter as she joined her parents waiting in the aisle. Her father gently offered his arm while her mother took her other one. A violinist in the gallery began to play the wedding processional as they moved solemnly forward.

Ed was waiting, standing with the aid of his crutches in front of the Speaker's dais as they advanced. The judge who had sworn Sally in as a House member was waiting beside him. She swallowed, suddenly shy.

They joined hands and faced the judge.

The simple ceremony took only a few minutes before the beaming judge decreed, "I now pronounce you husband and wife."

The chamber erupted in applause, the newly-weds sharing their first kiss before turning to face the audience.

EPILOGUE

Abraham Winters, the mayor of Wilford, was seated at his desk, working through a stack of bills and payments when someone knocked at his door. He looked up to see a gray-haired, well-dressed stranger standing at the open door and asked, "Can I help you?"

"Sorry to bother you. I'm Walter Castle, the new district court judge from Agate. I was told I could find the town magistrate here."

"I'm the mayor and magistrate. Have a seat." He waved at a straight-backed chair. "What can I do for you?"

The judge smiled wryly, "As I said, I'm the new district court judge. I wanted to become familiar with my new jurisdiction, so I've been combing through the court records of the past few years. In doing so, I've found some things I thought were rather unusual."

Mayor Winters' eyebrows rose.

Castle hastened to clarify, "Unusual. Not illegal."

The mayor asked, "What might they be, and what does it have to do with me?"

Judge Castle explained, "I've been reviewing the records of case filings for the last several years throughout the district. I found it odd that there has not been a single civil case filed in Wilford during the last three years, and only one criminal case of any kind. I'll grant this is not a high-crime town, but I'm mystified about why there hasn't even been a single civil case. I thought you'd be the best person to ask."

Mayor Winters smiled as he glanced at the clock on the wall behind the judge. He stood and began to move toward the window. "Come with me. In about five minutes I'll point out the answer to your mystery."

Baffled, the judge shrugged and followed the mayor.

Eying the street below, Winters explained, "They always go to dinner at the boarding house right at noon. We should see them in a couple of minutes."

Pedestrian traffic was light and the judge was starting to become irritated when the mayor suddenly pointed. "There they are! Do you see the young couple just in front of the newspaper office?"

The judge's eye followed the pointing finger to see a very tall young woman carrying an infant cradled in her arms. A much shorter young man accompanied her, walking with the aid of crutches, his body twisted as though by disease, a foot dragging with each step.

"I see them. What do they have to do with my question?"

The mayor returned to his chair with a smug look on his face. "We have two lawyers in this town. You just saw both of them."

The judge's eyebrows rose.

"Those two young people are probably the smartest lawyers in this state. Sally Storm, now Mrs. Edward Mason, almost aced the bar exam without ever attending college. She was trained by Squire Brown, one of the finest men in this state. When he died, she was appointed to fill out his term in the legislature."

The judge's attention was riveted on the couple. He had heard of the young woman. "She met her husband while serving in the legislature. They were married the day the session ended."

"That's right." The mayor's grin widened. "As I said, they're the only two lawyers in town. When someone has a dispute, each of them represents one side. They work with their own client, then sit down at home and work out a fair settlement for everyone involved.

"They always make clear they will take the case to your court if either client wants to do so. So far, no one has. What would be a court case in any other jurisdiction is treated as a contract, settled with minimal cost and hard feelings for everyone involved."

The judge stared in wonder. "So I've been rendered unnecessary by this young couple?"

"That's right. One reason it works so well is because everyone around here knows Sally. She was born here, and her parents, Sue and Ted, both served as United States marshals and are highly respected. Sally and Ed are so scrupulously fair no one has ever contested their decisions." He laughed. "At least everyone has accepted those decisions, even if they do sometimes complain."

"Maybe I should see about finding a place for her on the bench."

"You might have to wait a few years." The mayor's

smile softened. "She just gave birth to a daughter about a month ago." He suggested seriously, "I would not be at all surprised if she were the first female to become a judge in this state, and not all that many years in the future."